© Ken Goebel

Rivka Galchen received her MD from Mount Sinai School of Medicine, having spent a year in South America working on public health issues. She recently completed her MFA at Columbia University, where she was a Robert Bingham Fellow. The recipient of a 2006 Rona Jaffe Foundation Writers' Award, Galchen lives in New York City. This is her first novel.

Additional Praise for *Atmospheric Disturbances*

"Rivka Galchen takes so many risks in *Atmospheric Disturbances* that I opened it gingerly, back arched slightly, as if her first novel were a grenade.... Very, very funny... Galchen knocks out a remarkably apt ending to a story that defies even finding one.... Expect it to radiate under your skin."
—Karen R. Long, *The Plain Dealer* (Cleveland)

"Galchen's tone is addictive: playful, halting, intellectual, colloquial."
—*New York* magazine

"Rivka Galchen is clearly tuned, preternaturally, to the key of Auster, Borges, and perhaps Sebald.... By turns rueful, paranoid, melancholy, clever, and anxious ... Galchen's idiosyncratic, echo-filled sound comes through loud and clear."
—Stacey D'Erasmo, *Bookforum*

"Impressively clever... [Galchen] manages to appropriate the mystique of science, producing a novel that seems somehow grounded in fundamental laws, even while satirizing the confident function that science plays in modern life."
—Ron Charles, *The Washington Post Book World*

"Galchen, a Mount Sinai–trained MD, has a high old time, throwing an Oliver Sacks–style medical conundrum into a David Foster Wallace cosmology with a sideline in Tristam Shandy–ish humor.... Chock-full of erudite references, scholarly asides, and flat-out weird science." —Diane Roberts, *St. Petersburg Times*

"Funny, sad, and ingenious ... a Borgesian writer armed with a medical degree and a Rona Jaffe Foundation Award and intent on a rapprochement between art and science ... Witty, tender, and conceptually dazzling, Galchen's metaphysical tale of longing, grief, love, and the volatility of the self gracefully charts the tempestuous weather of the human psyche." —Donna Seaman, *Booklist*

"Galchen has created a heartbreaking puzzle of a novel, hilarious and daring. The novel tracks the way we seek to destroy our most precious love affairs and, in doing so, our own sanity. The hero, Leo, is like a brilliant mad scientist trying to prove that the earth is flat, because he desperately needs a ledge high enough to jump off of." —Heather O'Neill, author of *Lullabies for Little Criminals*

"[An] intriguing meteorological novel . . . a diverting and impressive debut."   —Jonathan Gibbs, *The Independent* (UK)

"Reader, you are holding in your hand one of my favorite novels ever: Rivka Galchen's divinely hilarious, heartbreaking tale of Leo's search for his lost wife Rema. This is a novel of Borgesian erudition, wit, and playfulness, though its obsessively pursued subject—as it rarely was in the Argentine's fiction—is love, the enraptured lover, and the mystery of the beloved, the intersection of love's fictions, realities, and pathologies. It is also as funny as any episode of *The Simpsons* (imagine Homer as a besotted and brilliant New York psychiatrist). The prose jumps with one astonishing observation, insight, and description after another. *Atmospheric Disturbances* delivers unforgettable joy."
                    —Francisco Goldman, author of *The Divine Husband*

"An excellent first novel . . . very funny . . . Meteorology, in Galchen's hands, becomes a fertile field, yielding insights into emotion and, in particular, the anxiety caused by knowing that we can never truly fathom the person we love."   —*The Guardian* (UK)

"Erudite and chock-full of heartache, Rivka Galchen's virtuosic 'debut' novel reads like the work of a cutting-edge literary alchemist who has created in her laboratory the Book of the Now. Part thriller, part romance, part autobiography, part psychological study, her book's sweetly skewed brilliance and stealth-bomb sadness will make you swoon with this realization: yes, these kinds of books are still possible."
                    —Heidi Julavits, author of *The Uses of Enchantment*

Atmospheric Disturbances

Rivka Galchen

Picador | **Farrar, Straus and Giroux** | **New York**

Designed by Jonathan D. Lippincott

ISBN-13: 978-0-312-42843-3

First published in the United States by Farrar, Straus and Giroux

First Picador Edition: May 2009

P 1

For Aaron

Since the first numerical prediction model we have witnessed a steady improvement in forecasting large scale flows. Yet on the human scale (i.e., the mesoscale) little to no improvement has been reported. Several reasons have been cited . . . yet the most obvious reason (to me at least) is: we cannot tell what the weather will be tomorrow (or the next hour) because we do not know accurately enough what the weather is right now.
—Tzvi Gal-Chen, "Initialization of Mesoscale Models: The Possible Impact of Remotely Sensed Data"

It may be that friendship is nourished on observation and conversation, but love is born from and nourished on silent interpretation . . . The beloved expresses a possible world unknown to us . . . that must be deciphered.
—Gilles Deleuze, *Proust and Signs*

Part I

1. On a temperate stormy night

Last December a woman entered my apartment who looked exactly like my wife. This woman casually closed the door behind her. In an oversized pale blue purse—Rema's purse—she was carrying a russet puppy. I did not know the puppy. And the real Rema, she doesn't greet dogs on the sidewalk, she doesn't like dogs at all. The hayfeverishly fresh scent of Rema's shampoo was filling the air and through that brashness I squinted at this woman, and at that small dog, acknowledging to myself only that something was extraordinarily wrong.

She, the woman, the possible dog lover, leaned down to de-shoe. Her hair obscured her face somewhat, and my migraine occluded the edges of my vision, but still, I could see: same unzipping of wrinkly boots, same taking off of same baby blue coat with jumbo charcoal buttons, same tucking behind ears of dyed cornsilk blonde hair. Same bangs cut straight across like on those dolls done up in native costumes that live their whole lives in plastic cases held up by a metal wire around the waist. Same everything, but it wasn't Rema. It was just a feeling, that's how I knew. Like the moment near the end of a dream when I am sometimes able to whisper to myself, "I am dreaming." I remember once waking up from a dream in which my mother, dead now for thirty-three years, was sipping tea at my kitchen table, reading a newspaper on the back of which there was the headline "Wrong Man, Right Name, Convicted in Murder Trial." I was trying to read the smaller print of the article, but my mother kept moving the paper, readjusting, turning pages, a sound like a mess of pigeons taking sudden flight. When I woke up I searched all through the house for that newspaper, and through the trash outside as well, but I never found it.

"Oh!" the simulacrum said quietly, seeming to notice the dimmed lights. "I'm so sorry." She imitated Rema's Argentine accent perfectly, the halos around the vowels. "You are having your migraine?" She pressed that lean russet puppy against her chest; the puppy trembled.

I held a hushing finger to my lips, maybe hamming up my physical suffering, but also signing truly, because I was terrified, though of precisely what I could not yet say.

"You," the simulacrum whispered seemingly to herself, or maybe to the dog, or maybe to me, "can meet your gentle new friend later." She then began a remarkable imitation of Rema's slightly irregularly rhythmed walk across the room, past me, into the kitchen. I heard her set the teakettle to boil.

"You look odd," I found myself calling out to the woman I could no longer see.

"Yes, a dog," she singsonged from the kitchen, still flawlessly reproducing Rema's foreign intonations. And, as if already forgetting about my migraine, she trounced on, speaking at length, maybe about the dog, maybe not, I couldn't quite concentrate. She said something about Chinatown. And a dying man. Not seeing her, just hearing her voice, and the rhythm of Rema's customary evasions, made me feel that she really was my wife.

But this strange impostress, emerging from the kitchen moments later, when she kissed my forehead, I blushed. This young woman, leaning over me intimately—would the real Rema walk in at any moment and find us like this?

"Rema should have been home an hour ago," I said.

"Yes," she said inscrutably.

"You brought home a dog," I said, trying not to sound accusatory.

"I want you to love her, you'll meet her when you feel better, I put her away—"

"I don't think," I said suddenly, surprised by my own words, "you're Rema."

"You're still mad with me, Leo?" she said.

"No," I said and turned to hide my face in the sofa's cushions. "I'm sorry," I mumbled to the tight wool weave of the cushion's covering.

She left my side. As the water neared its boil—the ascending pitches of our teakettle's tremble are so familiar to me—I reached for the telephone and dialed Rema's cell. A muffled ring then, from the purse, a ring decidedly not in stereo with the sound from the receiver in my hand, and the ersatz Rema thus hearkened back out to the living room, now holding the dog, and then the teakettle whistling, and, literally, sirens wailing outside.

She laughed at me.

I was then a fifty-one-year-old male psychiatrist with no previous hospitalizations and no relevant past medical, social, or family history.

After the impostress fell asleep (the dog in her arms, their breathing synchronous) I found myself searching through Rema's pale blue purse that smelled only very faintly of dog. But when I noticed what I was doing—unfolding credit card receipts, breathing in the scent of her change purse, licking the powder off a half stick of cinnamon gum—I felt like a cuckolded husband in an old movie. Why did I seem to think this simulacrum's appearance meant that Rema was deceiving me? It was as if I was expecting to find theater tickets, or a monogrammed cigarette case, or a bottle of arsenic. Just because Rema is so much younger than me, just because I didn't necessarily know at every moment exactly where she was or what, precisely, in Spanish, she said over the phone to people who might very well have been perfect strangers to me and whom I was respectful enough to never ask about—just because of these very normal facets of our relationship, it still was not necessarily likely—not at all—that she was, or is, in love with some, or many, other people. And isn't this all irrelevant anyway? Why would infidelities lead to disappearances? Or false appearances? Or dog appearances?

2. Around 2 a.m.

Amidst the continued nonarrival of the real Rema, I received a page. An unidentified patient—but possibly one of my patients—had turned up in the Psychiatric ER. Instead of phoning in I decided to head over immediately, without further contemplation, or further gathering of information.

It seemed so clearly like a clue.

I left a note for the sleeping woman, though I wasn't quite sure to whom I was really addressing it, so it was sort of addressed to Rema and sort of addressed to a false Rema; I simply let her know that I had been called to the hospital for an emergency. And even though this was slightly less than true, still, leaving a note at all, regardless of what it said, was clearly the right and considerate and caring thing to do—even for a stranger.

I took Rema's purse—the comfort of an everyday thought of her—and left to find out about this unidentified someone. A patient of mine, a certain Harvey, had recently gone missing; Rema had accused me of not doing enough to locate him; maybe now I would find him.

When I arrived at the Psychiatric ER, it was quiet and a night nurse was dejectedly resting his face in his hand and playing hearts on the computer. He, the night nurse, was boyishly handsome, very thin, his skin almost translucent, and the vein that showed at his forehead reminded me, inexplicably, of a vein that tracks across the top of Rema's foot. I did not recognize this man but, given my slightly fragile state, and my slightly ambiguous goal, I hesitated to introduce myself.

"You're late," he said, interrupting my dilemma by speaking first, without even turning around to look at me.

And maybe for a moment I thought he was right, that I was late. But then I remembered I wasn't scheduled to work at all; in an excess of professionalism, I was coming by extra early to follow up on the faintest lead that could have harmlessly waited until morning to be attended to. It was, therefore, impossible that I was late. Probably he was mistaking me for someone else—someone younger, maybe, of lower rank, who still had to work nights.

"Who's here?" I asked, while nodding my head toward the other side of the one-way observation glass. Over there: just an older man asleep in a wheelchair, wrapped from the waist down in a hospital sheet.

Not my patient, not Harvey.

The deceptively delicate-looking nurse didn't stop clicking at his game of hearts, and still without turning to make eye contact he began mumbling quickly, more to himself than to me:

"Unevaluated. Likely psychotic. He was spitting and threatening and talking about God on the subway and so they brought him in. He's sleeping off a dose of Haldol now. Wouldn't stop shouting about us stealing his leg. I'd leave him for the morning crew. It'll be a while before his meds wear off."

Then the nurse did turn to glance, and then stare—actually stare—at me. His look made me feel as if I was green, or whistling, or dead.

Furrowing his previously lineless brow, enunciating now more clearly than before, the night nurse said to me, "Are you Rema's husband?"

I caught tinted sight of my slouched figure in the reflection of that observation glass that separated the staff from the patients. I noticed—remembered—that I was carrying Rema's pale blue purse. "Yes," I said, straightening my back, "I am."

He guffed one violent guffaw.

But there was no reason to be laughing.

His Rema-esque vein pulsed unappealingly across the characterless creaminess of his skin. "I didn't know you worked nights," he said. "I didn't know if—"

I should explain now that ever since I'd gotten Rema a job working as a translator at the hospital, I'd come to understand—from various interactions with people I didn't really know—that many of Rema's coworkers were extremely fond of her. She does often manage to give people the impression that she loves them in a very personal and significant way; I must admit I find it pretty tiresome dealing with all her pathetic devotees who think they play a much larger role in her life than they actually do; I mean, she hardly mentions these people to me; yet they think they're so important to her; if the night nurse—apparently a member of Rema's "ranks"—weren't so obviously barely more than a child, then I might have wondered if he could help me, if I should ask him something, if he might have knowledge of the circumstances behind Rema's absence, behind her replacement, but I could divine—I just could—that there was nothing—nothing at all—to be learned from that man.

"We probably did take his leg," I said. On the night nurse's desk lay the patient's chart, open. Glancing at the intake page I had noticed the high sugar.

"What's that?" the nurse said, still staring at me, but as if he hadn't heard me.

"I mean, the funny thing is that, literally speaking, doctors probably *did* take that poor man's leg," I answered, explaining myself in perhaps a slightly raised voice. "We say amputated, he says stolen"—I was getting my voice back under my own control—"but that's not psychosis. That's just poor communication."

A beat went by and then the nurse just shrugged. "Okay. Well. Not exactly the irony of ironies around here." He turned back to his monitor.

"You shouldn't be sloppy with the label 'psychotic,'" I said. *Just because a man's in foam slippers*, I almost continued lecturing to his back. But as I felt an inchoate anger rising in me, an image came to my mind, of that nervous puppy the simulacrum had come home with, of the puppy's startled look of the starved, and I remembered that I had other anxieties to which I had intended to be attending.

Even if the unidentified patient wasn't mine, wasn't Harvey— as long as I was at the hospital, I thought I should look through Harvey's old files. Maybe there would be clues as to where he might have gone; Rema would have liked to see me pursuing that mystery. And a part of me clung to the hope that if I dallied long enough, then by the time I made it back home Rema would be there, maybe battling it out with the simulacrum, as if in a video game. Rema would be victorious over her other and then together Rema and I would set out (the next level, another world) in search of Harvey.

That, anyway, was the resolution that presented itself to me.

"I'll be in the back office," I announced, feeling, I admit, a bit unbalanced, a bit homuncular, and beginning to develop the headache that had earlier, unexpectedly, and without my even noticing, ebbed.

I did call up Harvey's old records, and I sifted through them, though I could detect no trends. But as I sat there, one Rema clue— or false clue—recalled itself to me. It was this: A mentor of mine from medical school had recently been in town. He had always been a "connoisseur" of women—this pose of his had always irritated, he had in fact once "stolen" a woman from me—nevertheless I admired him for other reasons and had been eager to have him meet my Rema. I had steeled myself against the inevitable jealousy of watching him chat her up—and I'd held my tongue when Rema put on a fitted, demurely sexy 1940s secretary style of dress—but then, all my mental preparations were for naught. Strangely, my mentor hadn't seemed much charmed by Rema. He'd behaved toward her with serviceable politeness but nothing more. It was odd. At one point he'd made a joke about the election and Rema hadn't followed. Maybe for a moment *I* wasn't charmed by Rema. As if she weren't really *my* Rema. My Rema who makes everyone fall in love. Case: the night nurse.

But back then it really was still her—I'm almost sure of it.

3. What may be highly relevant

I have mentioned my patient Harvey, but I have failed to properly discuss him and the odd coincidence, or almost co-incidence, of his having vanished just two days before Rema did. So, actually, most likely not a "coincidence." In retrospect I feel confident that the seeds of tragedy were sown in what I had originally misperceived as a (kind of) light comedy of errors.

a. A secret agent for the Royal Academy of Meteorology

When I first met Harvey just over two years ago, he was twenty-six years old, and for nine years had carried a diagnosis of schizotypal personality disorder. He lived at home with his mother, had been treated successively, though never (according to his mother) successfully, by eleven different psychiatrists, two Reichian psychotherapists, three acupuncturists, a witch, and a lifestyle coach. Additionally Harvey had a history of heavy alcohol use, with a penchant for absinthe, which lent him a certain air of declining, almost cartoonish, aristocracy.

Harvey's mother had called me after reading an article of mine peripherally about R. D. Laing. In my unintentionally lengthy conversation with her, with me practically pinned against the wall of some insufferably track-lit Upper East Side coffee shop whose coffee, she kept insisting, was "superior," I quickly came to understand that she had grossly misread my paper. (For example, she interpreted my quoting Laing on "ontological insecurity" and "the shamanic journey" as endorsement rather than derision.) But I didn't try to set right her misreading—that would have been rude—and I found the case of her son interesting. I could imagine entertaining Rema with its details. Also: it pleased me, the thought of telling Rema that a woman had sought me out after reading an article of mine.

Functionally speaking, Harvey's main problem—or some might say his "conflict with the consensus view of reality"—stemmed from a fixed magical belief that he had special skills for controlling weather phenomena, and that he was, consequently, employed as a secret agent for the Royal Academy of Meteorology, an institute whose existence a consensus view of reality actually would (and this surprised me at the time) affirm. According to Harvey, the Royal Academy dedicated itself to maintaining weather's elements of unpredictability and randomness.

"I would have thought the opposite," I said in our initial conversation.

"Everything we say here is secret?" Harvey asked.

I assured him.

He explained: Opposed to the Royal Academy of Meteorology was an underground group known as the 49 Quantum Fathers (*not* confirmable as existent by a consensus view of reality). The 49 ran self-interested meteorological experiments, in uncountable parallelly processing worlds, and it financed itself through investments in crop futures, crops whose futures, naturally, depended upon the 49's machinations of the weather.

I asked Harvey to clarify, about the parallelly processing worlds.

"Yes, well, the Fathers can move between the possible worlds," he said. "Like they can go to the world that is like this one but Pompeii erupts ten years later. Variables are altered. Like maybe in one of those other worlds you were hit by a produce truck when you were a kid and we aren't talking here now."

Perhaps my pressing irritated him.

He continued, "In one world it's a rainy spring in Oklahoma, in another world it's a drought," though I don't know if he was aware of himself trying to mitigate an aggression. "Normally the worlds remain isolated from one another, but there are tangencies that the 49 exploit, for muling data and energy from one world to another. I do wonder how they map them—that I don't know. You understand, of course, that knowing the weather means winning a war, that all weather research is really just war research by other means."

I didn't really know that, but I later read up on the topic on my own, and although one might argue that he was exaggerating, he was—even by a consensus view—off only in a matter of degree, not of kind.

"But," Harvey said, "I don't mean to aggrandize my personal work. I'm just the littlest butterfly. I handle mostly mesoscale events; I specialize mostly in local wind patterns."

The Royal Academy sent Harvey orders through Page Six of the *New York Post*; it wasn't that he saw text or images that weren't actually there; rather, he understood what was there as encrypted messages expressly for him. Early rumors of J.Lo's divorce had, for example, sent Harvey nearby to the Bronx, but often these orders—coded in a Hasselhoff binge or a Gisele Bündchen real estate acquisition—entailed Harvey setting off unannounced on missions across the country. Harvey's mom would learn of his whereabouts only days later when she'd receive a call from a distant ER or police station. Harvey's homecomings were often notable for cuts and bruises he could not explain, occasionally even signs of severe nutritional deficits, once including cerebellar dysfunction.

When asked about his absences, Harvey's elucidation tended to go no further than to say that he was "laboring atmospherically."

Arguably these disappearances actually endangered his life.

"From the moment I shook your hand," Harvey's mother said to me in her wet-eyed, well-wardrobed way, "I could just tell that you were different from the rest, that you were *superior*, that you would be the one to solve everything." She said this after my first meeting with her son.

Well, looking through Harvey's files, I saw that in the past medications had been thrown at him but, not surprisingly, to no avail. As far as I could ascertain, apart from his ideas of reference, he had no auditory or visual hallucinations and no compelling mood symptoms, so it was rather unclear what the medications would have been targeting.

In my next several meetings with Harvey, I tried to engage him in some reality testing. I asked him if he'd ever met anyone else who worked as a secret agent for the Royal Academy of Meteorology. I asked him how he had acquired his special powers for manipulating the weather.

He told me that his father had been a top agent for the Academy. He told me that his father had single-handedly prevented a major hurricane off the Gulf of Mexico meant to knock out an entire mango crop. That, Harvey explained to me, was why the 49 Quantum Fathers had abducted his father many years ago, stashed him away in a parallel world.

I chose not to pursue the father issue further.

I did make a few other efforts to gently instill in Harvey some creative doubt in the internal perceptions of his world—such doubt being the usual cornerstone of delusional treatment and the path back to the consensus view of reality. But I failed. My failure did not hugely surprise me. Reality testing is notoriously unsuccessful for schizotypals, and if taken too far—and too far is not that far—it will serve only to isolate the patient further and deepen his conviction that he alone understands reality. Then a downward spiral begins.

The day immediately following my fifth session with Harvey, he again went missing. Nine days later he turned up in a hospital in Omaha. There had been hailstorms.

b. An initial deception

I should explain about the lying.

It was Rema who suggested that I lie to Harvey. I did not come up with that idea by myself. "That you lie como una terapia," she emphasized. "You lie, but it is to benefit another. So it is a lie that is ethical. Isn't that fine? Didn't you tell me they used to hold the heads of disturbed patients underwater for the time it took to recite the Miserere? This treatment would be much nicer than that, this small lie carrying good intentions."

Rema began then, completely impromptu (and this is a perfect example of the kind of Rema-ness absent in her impostress), to propose and elaborate upon a scheme wherein I was to pretend that I—like Harvey—was a secret agent of the actually existent Royal Academy of Meteorology. But that I—unlike Harvey—was an agent of *superior* rank. Who was in touch with an agent of even more superior rank. "Psychotics very much respect ranking," she announced authoritatively.

"Yes, so does Harvey's mother," I added, not meaning to sound encouraging.

Rema paused and then added: "I'll call. I'll call to your office and you respond the phone and you listen very seriously and pass on the instructions that you will supposedly be receiving from a senior-ranking meteorologist. From me." Rema particularly liked that detail, of her being the senior-ranking meteorologist.

The instructions, primarily, would be that Harvey "labor atmospherically" at locations very close to his home. On street corners. In the park. Handling very important mesoscale phenomena in the greater New York City environs.

I remember, strangely, that Rema was eating kumquats as she explained this plan to me. The kumquats still had leaves on them, which made the orange especially vibrant. And within me, as I listened to Rema inventing, as I watched her thinking through an elaborate lie, an alarm was sounding. But all my life, so many alarms seem always to be sounding, and so it becomes near impossible ever to say what any particular alarm might be signaling, or what might have set it off, or if it in any way ought to be heeded. The alarm then could as likely have signaled simply the color of the kumquat—some perhaps atavistic and now obsolete warning of poison—as something more grave.

"Not only is it unethical," I said to Rema, "but your idea won't even work. Why should it? And if Harvey discovers the lie—well, then it's all over. The therapeutic relationship: over." And possibly my career as well, I didn't say.

We went back and forth on this for a good while, my doubts about the plan serving only to energize Rema more.

"Let's imagine for a moment that it is ethical," I said to her, as if in reconciliation. "And let's even imagine for a moment that this 'therapy' does work. There'd still always loom the possibility of being discovered, of being revealed as a liar. I wouldn't be able to go a day without worrying. I can't live like that."

"Oh," Rema answered with a small unimpressed shrug, "but that's what life is like all the time, no?"

Rema often made these broad, melodramatic declarations that seemed oddly heartfelt and sincere considering that they didn't mean anything. She was always nervous, though, that was true. She'd accordion-fold any scrap of paper that happened to be in her hand for more than a minute; at movie theaters she had often already decoratively torn her ticket before reaching the front of the line. Occasionally, though, her anxiety bordered on psychosis. For example, once in response to an essay of mine on pathological mourning, I received a threatening letter. It suggested that I didn't know what real loss was and that he, the letter writer, could teach me. Okay, it was worded more strongly than that, I admit, but it also evidenced such disorganized thought that it was foolish to believe such a person could actually set in motion a plan to cause harm. So there was nothing to fear. I brought the letter home to our apartment to show Rema mostly because of the inexplicable—and oddly beautiful—illustrations. There was no return address, but I thought it might be a kind of romantic mission to try to track down my correspondent. I imagined I might find a Henry Darger character on the other end. But Rema said that if the letter didn't worry me I should be locked up in an asylum. She began looking into our moving apartments. This even though (1) the letter had been mailed to the journal and not to me directly, (2) our address was unlisted, and (3) only a handful of people knew where we lived. Still, Rema was on the phone with brokers. I decided not to recite what I considered comforting statistics on how often, and which kind of, written threats are actually executed. But I did tell Rema that her response was ludicrously out of proportion. She must *actually* be worried about something *else*, I said. She had an endogenous mésalliance, I concluded. She said she didn't know what a mésalliance was, or what endogenous was, and that I was arrogant, awful, a few other things as well. I liked those accusations and found them flattering and thought she was right. Rema cried and hardly spoke to me for a few days. In bed at night she trembled.

But: it's curious that she could so easily imagine a catastrophe separating us. That did, after all, happen.

And yet she was completely comfortable with the risks, professional and personal, of lying to a patient.

"Nope. No. Definitely not. No on the lying," I said.

"Your choice of failures," she said. "In my neighborhood we had a name for people like you: parsley."

In the end—obviously—I decided to lie. Rema brightened considerably after that decision, and we had a sweet space of time, like the Medieval Warm Period, when wine grapes could grow three hundred miles farther north than they do today. Did I think then of the schemes that we would thus be swept into? No. I thought only of Rema.

c. An initial appearance

After I agreed to the plan, Rema suggested that I find the name of an actual scientist at the Academy, just in case Harvey looked up my superior's name or was already familiar with the members. I, she said, would have to emphasize that I was, like Harvey, a *secret*, and therefore unlisted, agent.

"Right," I said. "So no need to involve someone's real name, if we're talking about secret agents."

"The real is good for deception," she insisted.

And so.

Following Rema's advice I obtained a list of the fellows of the Royal Academy. I chose the name Tzvi Gal-Chen capriciously, or so I thought. It just seemed like an anomalous and gentle sort of name, somehow authoritative and innocent at once. I almost chose the name Kelvin Droegemeier. That name also had charm and a kind of diffident beauty. But in the end I settled on Tzvi, because I remembered that degrees Kelvin was a temperature scale, which made Kelvin Droegemeier's name, even though it was a real name, seem fancifully invented.

d. Initial anxiety (my mésalliance)

The night before I tried Rema's ruse on Harvey I had several straightforward dreams. In one I was unable to make a teakettle stop whistling, in another Harvey was a homing pigeon in a dovecote (though I'm not actually sure what a dovecote is, in the dream I did know), in a third I was wearing yellow pants that looked terrible on me, and in the last I was simply walking down a street— I was seeing myself from above, as if from a building's fire escape—and I knew that everyone hated me.

I woke inhaling the grassy scent of Rema's hair. I put a lock of it in my mouth. I tried to comfort myself: Rema and I had prepared a script of sorts together, rehearsed some canned answers, scheduled a phone call. Also I had on my side the awkward flightless-bird beauty of that name, Tzvi Gal-Chen. Just, I reassured myself, because I was capable of imagining Harvey standing on his chair and calling out *J'accuse*, this did not in any way actually increase the likelihood of such an event occurring. Pressing that salivaed lock against my cheek I told myself that if I failed with Harvey, then so I failed. He couldn't really get me into any trouble. If he accused me of posing as a secret agent for the Royal Academy, well, that would just sound like more of the same from him and I'd just deny the allegation. I decided that although I fancied myself afraid of failing with Harvey, my *real* fear of failure likely had to do with my cornsilk Rema. The whole Tzvi Gal-Chen therapy: it was Rema's, not my own, strangely translated dream, and yet I'd some-, how taken it upon myself to realize it.

I got out of bed (while Rema slept on) specifically because I felt within me an overwhelming desire to stay in bed.

"You're going to break some legs," Rema said to me later that morning, sitting across from me at the kitchen table with her hair, I remember, up in a tidy high ponytail; it struck me anew that I'd once thought that after enough time with me she would have put on a precious little potbelly and let her hair remain messy at home. I didn't think she'd be like my own mother, always so consciously assembled, as if still petitioning for the attention of other, unseen, imaginarily present men.

"You know you're saying it wrong, right? I don't like it when you try to be cute on purpose."

"I don't try to be cute."

"Rema, I have a very bad feeling."

Bad feeling *about this* I should have said. Or at least I *think* that would have been more properly idiomatic than just saying "bad feeling." But the little idiosyncrasies of Rema's language had already thoroughly sunk into me, and I couldn't hear so clearly anymore the space between what was Rema and what was normal.

Rema looked away from me and stared into the tea mug she held. "You ate meat too late. Lamb after eleven. That is the bad feeling. That is all. You should respect my ideas. You should respect your wife."

That is all *it is*. I remember wanting to correct her, to tell her to add *it is*. Wouldn't that have been closer to what she meant? I watched her touch her finger to the surface of her tea and then put her finger to her mouth and then suck on it, as if she had a cut there. She did this again, this very slow way of drinking that she had. (The simulacrum, she drinks like she's parched, like someone might take her drink away. Some mornings she's through her first mug of tea in three minutes, though I'll often find a second one left half drunk, grown cold.)

I did respect Rema, obviously I do. Though I know that she didn't believe or understand that, which I thought had more to do with her own self-doubt about who she was, or what she was doing, or not doing. She didn't have what one would call a "profession," but I didn't know why she particularly wanted one; it seemed like she'd been infected by a very American idea of identity, to think that who you were mostly consisted of what you did to get paid—that seemed silly to me. If I looked like Rema, if I had her ways, and if I weren't a man, I'd consider it profession enough to have streaky bleached hair, to wear a green scarf, to spill spicy teas, to walk (slightly) unevenly on high heels. What more is there to give to the world than that? I realize this sentiment of mine is currently considered appalling, but these days I find the popularity of ideas even more meaningless than ever before. I had told Rema once, when she complained of feeling aimless and amiss, that she was born in the wrong era and that she should consider just waking up every morning and *being her* profession enough. I told her she could be my duchess. She may have contemplated taking what I had said as sweet, but in the end chose instead—and I think "chose" is the right word—to be offended, because then she came out saying that maybe her problem was that she had been too happy to marry me, and that *that* had been good enough for too long, and maybe if she'd stayed lonely she might have made something of herself, even if something really dumb and superfluous, like a tax attorney, or a poet, and that would have been nice, to be able to say what one was. I said she was a Rema. I said, furthermore, that I didn't really understand what obstacle I posed to either of her mentioned goals, but she just said yes, I *didn't* understand, and I said that that was what I was saying precisely, that I *didn't understand*. But she was saying that it was that I didn't understand *her*.

So it was like that sometimes.

But about Rema's lamb after eleven comment. Although I didn't think she was right in that particular instance of my "bad feeling" before meeting with Harvey, I thought that her general idea—how we can misinterpret our own pain—I thought that was very right.

e. An initial (Pyrrhic) victory

You really look closely at a person before lying, or confessing love, or doing anything momentous. It is above all Harvey's outfit from that day that I remember well: navy blue suspenders hooked onto gray trousers (lightly pilling), a thin-striped button-up shirt (cuffs unbuttoned) with a dark ink stain like Argentina at the left floating rib and with sleeves too short and a collar strangely starched and flipped and seeming poised for flight. I don't know if Harvey actually had one arm notably longer than the other, but he gave off that impression.

Rema and I had planned on having her call near the end of Harvey's session. I was to have already introduced the fact of myself as a secret agent of the Royal Academy. I had failed to do so. I felt too conspicuous, as if I was as exhaustively vivid for Harvey as he was for me that day (his eyes are so improbably blue) and this even though I knew that in truth it was highly doubtful that there was anything remarkable about my appearance at all; that day, like all the previous days, I must have seemed to Harvey simply an unremarkable gray haze of overly gentle inquiry.

My feeling of conspicuousness—I'm certain—stemmed from an awareness that a ridiculous lie lay in wait within me; I'm not a natural liar, so I had very little faith in my competence as one. I don't mean to be smug by proclaiming my inherent honesty;

I don't think of my honesty as moral value, since I think of morality as involving choices, and I've never particularly *chosen* to be honest, have simply never been able to be otherwise, feel rather predetermined to fail at lying. Even as a child, in order to avoid saying thank you, upon prompting, for things I wasn't truly thankful for, I would bury my face in my mother's skirt. A smell of certain wools, the sound of a slip brushing up against hosiery, still recalls that emotion back to me. On the rare occasions when I have said I am busy when I am not, or that I like some item of clothing or person that I am indifferent to or hate, I am filled with unreasonable guilt over my "white" lie, and want to cry, confess, unburden. It's all a bit overblown, really, as if I've actually wounded someone, as if my small insincerity might actually matter. I even kind of like it when other people lie, when Rema lies, for example; it's a way of finding out, if the lie is uncovered, what she thinks is worth lying about.

So Harvey was saying something about El Niño, and dead fish.

Then the telephone rang, startling me far more than it startled Harvey.

"Hello?"

It was Rema, who, sounding inappropriately giddy, called me Dr. Liebenstein and asked me what I was wearing.

"Oh yes hello," I said, staring at the lines at Harvey's cuff, watching them blur.

Rema chatted comfortably about what she wanted me to pick up for dinner, urging me not to be cheap about the fish—everyone with the fish—asking me also could I pick up the thin almond cookies that she liked, the ones she liked to dip in her tea, did I know which ones she meant? Through all this I nodded sagely.

"And these El Niño winds?" I asked.

She talked on, saying I'm not sure what in her beautiful mint-pitched voice; eventually she suggested that she get off the phone. I said that of course I would pass everything on faithfully.

"Well," I throat-cleared to Harvey, "I apologize for that interruption, but I can now say something rather important to you. Are you familiar with the work, the public work that is, of Dr. Tzvi Gal-Chen?"

Preplanned words exited my mouth hastily, stumblingly, and I heard them as if they were not my own. Blushingly confessing myself a secret agent, I passed on to Harvey Dr. Gal-Chen's assignment—a cold front approaching Manhattan. And as I spoke—my gaze fixed on the stain on Harvey's shirt—I further estranged myself from myself, so that while one part of me talked to Harvey, another part thought about a certain shade of pale green that happened to be the exact shade of pale green that the newspaper once published as having been calculated by astronomers to be the color of the universe, after which a correction appeared in the following week's paper stating that a math error had been made, and that the astronomers now realized the universe, if you could stand outside of it and see it, was actually a shade of beige. (Willed depersonalization is entirely normal, a valid, even laudable, coping technique. Only unwilled depersonalizations would be a cause for concern.)

After I stopped talking there was a brief or long—I'm not sure which—moment of silence.

"How long have you been working for the Academy?" Harvey asked.

I told him that there were very few details of my work that I was allowed to disclose.

He asked me if I could tell him if I'd received any awards, in particular the Symons Gold Medal or the Carl-Gustav Rossby Medal.

I said it was lonely having secrets and that Harvey probably understood that loneliness.

Then Harvey smiled shyly, and talked a few minutes, in a comradely way, of the difficulty and delicacy of meteorological work. It's never ceased to amaze me how, if you're calm and quiet, others fill in any gaps in your story. Harvey pulled out his compact mirror and smoothed down his eyebrows, and then began to explain something about this instrument of his, which he used, he said, to alter vectors of light and sound.

I noticed spidering burst capillaries across his cheeks. I remember well the dejected feeling of having, apparently, succeeded. I wanted to reach across to Harvey and just touch one of his sleeves. I don't know why, not precisely. Even a well-intentioned deception leaves a metallic taste in the mouth.

Did I think I'd ever partner with Harvey in order to find Rema, rather than partner with Rema in order to control and deceive Harvey? I did not.

f. An unusual initiation of a kind of friendship with Tzvi Gal-Chen

Relaying Dr. Gal-Chen's instructions to Harvey became easy, ordinary, domestic. The phone would ring, Rema would often recite a grocery list, and I would tell Harvey that Dr. Gal-Chen says high-pressure systems are coming in from the north and Harvey's assistance is needed locally.

And following the initiation of the Gal-Chen therapy, for the next nineteen months, Harvey didn't go missing even once. He followed strictly Tzvi Gal-Chen's orders to stay for work in the city. He deregulated tidal winds off the Hudson River estuary; he finely negotiated the chaos of an incoming tropical storm system from the corner of his own street. As for me, Harvey's mother regularly sent me grids of artisanal chocolates, each chocolate with its own transfer textile type pattern atop—and, well, this made me feel good about myself.

Rema also was very pleased—probably more pleased than me—with the success of the Tzvi Gal-Chen therapy. At least in the beginning, at least for a little while. She took to calling herself Dr. Rema, and she often held my hand and pressed the back of it against her cheek. Once, when the weather report interrupted the news, she squeezed my arm and leaned over and kissed me and laughed. She was the kind of happy that made me feel that she would love me, and me alone, forever. But maybe it was just that successful deceptions made her euphoric. "Why," I asked her one evening, "did you say the corner store was out of clementines when in fact it wasn't?" In response, she eyed me suspiciously. "I found the receipt for that blue sweater you bought me," I said, "and you understated its price by eighty dollars." She ignored me, remained unaffected in her bout of cheer. It was nice, though; contrary to my nature as it was, happiness grew in me.

Gal-Chen therapy language made its way into our apartment, first teasingly, but after a while who could say? When Rema and I disagreed, I'd invoke our meteorologist: "Dr. Gal-Chen prefers the green wool," "Dr. Gal-Chen says no to imitation Nilla Wafers." Or sometimes, more intimately: "Tzvi wouldn't be pleased about your not wearing socks," "Tzvi thinks you should return the movie," or "Tzvi thinks you should plump a little." Rema may have tired of this, but, after all, the specter of Tzvi had entered into our lives on account of her therapeutic invention, not mine. I thought of Tzvi as a stranger, certainly, but one whom I felt in some way shared our life, as if he returned to the apartment late, after Rema and I were asleep, and snacked on leftovers from the refrigerator, watched the television with the volume down low, left tea mugs in the sink.

One free afternoon, I came across a photo on the Internet of Dr. Gal-Chen with his family; I e-mailed it to Rema. She printed it on a color printer at the hospital, brought it home carefully tucked inside an empty patient folder, and then magneted it onto our refrigerator.

"That was nice of you," I said.

"Oh, I just did it for myself," she responded, maybe a tiny bit irritated.

I recall, at the time, having had certain interpretations of this action, this posting of a family photo on the refrigerator. But in retrospect, with all that has since happened, those interpretations now seem too simple. I admit that I had rather unsophisticatedly read the photo in our home as symptomatic of a longing for children, though I wasn't certain if the longing was Rema's or my own. Or if really the longing was just for a return to Rema's own unremarked-upon childhood, or to an alternate of her own childhood. Or maybe the longing was for something else, for someone else. But whatever that photo was, I don't care, it doesn't really matter, it was also, and above all, just an amusing photo to look at when one went, from hunger, to let the yellow light and cold out of the refrigerator.

The butterfly collar and tinted glasses on Tzvi, the eyeleted cap sleeve with trim on his wife, that stolid Izod polo on the son— it was pleasing to travel back in time like that, falling through those mode details. And that little Bavarian mock-up on that tidy little chub of a child, well, that was just precious. "Why do you only notice clothing?" Rema asked, as if pointing to a moral flaw.

But when I pushed her as to what she noticed, she could only point out the creamy crooks of the elbows on the mother and son. Sometimes I wondered at the necklace on the wife, other times at the inscrutable pale blue square on the shirt of Tzvi Gal-Chen. And once Rema and I had a long argument about whether Dr. Gal-Chen's shirt showed a button or a snap. I argued snap quite heatedly, on the basis of context. She argued button on the basis of visual details that I apparently couldn't see. But look at the way the light catches on that snap—it's pearline.

It was strange, now that I think about it, how I never tired of that photo.

Even though I know better than to trust appearances, especially posed, studio-airbrushed, heathered-backdrop appearances, still: the Gal-Chens had the look of a *happy family*. Maybe not particularly sophisticated, or good-looking, or fashionable, but still, happy. Even now I do not know if that was, or is, true or not. If they were, indeed, happy. But who can ever really know about anyone's happiness, even one's own? And if another woman can have the appearance of Rema, then perhaps I should by now be giving up on appearances entirely. But with that photo it was more than just an appearance, it was also a feeling, a *family feeling*. A feeling that at least seemed to be responding to something beyond mere appearance, though at times such "feelings"—such limbic system instinctual responses—are the most superficial and anachronistic of all, like the feeling a baby duck must have when it responds more strongly to a stick painted red than to the beak of its own mother.

4. A mysterious knuckle

So that was the state of affairs with Harvey—he was again missing—but I did not immediately connect his most recent disappearance (or Tzvi Gal-Chen) with Rema's replacement, even though I had (as if a part of me knew something another part did not) immediately expected to find Harvey when I was paged shortly after the simulacrum had fallen asleep. When I returned from the hospital where Harvey wasn't to the apartment where Rema wasn't, I put Rema's pale blue shoulder bag underneath the sink, for safekeeping. It was 5 a.m. and my new houseguest was not yet awake. She was hidden beneath Rema's ugly old yellow quilt, with only one indefinite tan arm and a few tickles of blonde hair showing. I pulled the quilt back a bit; she didn't stir.

It was a little uncanny, the feeling I had, looking at that lookalike. I was reminded of how I used to feel before I actually knew Rema, reminded of the winter when she was still a stranger and I would notice her, nightly, coming to the Hungarian Pastry Shop, wearing nubbly red mittens and her same wool coat with oversized buttons. She always ordered the loose-leaf teas, and when she would sit at a table near mine I liked to watch her try to pour from the little metal teapot without spilling, which wasn't easy, since at almost any angle the water's path of choice was to travel retrograde along the outside of the spout and spill on the table. Rema would then pat the table dry with her napkin and then get up and get more napkins, and this was every time, as if she couldn't have anticipated and stocked up on extra napkins from the beginning. This—and her cornsilk hair, and her slightly clumsy gait, and I don't know what—I loved her already then.

Leaving the sleeping simulacrum to herself I lay myself down on the sofa, experiencing the unhappy déjà vu of having lain myself down in just the same way not so many hours earlier, expecting Rema's imminent arrival. I tried to rest. But although the phone did not ring—it was always ringing of late—intrusive thoughts, rising as if carbonated, disturbed me from sleep:

- a movie dimly recalled from childhood, with a blind samurai who can't see that the man pursuing him is his double
- John Donne meeting his wife's doppelganger in Paris, and this portending his baby's death
- Maupassant seeing his own doppelganger, and it portending his own death
- Rema asleep on my shoulder at the movies
- a guff of ugly laughter

This is just a problem I'm trying to depersonalize, I told myself. Probably just some very normal problem dressed up as a strange one. An ordinary problem masquerading as extraordinary. My mother used to say that almost any problem could be solved by one of the following three solutions: a warm bath, a hot drink, or what she called "going to the bathroom," though she never specified what was to be done there. I was thinking now how I can't really recall any episode from my childhood when her advice didn't work. Our bathtub was in the middle of our kitchen, and the bathroom was a thin-walled room just on the other side of the kitchen sink; both rooms had the same houndstooth hand-layed tile floor, and one always heard water coursing through pipes, or braking, or boiling.

The sound of something like Rema walking by woke me from what couldn't have been much more than an hour of sleep, but an awkward hour, from which I woke—starbursting pain—with a numb and tingly left hand. After again catching sight of the decidedly not Rema's face, and during the achingly familiar sock-footing about in the kitchen that followed, I decided that I couldn't just wait around feigning normality; I had to go and search for the real Rema. And though I didn't know quite what that meant— would I don a cap, grab a magnifying glass, and go dusting for fingerprints?—I knew it was the proper next step to take.

Over red zinger tea with honey, I told the ersatz Rema of my plans. Or, at least, I mentioned to her that I thought I'd spend the day—which I could see out the window was another very gray, precipitous day—out walking.

"A walk sounds nice," she responded expectantly, looking across the table at me with her dove dark eyes. "That sounds," she continued, "like exactly what would please me. You and me and the gentle dog and we'll—"

"I'd rather walk alone," I braved.

"Oh." The dog lover frowned. The red zinger had stained her lips a pretty pink. "I only offered to join you to be kind. But really the weather is ugly. What does the weatherman call this? Wintry mix? That makes it sound like dried cherries and coconut and pecans. But actually it is not so nice like that at all."

As she spoke I was staring at her hands, both wrapped around her tea mug, staring at the little elephant-knee patterns of lines at the finger joints. I could see the divot in the knucklebone, the grooves that reveal the finger as but a line-and-pulley system. The longer I stared at that knuckle the more it grew foreign rather than familiar. Pretty hands. Pretty knuckles. Pretty little way of holding a tea mug.

"Wintry mix," I finally said, slowly, copying the woman's copied language. My tea had meanwhile grown cold. When red zinger gets cold it tastes too full of tannins and makes me more rather than less thirsty. "That is kind of a euphemism, isn't it?" I agreed, trying to sound chummy and casual. But I couldn't make eye contact with the impostress. It was as if, by not admitting that I planned to go out in search of Rema, I was cheating on her, on this alternate Rema.

"Where," I tried, "is the puppy?"

"Bedroom," she said. "You were sleeping." And she got up from the table not aglow with happiness, not placated at all, in fact perhaps rather irritated. "And she's not a puppy. She's a dog. She's an adult. In a new and stressful situation and so especially in need of love and attention," she concluded, beginning to walk away from me.

"Why did you bring her home?" I called out with a desperation I didn't expect.

"Why did you not bring her home?" she said. "Why do you not do anything at all?" she continued, not looking at me, and almost out of the room.

She was wearing Rema's green nightie boxers. Her legs were pretty, a faintest blue. And also they were long, with one hip ever so slightly rotated inward. Like Rema. I was proud of myself for having had the strength of character to leave behind such an attractive woman. I wish Rema could have witnessed that. I just would have liked her to enjoy the spectacle of how obviously and entirely and singularly I loved her.

5. An initial search

How did I search the city for Rema? I found myself standing in front of the Hungarian Pastry Shop, in front of its fogged windows into which no child had yet traced patterns. Below the windows: the pastel mural of slightly deformed angels. To the left: stacked white plastic chairs. To the right: a man descending into the sidewalk cellar holding a tray of uncooked dumplings, the wrappings pinched and pointing to the sky. And, still standing outside, reflected in the glass, was—and for a moment I didn't recognize him—me: hairy handed and slope shouldered and not as tall as I like to think I am. With a rising sense of ridiculousness, the thought surfaced: this is how I search for my wife? This was probably the one place she almost certainly would *not* turn up. Like the most gumshoe of all gumshoes, I'd gone where I wanted her to be, not where there was any reason or unreason for me to believe she actually would be.

I went inside anyway—it was warm and humid, like a room for leavening. Near the pastry display case, a young boy was patting at the pocket of his mother's (I assume his mother's) coat shouting *biscotto! biscotto!* A skinny vulture of a man—he had terrible eyebrows—watched from the table; he was a regular who typed pompously, and flirted with the waitstaff, and I'd once overheard him say he was into meditation, and I thought of him like a disease. A little farther back I saw the crowd I thought of as "the dirty kids": two messy girls who seemed always to have just left a medieval fair—eternally in old velvet or silk or lace—and a young man, with unwashed hair and a small cartoon bear nose, who perpetually wore a shapeless too-short leather jacket. He looked sad that day; the girls were consoling him. Also I saw a pretty wavy-haired undergrad with her thin arms bare. A little boy was crawling under her table and he picked up and turned over a pale green scrap of paper.

Sometimes it terrifies me, when I sense the exponenting mass of human lives—of unlabeled evidence of mysteries undiscerned—about which I know nothing.

"What did you say?" someone said maybe to me.

"Nothing," I said to almost no one.

Having pined for Rema in the past in this very place (her tea's leaves would stack up in the sieve and look like topiary) I felt my new loneliness echo against the anxiety I used to have watching the door wondering if Rema would walk in, and that feeling was then echoing against the haunting vision I used to have of Rema's cornsilk hair, which was echoing against the memory of that first day I saw Rema see me notice that she had looked at me after which she had then quickly looked away, all of which echoed against a sensation of her kissing my eyelid, which made me shiver.

It was very bad, the acoustics inside of me.

I wanted, suddenly, to leave.

I ordered a coffee to go—a terrible coffee that pleases only for bearing the name coffee and for being hot. I walked over to Broadway, went underground, boarded the number 1 train heading downtown. Each time new passengers came on, I watched expectantly. Near the bottom of the island, I exited, ascended, crossed the street, redescended, waited, and reboarded the subway going uptown. At the third stop, a man entered the subway car and announced loudly: "I had already apologized, for those of you who did not know." Then he said those same words again, and again, and again, so I realized he wasn't speaking to me, at least not in particular. But I anyway couldn't help but feel that what the man really meant was that *I* should be sorry, that *I* should apologize. Maybe everyone on the train felt as I did, that they were the point of all this, of everything. It was like when the music comes on at the Chinese restaurant and suddenly even the random movements of the fish in the aquarium seem choreographed, thick with meaning; then the music pauses and meaning abruptly disperses. The fish seem dumb, as do all the diners.

At the 110th Street stop I exited and began a repeat of the whole cycle. Later I did sit for a few hours at the coffee shop, made some drawings of sugar cubes, and of an upside-down cup, and of the pattern that a small coffee spill made when it was soaked up by a napkin, a pattern like an archipelago.

Though my initial progress did not look or feel like progress, I believe it was a kind of progress, that of just staying in place, of not slipping backward into despair.

6. An alleged orphan

Walking, finally, home, I comforted myself with the likelihood that I would very soon see Rema, that she—the selfsame girl I'd picked up at the coffee shop years before—would be right there at home, russet dog or no russet dog. Maybe she would be shelling pecans. Or reading the newspaper. Maybe she would be very happy to see me.

I put my key to the lock, I heard scratching at the door, I opened the door and I found myself being lavished with affection, from the russet dog. Then the dog undid my left shoelace. I heard a voice coming from the bedroom and I heard a hanging up of a telephone. Meanwhile this dog still had my shoelace between its teeth and was shaking its head back and forth madly, behavior that may appear playful but that is quite clearly a manifestation of the instinct to break the neck of caught prey, a manifestation that we refer to as cute. It's just like how we have so successfully forgotten as a species that a smile was born as a masking afterthought to the sudden baring of teeth. At least that's the most convincing smile theory I've heard.

Then the woman emerged from the bedroom. I smiled. She was the same. The same false vision of Rema from before.

"The dog makes you happy?" substitute Rema asked, and what could I answer except no. The dog then left me (left my shoelace) for her; she picked that dog up in her arms, snuggled the dog with oversized gestures, as if performing onstage. She told me she didn't care what I thought about what to name the dog, that she was going to name her without me. I said I didn't care what she named the dog, the dog that was licking her face with dedication.

"But I got this dog," she said to me, "for you."

The dog had dark, wet eyes; the woman's eyes were similar. Then I noticed that she—the simulacrum—had fine lines of age on her face. Tiny crow's-feet, and not just when she smiled, since I could see them and she was not smiling. This look-alike Rema, I began to realize, was not such a perfect look-alike; it would seem Rema was being played by someone older, or who at least looked older. Someone pretty, but not as pretty. Not that there's anything wrong with an older woman—there is nothing wrong with a woman my age for example, I just don't happen to be married to one.

"You said dogs are brilliant," she said, her voice supersaturated with emotion. "You said Freud's dogs could diagnose the patients."

But Rema knew Freud was essentially demoted (in a few specific passages promoted) out of my notion of an ideal psychiatry. As the impostress talked on I wondered: was Rema kidnapped or did she willingly leave? Which would be worse? Determined not to let emotion crack my voice, I tried to avoid speaking altogether. The simulacrum, fortunately, seemed to have the same talent as Rema for filling up silent spaces, and she went on: "You said Freud's dogs knew when therapy was over, and knew who was psychotic and who was neurotic, and that when memories were recovered the dog would wag its tail. You said you would have liked to have such insight, such dog insight, that it would be better than your own, and so there I was at the hospital, and this poor dog was left orphan, and it seemed like a sign, like not just random, like this dog was sent to us, for us to save her and for her to save us, silly I know, but no, you just look at me strange." The russet puppy— I mean, dog—was licking tears from the doppelganger's face.

"But Freud's dogs," I said, "they were chow dogs."

It was all I could think of to say. I turned away from this woman and went to the bathroom, where I ran hot water over my hands, which is something I like to do in the colder months, it just makes me feel a little bit better. Then I touched my face with my warmed hands. It calms me down, it's just this very normal thing that I do.

Over the sound of the running water I could hear that Rema-like voice calling through the door. She didn't sound pleased. I was thinking, *Does Rema know this twin of hers? Did Rema complain about me to her?* There were difficult aspects of Rema, I can't deny that—a lot of this arguing through a bathroom door had been going on of late.

The Rema-ish voice came though the door with something about being tired of it always being her getting stuck with the label of unreasonable, irrational, crazy. I thought to shout back that of course it was her getting stuck with that label, and that furthermore I'd only ever said irrational and unreasonable, never crazy, and that it was she alone who was assigning normative value to those labels and, listen, she couldn't even let a man just wash his hands in peace, but I stopped myself, instead said nothing, thinking to myself: *This fight is stupid. This fight is ridiculous. And to have it with a woman I don't even know—that is even more ridiculous.*

Older, wrong, and no more manageable, this replacement wife. I heard the front door open and close.

7. I am contacted

After finishing my private peace of running hot water in the bathroom I came out to find that the simulacrum and the unnamed dog were not in the kitchen, not in the living room, not in the bedroom—they were gone. Which meant, I decided, that I could think and plan in quiet, which I proceeded to do in a prone position on the sofa, which meant that I was promptly asleep but without knowing that I was asleep, a fact that I did not discover until the phone roused me from my poor and hectic slumber during which I'd suffered a dream in which what was happening to me was exactly what was actually happening to me. Because I woke up with a sense of relief, I had the clawing hope that Rema's replacement had been not also but only in my dream, a bad dream induced simply by indigestion, or a cold draft, or a foot cramp. That was the stage of loss I was in then I suppose, like the first days after someone dies, when you bend down to pick up every piece of lint, and you wonder what the dead person, when you meet her next, might have to say about her death (or about lint), and you worry, a little bit, about how that is going to be a very awkward conversation, the conversation with the recently dead.

Again the phone rang.

"Hello," I said, bringing the cold plastic receiver to my face.

"Leo Liebenstein."

"Yes," I said, not even rising from my reclining position because I didn't want to lose the warmth I'd invested in the cushions of the sofa.

"Leo Lieben—"

"Yes," I interrupted sleepily but louder.

"To whom am I speaking?" the voice on the other end said politely, in a strange accent. Or what seemed like a poor imitation of a strange accent.

And I began to feel more awake. "Who is this?" I asked.

Muffled bickering came through the line; then it sounded like the phone dropped. Just as I was about to hang up, a new voice came on, this time thin, sandy, and ambitious.

"I'm calling from the Royal Academy of Meteorology; we'd like to invite you to become a fellow. Would you—"

"Harvey?"

"Sir, I'm calling from the Royal Aca—" Again I heard a tussle over the phone. Then I heard Rema's voice, though I couldn't make out the words. I thought the voice was coming to me through the phone.

"Rema?" I called into the phone loudly, startling myself.

"The teakettle!" answered Rema's voice—now clearly traveling directly from the bedroom—and I could feel the hot atmosphere my own voice had made near the phone's mouthpiece.

"We'd like to make you a fellow," I heard. "Do you understand? It's a tremendous—"

I hung up.

I looked around the room: rocking chair, scratched wood floor, *Godzilla* poster—my familiar life. And Rema? I crossed over to the closed bedroom door, leaned against its unsmooth grain, and listened. I heard just that sound of cupping a hand over an ear. Of a distant ocean marked with a yellow flag, of my own ear anatomy breaking up the trajectories of randomly moving molecules of air, hearing its own little self-made sound universe. And suddenly I sensed my ridiculousness—pressing a cupped ear against a door in my own apartment—sensed, with a rising sadness, my familiar space growing foreign to me.

I abandoned the sounds of my ear cupped to the bedroom door. I went to the kitchen, turned the click-clicker of the gas stovetop—blue-orange burst!—filled the kettle with tap water—a nice contact sound!—and rested it on the flame. I love the different sound stages of water on its way to boiling. I like listening to the teakettle's tremble. Our teakettle's handle is slightly loose, and its shaking adds another harmonic layer over the tremulousness of the metal.

"Who was that?" came the voice.

I turned and saw her, under the kitchen's lintel, wearing my button-up and her little boy shorts, thigh slightly rotated inward, holding that russet puppy—dog—in one hand. She walked past me, leaned against the counter near the stove; Rema had always liked leaning there, in just that way, so she could feel the heat, and so she could turn off the flame before the teakettle's whistling had ever really begun. Maybe on account of that lean, despite that dog-puppy, I began silently to argue to myself: this must be Rema. This must be her. Believe this Rema like you always do. Look at her. Is she really more strange today than any other day? The hair, the eyes, the long legs leading down to slightly pigeon-toed feet. Who else could it be? Believe this Rema like you always do.

But I knew that my reasoning was post hoc, and another voice came in, mocking me, reminding me that post hoc reasoning is the consolation of the psychotic—all evidence interpreted under the shadow of an axiomatic belief that one is Jesus Christ, or the king of Sweden, or made entirely of glass.

Why should I believe, just by fiat, that this woman was Rema, when that ran contrary to the phenomenology?

The simulacrum tilted her head at me, like puppies tilt their heads.

And a high-pitched pain, like a thousand tiny moths, began to collect behind the front of my skull, accelerating, advancing. Something was wrong. I reached out and put my hand on where I expected her abdomen to be, because I had a feeling my hand might pass right through her, as if she were a hologram, as if only the clothing were real. But I was all wrong about what was wrong. My hand did not go through her abdomen, which was real, or appeared to be so, as solid, anyway, as anything else I know, though I suppose they say it's almost all empty space, the building blocks of matter—a moth in a cathedral?—but one shouldn't take the extension of such metaphors too seriously.

She looked at my hand on her abdomen. Then she squinted at me, as if to put me in focus.

"Wait, who was that on the phone?" she asked again.

The pain in my head had grown dizzying so I sat down on the cool blue tile floor, sat by that woman's foot, and looked at the blue vein there across her arch. For a time during my medical training, on account of so often drawing blood and placing IVs, my eyes would travel, of their own accord, to plump veins. I would search feet and hands and wrists and crooks of elbows, and it would be difficult for me not to reach out and place the pad of a finger on those veins and feel the blood coursing through. It's like a ghost living in us, our blood, that's what I think it is like, having something within us—like our blood, like our livers, like our loves—that goes on about its business without consulting us. I touched that vein there on Rema's foot. I feel like I can say that, that the foot at least, that foot was really Rema's. Or probably not really. Or so only in that every foot becomes, in my mind, Rema's foot slightly varied. And Rema's foot is like Rema entire; her foot alone is enough to recall her to me whole. I don't know, I was very confused then.

"Leo," this woman said to me gently. "Leo, are you all right? I'm sorry I was angry earlier, I didn't mean to hurt your feelings about Harvey's leaving. I think that is what this must be about. I don't think it is your fault. Only you think it is your fault. Maybe it is my fault. Is that what this is about?"

I was petting her pretty foot. The teakettle's trembling had advanced somewhat. I could hear the puppy, the dog, in her arms, above me, panting.

"What," I asked her—and I asked gently because even if she wasn't Rema she still seemed like a very nice person—"would you say if I told you that the Royal Academy called me?" I pressed on the arch's vein very lightly, and watched its world go white.

"The Royal Academy?"

"You know which I mean," I said quietly, wondering if she knew what I meant. I leaned down and kissed her foot, which was cold and dusty, as was the tile floor that I then stretched myself out upon more fully. "Of Meteorology."

"Leo?"

"Where Tzvi Gal-Chen is a fellow," I said, gesturing with my head toward the refrigerator, though Tzvi's family photo was no longer there, I don't know where things like that disappear to, the kinds of things one has on one's fridge. These things are not just under the fridge like you might think, because I could see under the fridge and I saw only a curled fruit label sticker and a child's jack.

The woman turned the kettle off. It wasn't—by sound stage— even near boiling. She set down that animal (who began licking my face and disturbing my peace) and sat down next to me. "Jokes aren't funny," she said to me, "when they need lots of explaining. Are you feeling well? You look sad, Leo."

A prominent vein tortured across her hand too. I could press on the vein and it would fade to white and then return again, to that very particular blue.

She said, "Your walk. Do you want to tell me how it was? It's a cloud out there."

I thought that she was right, not just about the cloud, but about how jokes did lose their humor when they needed explaining, and I thought that *maybe I had been making a joke*, and that it hadn't been the Royal Academy that had called. Later, when the phone rang again, I insisted that neither of us pick it up. We sat together on the sofa that evening and I kept my eyes on the floor and at one point I told "Rema" that I missed her, and I leaned over and bit her ear gently, and then I kissed her hand and the inside of her wrist, but that dog was running about, and quietly, in my thoughts, I apologized to Rema because I had wanted to hold that other woman. I think you can imagine the feelings that I had, and their strangeness to me.

8. Single-Doppler weather radar

In the salad days of Gal-Chen therapy I used to like to watch NY1 weather and think of Tzvi as the man behind the scenes, the unsung hero who made it all possible, deploying Doppler radar technology and interpreting the data at record speeds, simultaneously forecasting for all five boroughs. It was a light thought, a happy hyperbole, one of the many childish banalities that made up my daily secret life. Not much of a secret life, but enough. Enough to let others—Rema, I hoped—project something grander onto those private spaces. But my projections onto the unknown Tzvi—it turned out they were insufficiently ambitious, palest shadows of the truth.

Tzvi Gal-Chen's contributions to the field of radar meteorology include a series of "retrieval" papers, all of which confront the problems of translating Doppler weather radar data into real-world, and eventually real-time, information. Familiar enough. But Tzvi focuses in particular on how valuable data retrieval can be accomplished with a single-Doppler radar; in this way his research represents a break from more conventional retrieval methods involving dual-Doppler radar systems: two radars, distant from each other, looking at more or less the same volume of air from perpendicular angles so that real-world information can then be divined through triangulation. Why not stick with dual-Doppler radar systems? Tzvi describes his motivation for developing single-Doppler retrieval methods thusly: "Perfectly coupled radar systems are rare, if they exist at all." And "dual-Doppler analysis requires accurate calibration of radar antennas and simultaneous operation of both radars."

Whereas I was genuinely alone. The therapeutic relationship, like, for example, the mourning process, is inherently asymmetric. I suppose I had let that sort of asymmetry leak into all aspects of my life, so while I had a number of pleasant professional relationships, I had no one I could really turn to for advice about Rema's replacement, no one whom I could simply call upon as a friend, as a second. Except for Rema, and Rema wasn't there. I admit that it's generally better to consult another person, to adjust for a limited perspective, for the distortions of perception. If I'm wondering, for example, "Do I look haggard?" it would be useful to have another person's eyes on me; between the two of us we might be able to settle the question near the truth.

But given the particulars of the situation, corroboration was an unreasonable expectation. I'd have to proceed on my own.

The limits of my knowledge and education inevitably restrict my comprehension of Tzvi's work, so far outside of my own discipline, but I have come to understand the basic ideas quite well.

Doppler radar turns to advantage what is known as Doppler effect, an oft-misunderstood concept. Doppler effect describes an apparent—as opposed to actual—change in frequency or wavelength. It is the change perceived by an observer who is, relative to the wave source, in motion. Textbook example: as a speeding car approaches, the sound it emits appears to go up in pitch, in frequency. But in actuality, the emitted frequency—the car's trembling of the air around it—does not change at all. It only seems to change.

Let us imagine a source from which a Rema look-alike emerges every second.

If the source is stationary, and I am stationary, then every second one of these Remas will pass me by.

But if the single observer, again let's say me, begins walking toward the source of Remas, then a Rema will pass by me more frequently than every second, even though Remas are still exiting the source at the precise rate of one per second. From my (walking) perspective, there is now less spacing between the Remas, and therefore the wavelength has been affected, the perceived frequency of Remas has changed, has increased.

One might also consider the case of my remaining in place, and the source of Remas moving toward me. Or the case of myself and the Rema source both moving. Any frame of reference will do. If in the sum of movement vectors, the source and I are moving away from each other, then Remas will pass by less frequently, the perceived frequency of Remas will have decreased. (A lower pitch will be heard from the receding car.)

Being aware of this distortion of perception allows scientists to take advantage of the distortion itself in order to gather accurate data about the actual, and not just the perceived, world. In fact, more and better data than could be gathered if the distortion did not exist. Doppler effect refers to these distorted perceptions, and Doppler radar's utility relies on savvy interpretations of these distortions that, properly understood, enable a more accurate understanding of the real world.

More or less, that is the Doppler effect, most famously used to come to the conclusion that the universe is expanding, since no matter which way a radar is pointing, it detects a redshift, the visual manifestation of wavelengths bouncing off of a receding source. That had been a surprise: the universe, in every direction, was leaving us (and apparently looking beige while doing so). I'm not sure if it's wrong or silly to feel more sad and lonely on account of such facts, facts like the universe's expansion, but somehow I do feel that way. But back to the point: Doppler effect. Or as I have come to call it in my more personal experience of it: Doppler-ganger effect.

9. Dopplerganger effect in effect

She said to me: "Anatole, I am worried about you."

Anatole? I felt for a moment like I could sense my own skin desiccating, that all those people I'd seen in the coffee shop were members of my own self, in masquerade, laughing at me, that I could sense water molecules moving not toward boiling but doing the opposite, colliding together out of the air. What came out of my mouth was: "What?" I saw red. Or beigey stars with red auras, receding.

She answered in a very quiet voice, "Well, I said. I said: Well, that I am worried about you."

"You said Anatole," I said, turning my head to look up at her face. From down below like that—I was still on the floor of the kitchen—her lips looked like bas-relief, exaggerated and grotesque.

"For a toll?" She said. "No, no I didn't say that."

I could still sense the dog in the room, but it was as if she were unfathomably far away, as if her tail were metronoming over a distant horizon.

"You said," I said again, "Anatole."

Her eyes were watering. "No, I didn't. I said just, oh, that I am worried about you."

"I heard Anatole," I said again, unembarrassed, because after all she was a stranger. I lifted myself off the cool, dry, dusty floor— feeling somehow a small loss at no longer being able to see the lost jack under the fridge—and I sat myself up next to the woman. "Anatole. Is that the name of the night nurse?"

She kept crying very quietly and did not answer me.

"Is he your boyfriend? *Is he in on this?*"

She wiped her face with her sleeve. "So stupid," I heard her mumble.

"What?" I said. And one might fault me for not attending to this woman's suffering—but I myself was still in such shock, under such duress.

"No, silly. No, not what you might think at all," and she began to laugh a little bit in her tears. She stood up then, from the ground, the floor I mean, and walked to the bedroom.

I did not follow her, not right away.

I went to sleep knowing that if I was somehow wrong, if this really was Rema, then in the morning we'd pretend none of this had happened. That's how things were with us. I liked that, our mutual commitment to delimiting our intimacy, that commitment, in its way, a supreme form of intimacy, I'd argue. I often miss that very particular habit of ours these days, when it seems everything I've said or done or eaten or worn the day before is being made reference to, is being discussed. People need secrets. Anyway, that night I slept at the very edge of the bed; the woman did not seem to mind. She slept with her back to me. She held the dog in her arms and did not touch me.

I also let her remain alone.

10. I walk the dog; the dog walks me

At some point during that night—after the naming-of-the-dog fight and after Anatole and the foot estrangement, when Rema was still not Rema, and the Royal Academy had either called or not called me, and Harvey was either dead or just missing again—I woke that woman sleeping next to me with her arm around a new animal and I asked her if I was talking in my sleep. She mumbled: *You are talking right now but I don't know if you are sleeping.* I shook her again and she said: *But I am sleeping, viejito, please please leave me alone.* I didn't know what to make of that. I breathed in her hair, which smelled just right and made my eyes water. And I put my hand on her sleeping forehead, which felt just the right shape. And I carefully reached my arm around her waist to find the handle of her far hip and it felt just like Rema's hip, though maybe a little bit bigger or a little bit smaller, or something—I was having such a hard time articulating my perceptions, even just to myself. I tried to fall back asleep, and I think I did, but it was the kind of sleep where one later wakes up exhausted, with the conviction of having slept not more than minutes.

When I finally awoke, the simulacrum was not in the bed.

·I found a note, written in a slightly undersized Rema-ish script, magneted onto the refrigerator, where the Gal-Chen family photo used to be.

PLEASE TO WALK THE DOG BEFORE YOU LEAVE

Well: it was something meaningful to do while I tried to conceive of a better method—I didn't have one yet—of searching for

Rema. Even then I knew I couldn't just ride the subway all day long. And although I was not yet explicitly thinking of my situation in terms of research into single-Doppler radar retrieval methods, I was already aware of the need to overcome the confines of my lonely point of view. I couldn't yet imagine how to make deductions from my restricted knowledge without it being like trying to determine the position of a star without understanding parallax, or, perhaps more to the point, like trying to determine the actual frequency of an object moving away from me at an unknown speed and in an unknown direction, and not knowing whether it in fact was me or the object doing the moving.

I found the nervous russet dog in the closet, jaw on dusty floor, one paw possessively in a yellow high heel of Rema's. "Okay, little orphan," I said to her quietly. When she saw me, she thumped her lean tail clumsily and whimpered. "You have no idea," I went on, trying to lean down toward her slowly, without frightening abruptnesses, "why you're here, why you're not at home. Maybe you think I smell odd. It's very important, did you know, for getting along, for falling in love, to like each other's smell, even if you're not aware of noticing it." She gazed at me steadily. I felt she was calmed by my Rema-like chatter. "Rema smells like cut grass and bread and lemon," I said.

Leashing the pup felt wrong.

I walked her over to the steps of the Cathedral of St. John the Divine. She received numerous compliments, the pup. I received none. I used to sit on the cathedral steps, waiting and waiting for Rema—by chance—to pass by. This was before we were together. Sitting on that cold concrete I inevitably felt like the worst kind of fool—winter and not even a hot drink in my hands or a spiritual temperament to my mind to excuse my presence—and waiting there, exposed to the elements, a part of me vehemently hated the innocent Rema, hated her for taking up my time, for occupying an unclosing preoccupative loop in my mind, but, of course, another part of me loved her, ecstatically, for pretty much the same reasons, with profound gratitude toward her not just for her herself but also for my obsession with her, which rescued me from my unceasing progression of unpunctuated days, because one thing my obsession did, if dizzyingly, was punctuate. And get me out of my apartment, and my habits. And I did occasionally actually see her. And even just that much of Rema, brief sightings of her, would have been worth all my devotion; she's a finer world.

The pup seemed uninterested in ascending the steps; they didn't mean to her what they meant to me; we walked on, proverbial man and beast, and then, in the reflective glass of a Korean dry cleaner's window, overlapping with a faded sign showing a shoulder-padded '80s woman and with the text *Modern women wear white too!*, I caught sight of an adorable dog leading an old man whose coat was buttoned up wrong.

Twice now. I needed to look at myself on purpose, I resolved. Not by accident.

I readjusted the buttons of my coat.

I looked again in that reflective glass and saw a more distinguished man.

And it struck me—as if it hadn't struck me before, or with more particulars than before—to analyze my situation as if it were not my situation but, instead, a patient's.

This simulation of there being two observers looking at the same problem (my life) without there actually being two observers echoes—though I didn't realize it at the time—the solution that Tzvi came to in his research into single-Doppler radar retrieval methods. I was deploying Tzvi Gal-Chen's solutions even before I properly understood them to be his solutions, as if his ideas were already coursing invisibly through my veins, which perhaps they were.

So the plan came to me, as if flooding into my hand from that leash, to do just what I did with my patients. I would accumulate data, do a literature search. Though on exactly what I wasn't certain. I would simulate the addition of another radar into the equation, if not a perfectly coupled one. There'd be two of us. An I and a me, I might say, if I felt like being cute about it. Like that interrupter Lacan's changing of the comma to a semicolon in Descartes' famous formulation, about thinking and being. I think; therefore *I* am.

That, anyway, was my resolution; or at least that was my hope.

I called my office, asked to have my appointments canceled, said I was sick, terribly sick, and left for the public library to research the state of me.

11. Paradigm shift

The way I proceeded with my investigation might cause me to lose credibility before mediocre minds. And I should admit that I've always simply loved the New York Public Library, so arguably my motivation for going there that day was not just to find more information but also to be comforted, to see the light pouring in through the enormous windows in broad cones as if from giant parallel movie projectors. Maybe—but really the meekest of maybes—I was pursuing the sense I used to have as a child, when I'd see the illuminated dust shimmering and winking and—this was back when the library was always warm—I'd feel myself safe in the belly of an enormous and unknowable beast. When I was ten or eleven, my mother used to take me with her to the library almost every day. She was researching the legal proceedings related to eviction. Or maybe she was researching a family tree. I don't really remember, so probably both of these things were, at different times, true. She did always believe that some outsized inheritance was seeking her; she'd stand at the newsstand and search the "Seeking" section of the classifieds, and then refold the paper and return it to the stack.

But it's not as if, in obedience to some zeitgeist Freudianism, Rema dimly replaced my mother; if anything Rema made my mother, retrospectively, seem a pale shadow of an original love yet to come.

At the library that day I knew that in adopting my new methodology, the logic I was familiar with would inevitably fail me. Certain rules can be said to hold, but only under a very specific set of conditions, conditions even an approximation of which had rapidly receded from me. What rules could be said to hold in my new world? I didn't know. But I've always been logical, quite traditionally so, for example I put my least frequently worn clothing in the bottom drawer, which is the most uncomfortable to reach. And I had my office carpeted in pale blue because it is one of the few colors that are masculine and feminine at once. And when I first got Rema's number I purposely didn't enter it into my cell phone so as to keep myself from calling her too often. Instead I taped her number onto my refrigerator, which meant I could have lost it—it could have fallen, been swept away—but I knew the risk was an essential one and so, being rational, I took it.

But those old logics of mine had grown suddenly antique—to abandon them for something new was only reasonable.

I sat myself down at one of the library's long communal tables. I pulled the beaded cord of the desk lamp. I stared at the illuminated green lampshade. I was waiting not for me to come up with an idea but for an idea to come up with me. This went on for a while, how long I am not sure. As I sat there, attempting patience, I became conscious of a faint ringing just quieter than the ventilation system, an alternating two-tone ringing of irregular rhythm. Looking around failed to reveal if anyone else heard this, or was disturbed by this, or if it was just me.

Along the spine of the long table lay stunted pencils and old beige card catalog cards. I watched myself write—the lead of the pencil was soft and pressing it down against the note card inevitably made me think of Rema applying eyeliner, her gaze up and out— one term on each of three separate note cards: LEO LIEBEN-STEIN (ME), DOPPELGANGERS, ROYAL ACADEMY OF METEOROLOGY.

A plan came to me: to select a note card at random and to begin my research in the direction thus dictated. Again I stress, it is precisely because I am intensely logical that I recognized that in order to determine how best to proceed I needed a new kind of logic.

I had not, however, abandoned my faith in experimental controls. I quickly wrote three more note cards: HERONS, WOOL PROCESSING, HEMOCHROMATOSIS. Those would be my red herrings. Maybe I'd chosen herons with that obscurely in mind. Regardless, I turned all six note cards over and shaped them into a stack, shuffled them, then spread them out on the table. It was difficult for me to convince myself that I didn't still know which card was which, so I gathered the cards into a pile again, then left for the men's room, where I washed my hands with horrible bubblegum pink liquid soap and dried my hands on mealy paper towels.

This picking of the card would have to be truly, not just apparently, random. Otherwise I ran the risk of being guided by plans that only seemed like my own but that were actually determined by whatever ideas had been seeded into the air, intruded upon me.

I returned to the table; I shuffled the cards once more. Sitting across from me was a double-chinned, mustachioed man; he didn't even glance at me but his left hand kept drifting to just behind his ear, to rub something there, and this somehow made me feel self-conscious and awkward and ugly, as if he were me. Leaving the cards scattered, I rose once more from my seat—the sound of my chair scraping the floor reverberating in the belly of that whale, of course I had doubts—and I took a walk down the long center aisle, looked at a spine on a book shelved at the far wall (*Who's Who in Scandinavia, 1950–1970*), touched the gold lettering like a home base, then returned—in that cavern—to my seat.

The mustachioed man's hand was again behind his ear. His earlobe was large and pale, but the antitragus was bright red.

I re-reshuffled my sense and nonsense cards, re-redistributed them across the table in front of me, and, finally, picked one. I turned it over: ROYAL ACADEMY OF METEOROLOGY.

No red herring!

So: I would do a literature search on the Royal Academy of Meteorology.

12. My second search, objective unknown

Only very briefly did I panic, when, in my aloneness, I realized that the one reference database I knew how to use, besides the now dead and dismembered card catalog, was Medline.

That realization, being surprised by my own inability, shook me up in a way that reminds me of the first trip Rema and I took together, walking hut to warm hut in the Austrian Alps. This was relatively early on in our relationship, and I had told Rema that I knew German "more or less." In truth I'd once taken a two-week German class. I'd retained maybe four phrases: *milch bitte, Ich bin ein Berliner, die Zukunft einer Illusion,* and *Arbeit macht frei.* But I wasn't quite lying to Rema when I'd said I knew German "more or less," because I did truly *feel* that once I got to Austria I would "remember" German. We need to develop a better descriptive vocabulary for lying, a taxonomy, a way to distinguish intentional lies from unintentional ones, and a way to distinguish the lies that the liar himself believes in—a way to signal those lies that could more accurately be understood as dreams. Lies—they make for a tidy little psychological Doppler effect, tell us more about a liar than an undistorted self-report ever could. Well, I thought I'd remember German despite having never actually forgotten it, having never—as I vaguely felt I might have—listened to German radio broadcasts, or spoken German as a child. But we get these wrong feelings sometimes, feelings like articles slipped into our luggage but not properly ours. I think of it like vestigial DNA. Code for nothing, or the wrong thing, or for proteins that don't fold up properly and that may eventually wreak great destruction. I talked about this wrong luggage thing with the simulacrum the other day, explained to her how maybe she really did *feel* that she loved me, as if she were actually Rema, and not just "Rema." Anyway, at the desk of our pensione that evening, I opened my mouth and was genuinely shaken to realize that no German words came to mind.

"Help finding?" I said, leaning over the reference desk.

"Collected papers?" the gentle fernlike woman there answered me. She then tapped on her computer, then wrote something down, then translated from one call-number system to another call-number system, to a particular location, and then, taking me almost by the hand, she delivered me to five oversized, clothbound aquatic blue volumes of compiled papers from the past twenty years of annual conferences of the Royal Academy of Meteorology.

"I'm eternally grateful," I found myself saying.

The fern nodded politely, but I could see she appeared little interested in the investigation into which she had launched me. She didn't even ask me if I was a meteorologist. She padded away, as if I were utterly forgettable to her.

Not knowing what else to do, feeling perhaps overly bereft after my fern friend left, I took one of the volumes in hand, sat myself down on the floor. The light was on over my aisle alone, and I could hear its ticking, as if it were on a timer, which maybe it was. I began to hum a little Rema ditty whose words I could not recall, began to turn thin newsprinty pages, then more and more pages, somewhat randomly, not one by one—*flipping through, I believe they call this*, some part of me said to the other parts, as if to diminish by chattiness, by music, by anything, the sense of serious portent I felt taking me over. The tiny font of captions, the murmurous italicizations of abstracts, the pridefulness of columns, the unassuming data plots. Hearing those thin pages micro-skid across the grooves of my finger pads was such a comfort I almost forgot my original purpose; that almost forgetting was probably a comfort as well.

I'd thought you didn't even love her that much anymore, some part of me taunted. Some parts of me are so mean.

Suddenly I was looking at something beautiful. Or something beautiful to me, though I couldn't say why, something that seemed potent with form, but a form I could not classify. Intrusive beauty, like the cornsilk of Rema's hair—which is not necessarily unanimously considered beautiful, streaky as it is, and uneven, and sometimes greasy—a mesmerizing, unsolved kind of beauty. An irritant, actually. Something irritatingly beyond category—sublime, the melodramatic might say.

I can reproduce the image here. But I'm unable to reproduce the effect, the effect the image had on me, which was, well, uncanny, like those dolls whose eyes seem to follow you around a room. I felt like I had seen the image before, though what are the chances? Beauty, maybe the sublime, and déjà vu combined, is that what stopped me? Like I was looking at a topographical map of a landscape I knew only from close up. Some sense of concordance, and meaning, of a pattern both inscrutable and yet, at some almost

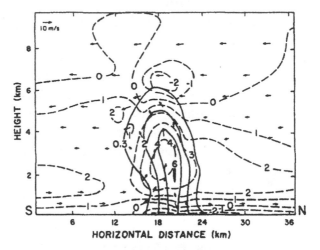

FIG. 3. Vertical y-z cross section at 90 min. at x = 14.25 km through the model storm showing the rainwater mixing ratio contours (g kg⁻¹, solid), the velocity vectors in the plane, and the potential temperature change from the initial base state (°C, dashed). South is to left and north to right. Wind speed proportional to vector length; areas void of vectors indicate very little flow in this plane.

cellular level, detected. I wonder: if I saw my own DNA denaturing in some petri dish, would I experience the slightest spine tingling of recognition? What if I passed my father on the street, would I recognize him, or him me, or would we just have an uncanny feeling, one that we might or might not ever decode?

Anyway, I would be curious to know what this image recalls to others.

After an uncertain length of time spent staring—I heard footsteps in a nearby aisle—I flipped back a few thin pages to the cover page of the article that contained the arresting image.

The first author: Tzvi Gal-Chen.

The paper was originally presented at a conference in Buenos Aires.

Buenos Aires being Rema's hometown.

And Tzvi Gal-Chen being Tzvi Gal-Chen.

And the article was about retrieval. Specifically: "Retrieval of Thermodynamic Variables Within Deep Convective Clouds: Experiments in Three Dimensions."

My pulse rose; my fingers went cold. Then the light went out; I crawled along the shelving to turn it back on. I know the ordinary often masquerades as the extraordinary, that if you put thirty people together in a room, the likelihood that two have the same birthday is over ninety percent, that when you learn a new word and it then seems suddenly ever present it is only because you have just begun to notice what was there all along. (This once happened to me with the word *cathect*. Also *Rosicrucian*.) Maybe that's all that this find of mine was. For all I know, maybe Tzvi Gal-Chen and Buenos Aires were both already pervasive terms and I'd simply stumbled across two examples of Baader-Meinhof phenomenon. But the fitting together of so many elements—sometimes that really happens, a stray orange peel, a necklace, and a certain joke about iceberg lettuce once converged to reveal a girlfriend's infidelity—convinced me that I was perceiving something real, that I was not myself in any way cracked, that only my world suddenly was.

So I would go to Buenos Aires. I'd return to Rema's beginning, a place I'd never been. Why Rema might have gone south—or if she'd been taken there, or if she was still there, and what her connection to Tzvi Gal-Chen might or might not be—I had no idea. But it was that afternoon in the library, in those dusty aisles with the lights always threatening to turn off, when I had only the faintest of knowledge, that I knew with the most certainty what to do next. Like how it is on the foggiest of nights that radio signals come through most clearly and from seemingly impossible distances.

13. We exchange words, not pleasures

The dog lover did not take it well that night over dinner—a heap of lentils and bacon and spinach with a facedown sunny-side-up egg on top, I always loved our messy pile-on meals—when I said that I'd be leaving for an indefinite length of time. She asked me why I was leaving; I said because something had changed and I just needed to get away. She asked what did I mean by leaving and I realized I didn't quite know, so I decided to be cautious and say that I was taking a personal vacation. Those phrases, *something has changed*, *just need to get away*, *personal vacation*, were not really my words but TV words, movie words, pollen in the air. Not even aliens from within me, but aliens from without. More luggage. She: leaning on an elbow, holding her fork aloft and still, with nothing on it, asking, What did I mean by "changed"? Me saying I wasn't quite sure what I meant, that I hadn't found words for it yet. She: asking, Where, exactly, was I going? Me telling her that as nice a person as she seemed to be, I didn't really feel comfortable telling her. "Not yet," I clarified. "But maybe never."

She pressed the empty tines of her fork against her bottom lip. Then she set her fork down. She was very sober, and very calm, very unlike Rema.

"Are you seeing someone?" she then asked, which struck me as funny, because there are so few people in the world that I like even a little bit.

I may have cracked a nervous smile. I shook my head no.

"Are you playing a joke?" she asked.

Again I shook my head.

"Is this related to, are you relating to, um, yesterday?" she asked.

"I don't think so," I said, which was as honest an answer as I knew.

"Or Harvey?"

"I don't think so," I said again.

"I don't understand," she said, putting down her fork, which, touching the plate, sounded a gentle reverberating *ting* like a creeping chill. Her tines then disappeared into the lentils.

"I don't understand either," I said, and I also put down my fork, as a gesture of respect, even though I was still hungry, and even a little bit happy, since I had a kind of plan. I could almost see the pulley system—something made of thick gray rope and metal coated over with a chipping white paint—by which my life's getting better would make this other Rema's life worse, and just having that thought moved the ropes back against me, for her.

We were quiet for a little while. I looked at her and then when I saw her look at me I looked back away, down at my plate. The lentil dish we were eating that night was made with tarragon, which I always forget smells like licorice until I close my eyes and ask myself why I have an image of myself lying under a patchwork quilt and coughing. I wonder if Rema, or her doppelganger for that matter, experiences silence (or tarragon) the same way I do; for me silence is like a humid swelling of scents, originless clicks, phantom elbow pains, a puff of air near the eyes, a sense of grass pushing up through the earth somewhere, or everywhere at once. I've never asked Rema about this.

The simulacrum scooted her chair back, went to sit on the sofa; the russet dog joined her. "You are trying," she said, not actually looking at me, "to make me say I love you and beg you to sleep with me, but I am not here to perform for you, you can go through your preoccupations on your own and talk to me on the other side of them."

I said nothing. I just looked at her. There on the sofa, unnamed pup at her side, she was running her fingers perpendicular to the wale of her corduroy skirt. Then parallel to the wale. Then perpendicular. Just by watching, I could feel the grain of the fabric, which made me think of the grooves that make our fingerprints, which made me think of the fingerprinty look of that meteorological image in Tzvi Gal-Chen's paper, which made me think of the myth of fingerprints, of one of the few things that I remember my father telling me, that really all fingerprints were the same. And snowflakes? I'd asked. And snowflakes, he'd answered.

The russet dog nose-sighed, turned a tired gaze toward me.

"Is it your plan," the simulacrum said, "to say nothing? You're not really going to leave. You're just imitating a drama of me, a show I might put on."

Despite a certain type of certainty, I remained very unsure as to how conscious this woman was of being an impostor, or perhaps an alternate. As far as I knew she might be like an understudy who's been lied to and believes that the show goes on only on Tuesdays, and that she is really the only star. Maybe this woman also felt that something was somehow wrong, that she was with the wrong Leo; maybe she, like me, could not articulate precisely what was wrong, but unlike me she did not trust her feeling. Maybe at some point in time, in some place, an other Rema and an other Leo were living together very happily in a whole other parallel possible world. A world not unlike the ones Harvey so often talked about. It was possible.

Again the dog's nostrils flared.

And I found myself saying to this other Rema, calling out to her across the apartment—and this too felt like clichéd speech that had infected me—that I wanted to tell her *the whole truth.*

"Okay," she said, returning her gaze to me.

So laconic. It was details like that that made it clear to me that I was not speaking with my Rema. But even so, the doppelganger, she had a wintry kind of pretty about her that day, chapped and rosy like freshly sanded wood. Even if she wasn't my wife, I still felt sorry for her. My heart always goes out to beautiful people, which I realize really isn't fair, but at least my heart goes somewhere.

And at least, unlike the previous day, I did not feel that I wanted to hold the impostress, though I was surprised and perhaps a little offended that she didn't—even as a kind of ploy—try to seduce me. But once I realized that I didn't want to hold her, I realized that I had nothing further to say. She was still waiting for my promised explication. But I did not know what "the whole truth" was. I cast about for an explanation with the sense that it would arrive *whole*, entire, like a forgotten memorized poem, if only I could recall the first word or two. Again like my sincere belief in my nonexistent German. But I couldn't find my way out of the crisscrossing thought: either I tell her she's not really Rema and she thinks I'm crazy, or I tell her she's not really Rema and she doesn't think I'm crazy, because she already knows she's not Rema, in which case why should I let on that I know? Those weren't really the only two options, logically speaking, but I got caught within that syllogism, like in the still place inside of storms.

"You aren't speaking?" she asked.

Even though the vein on this woman's forehead had not been prominent before, it became ghostly blue prominent. Like her maybe lover's, the night nurse's.

Then the phone rang.

14. Pleasures past

The first time I actually spoke to Rema: she was again sitting right in front of me at the Hungarian Pastry Shop, and I had leaned forward toward that hair, and I actually tapped her shoulder, but then what was I going to say if she turned around? I had no plan.

She did indeed turn around in her chair, her profile showing off her long, gently fluted nose and the tendons on her neck.

I found myself asking her if she was Hungarian.

During the silence of indeterminate length that followed I fixed my gaze upon her forehead, since I couldn't possibly look straight into her eyes, and what I eventually heard, in a lilting long-voweled accent, was: *Why do you stare at me?*

Over the sound of milk being steamed I asked, alarmed, "Do I stare at you?"

"*You* are from Hungary?" came from her, now in a louder voice, to the sound of silverware being sorted.

"No, no."

"Oh."

"Though my mother. Actually."

"Oh?"

"But no. Not me. A mistake."

"A mistake."

"Do you make these cakes here?" shouted a surprisingly tiny woman across the nearby counter.

And I remember it striking me then (as my mishearing had nearly become conversation) how in my line of work the fact that I sometimes can't hear so well—I just have trouble disarticulating sounds—is almost a plus, since people give out so many clues about what's ailing them that are so much more important than the actual words they say. But in all other aspects of my life this "quality" left me fairly crippled.

"So where *are* you from?" I asked, and somehow our conversation hobbled on from there. I don't know why she was so willing to talk to me; she had not been in the country for long at that time and I believe she must have felt alone, and Rema does not luxuriate in feelings of aloneness, and she tends to be kind of catholic in her interest in people, at least for a little while.

"Really?" Rema said when the fact that I am a psychiatrist came out. "Did you know that Argentina has more psychoanalysts per person than has any other country?"

I did already know that fact about Argentina, about its psychoanalysts, but I said:

"No, I didn't know that. That's so interesting." Also: normally people's conflation of psychoanalysis with psychiatry irritates me profoundly—I could never be an analyst, those people are too unpleasant, too passive-aggressively authoritarian, and, yes, all crazy, and out of fashion to boot—but when Rema conflated the two, I was not irritated.

"And the south side of Buenos Aires—it is the inconsciente," Rema explained. "Or so they will tell you, no? You see there is Avenida Rivadavia, and it cuts the city, the north from the south. When the streets cross Rivadavia, their names change. From north to south, Esmeralda becomes Piedras, and Reconquista becomes La Defensa, and Florida becomes Peru. That is cute, no?" She brushed unseen hairs off of her face.

She had a somewhat manic speech pattern, with increased rate and rhythm, though not volume. Also her hair was cowlicked at her temple. Looking at her I had the urge to tell her what I often feel impelled to tell a beautiful person, which was that she really didn't need to say anything at all, and that she shouldn't worry, and that it is not just me who will be helplessly devoted to her regardless of what she says. But I didn't tell Rema that. Pretty people often actually don't like to hear that kind of thing, I've found.

"And even the whole of Argentina," she went on, "it is the geography of a mind. Patagonia, in the south, is the savage and inhospitable inconsciente. Or so people say. And on a small scale, like snow globe, my neighborhood in Buenos Aires, it is named Villa Freud." She smiled at me. "You must think this is very silly what I am saying." Then she looked down at her napkin, which she began folding into triangles. "I also think it is very silly; maybe it is thinking like that that made me want to leave. Everyone so interested in how they are feeling, and who they maybe really are; even the newspapers, they print passages from psychoanalysis." Then: "Have you been? To Argentina?"

I told Rema the truth, that I had not been. I thought about saying something about Borges, but I know that I have a problem with coming off as pretentious, and I was worried that bringing up Borges might appear showy, even though every introverted schoolboy reads Borges, so it's rather ambiguous what such a reference would or should indicate. Another reason I generally don't like to mention Borges is because often a response will be to the effect of *he has no emotion*, and I hate hearing that said, because it is so wrong, and it's not a discussion that I like to get into. In retrospect I know that Rema would have agreed with me, but back then, I wanted to protect Rema from saying anything that might make me not like her.

"If the Argentines are generally like you, then it must be a lovely country," I said, immediately regretting my banality.

"You will have to go," she said firmly.

"Oh I apologize for troubling you," I said.

"Yes, you will have to go to Argentina. Unfortunately I can't go myself now, they might not let me back here, you know? What is that: what is easy to get into, easy to get out of, but almost impossible to return to? It is some very big answer, I think, something like life, or love. Something silly like that. For me, it's this country."

The way her bangs were parted made me think of an ink brush.

We never went to Argentina together, Rema and I—or, not really. Thinking of that now, I can't help but wonder if Rema had hid Argentina away from me intentionally, like some token from another lover. But Rema wouldn't try to hide an entire country. She hid much smaller things. I'm thinking about the time we went to have a slice of pizza together. It was like this: just in front of that mural of deformed angels, the mural at the pastry shop, Rema and I decided to get a bite to eat. And she said, well where should we go? And I, not wanting to look as if I were trying to impress, and not wanting to seem as old as I am, said, well we could go to Koronet for pizza, to which she said, sure, I'm happy with anything. Which I've always taken to mean the opposite. And indeed it did mean the opposite. She stopped then a moment—that day she was wearing a yellow jumper with a navy blue cardigan, she looked like an airline stewardess on some small Eastern European line—and said, oh I don't want to eat there, can we eat elsewhere? And I said that we could have a slice at the Pinnacle—but she said that she didn't like that pizza—or at the Famiglia—which also she said she didn't like, that the crust was so thick, and the cheese "unhappy," and she added, "Oh I'm sorry, you see I said I'm happy with anything when actually the opposite is true, I'm never satisfied." I blushed and shrugged my shoulders. Indecisiveness, capriciousness—these qualities in Rema never irritated me. I've always thought of my own mind as an unruly parliament, with a feeble leader, with crazy extremist factions, and so I don't look down on others for being the same. Maybe that's what "our humanity" means. My mother was like this also: often she'd run bathwater, set the kettle for tea, and go out for a walk nearly all at once, and when she did this it was usually I who had to stop the bathwater's running, turn off the kettle before the whistle blew. So Rema and I stopped there a moment on the sidewalk, and stood silent, and then Rema said, "Yes, let's go to Koronet. I do like it there. I just can't ever finish the slice and then I feel I am wasting and I feel sometimes a little bit sad—that is silly, no?—but I am very hungry tonight, I am sure I will finish, and the crust is nice and thin and I like the people that work there."

In retrospect, I can't help but wonder if maybe she was avoiding someone, what with all the nervousness and mind changing.

We went there, to Koronet, where I'd originally proposed. But for having fallen out of the plan and then back in, it seemed like a place anew, and if my spirits had been lagging earlier, inevitably disappointed in this woman for agreeing to spend time with me, I now was infatuated with her again, through my standard mathematics of love, a sort of dynamic stability, with Rema being now a new Rema, an always and ever renewable Rema, whose parts never quite added up. What can I say—why should I expect my inner workings to be different from anyone else's?

Rema ordered a slice of cheese, and took a plastic fork and knife, and I watched her slicing her pizza. I then took a fork and knife to my own pizza. I sliced the whole thing to pieces before taking a bite. Rema and I sat along the counter where there is a mirror, and I stole glimpses of us, of our reflection, where we looked like a happy blushing pair, and I had a little moment of imagining being over there on that side of the mirror, the side where we were happy and new and now forever.

We had such nice early days. Everyone looked at Rema, but Rema always complimented me and seemed to notice other men only so as to point out how they paled in comparison to me, how one might be handsome but not clever enough, another clever but not boyish enough, another boyish but without depth. She made me small gifts—elaborate origami boxes, uselessly small pillows, socks with my initials embroidered on them—always getting these gifts to me in a hurry, as if there weren't time enough to finish them, as if our relationship were always on the cusp of ending suddenly, unforeseeably, as if by natural disaster.

How odd, now that I think about it, that she loved me.

15. An object that will not be permanent

I turned my back on the corduroy-petting simulacrum—waiting there for the whole truth as she was—and I answered the ringing phone.

The other line hung up.

How random.

Although a series of hang-ups, I suppose that's not so random.

"Who was it?" she said.

"Who do you think it was?" I said.

Maybe she was waiting for a call from Anatole. Or the night nurse. Or the Royal Academy of Meteorology.

"The whole truth," she said with disgust, getting up to turn on the television. She quite obviously didn't really think that I would leave, didn't really believe that I was on to her.

And I admit that I didn't entirely believe myself either. If I'd looked up at the ceiling and saw in the drips there an arrow pointing me out the door—well, then I would think I was imposing a self-deluding order onto chaos. If I'd seen three fallen buttons on the floor and perceived them as a triangle pointing me in a particular direction—again I wouldn't have trusted my perceptions. If I heard voices. If I had a fever. Or any neurological signs. Or feelings of grandeur. Or if all the articles in the newspaper seemed to bear messages especially for me. Even just if the weather had been on when the simulacrum turned on the TV, and if I took that fact too seriously—even then, I would have doubted myself, wondered about the selectiveness of what I noticed. But none of that was happening.

"You're like a different person these past couple of days," she said. "Maybe months." And there couldn't have been a more bold, if tacit, acknowledgment of the situation than that. A fresh vision crept over me: myself at an airport desk, in much better shape and younger than I actually am, casually asking to be put on "the next flight to Buenos Aires." Hurried keyboard tapping, a negotiatory phone call, an underling being sent ahead to the gate to ask them to *please hold the door!* A seed of happiness in me: at the thought of being a player in some tragedy or comedy so much larger than myself. Surely I was emotionally suffering terribly, but of course our minds play tricks, dress up our emotions in masks, hosiery, feathers. That can be very useful. It was good to feel kind of good.

I waited for the woman to fall asleep, so that I could leave in peace. I packed a suitcase quietly, filled it with my clothing, and a bit of Rema's clothing as well, so that I'd have it to bring to her. I kissed the dog goodbye. At the airport I called my mentor, who had been through town and who had reacted to Rema so strangely. I mean sort of strangely. I tried to ask him about his reaction to her, if he thought something was "off" with her; I tried to ask him somewhat discreetly. But this is what he said to me: "You used to just be jealous. Now you've converted your jealousy into a psychological gain, some narcissistic pleasure in believing that everyone else wants what you have, wants to sleep with your wife. You should grow up. It's not healthy."

His response was neither random nor spontaneous; it was predetermined by his previous ideas about me; habits of thought are death to truth; I was outside of my habits; and he—he was wrong.

16. I contact a third party

Although the elaborate latticing of the ceiling had given me a kind of confidence in the country's infrastructure, still my suitcase (Rema's suitcase) did not arrive on the carousel at the airport in Buenos Aires. An attendant—a thin man with pockmarked skin and longish hair and a Roman nose and a filmy oxford shirt through which I could see his undershirt—told me not to wait but to return the next morning, that nothing could be settled until then.

"I have important things inside," I said in my poorly accented Spanish. Maybe it sounded like I was talking about my feelings. That first burst of language made me feel like a child, unable to find more precise, or more polite, words.

"I understand," the attendant politely lied in response.

"Shouldn't an investigation be started?" I asked.

He reiterated that I should return the next day. "You are not having an unusual experience," he emphasized, then looked past my shoulder to the woman behind me.

So luggageless, I set out into the city. I began my search for Rema by settling on the most direct and reasonable of plans: calling her mother. A more bold notion than it might appear. Not only had I never met Rema's mother, Magda, but she didn't even know—as far as I knew—that Rema was married to me. She didn't even know I existed at all. Rema was estranged from her mother, or her mother from her, or both. I didn't really know the whole story, not even the whole Rema version of the story. (And about Rema's unmentioned father—I never even asked. I presumed one of several sad variations. I'm not the only psychiatrist who advocates occasionally leaving silences silent, not confounding confession with intimacy.)

I found a public telephone, a glass and red-painted metal take-off of a London phone booth. Stepping inside—why did Argentina look so wrong? where were all the beautiful people? why did the architecture look like it belonged in Tel Aviv?—I flipped through the phone book and found her number—so easy! Then I breathed on the glass, then smudged my breath, then breathed again, smudged again, such that I was looking at a saliva-rainbowed distorted reflection, which at least gave me something to look at while I held that phone inevitably infested with the invisible germs of a thousand strangers.

A woman answered, and I introduced myself as "a friend of Rema."

On the other end: "What?"

I cut to the proverbial chase—very proverbial, I was feeling—with, "Listen, if you don't mind my asking, when was the last time you saw Rema?"

She asked, "With whom am I speaking?"

"This is Leo. I'm a friend—"

"What," she interrupted in an anxious blushing voice, "are you asking me about Rema?"

"I'm in Buenos Aires—" I began, but then I couldn't remember what I had thought I was going to ask Magda; I could remember only—as if my brain had monochromed—how much I hate speaking on phones. "And—"

"You know where Rema is?" she asked.

"Well," I said, feeling vaguely distinguished and proud, "I do believe I saw her as recently as three days ago."

"Here?"

"No. In New York—"

"Oh. Yes, yes. I knew that. You are an American friend?"

"Okay. Yes."

"But you are in Buenos Aires?"

"Yes. In this strange red phone booth actually—"

"And you are Rema's friend," she said again, the repetition seemingly undermining the truth-value of the statement. Maybe Rema doesn't consider me a friend. That's possible. "Well," Magda continued, now in a fresh vanilla kind of voice, "you should come over. You should come over anytime. You should come over right now. Would you like to come over right now? We will have a coffee, sweets—"

"Well—"

After giving me street names, and after describing to me the front of her home, she concluded with: "And don't worry about the dog." She gave a little cough. "Despite appearances, he really is very sweet and there is no reason to be afraid."

Everyone with their dogs.

17. EigenRema

Far more dogs than I was accustomed to promenaded through Magda's neighborhood; many dogs appeared unaccompanied; some attended playgroups of others of an equivalent size. It was as if decoys had been deployed to diminish the conspicuousness of the primary clue of the doppelganger's dog. But also maybe—maybe even probably—there were just many dogs. Consequently much feces. Some of it obviously stepped on. This in contrast to the fresh paint on the low-rise buildings, the potted plants on balconies. As I nearly failed to evade a particularly sculptural pile of feces, the thought came to me of who house-trained the pup now living in my apartment. Someone now dead?

Soon a woman, dressed in heels and a high-waisted cream dress with a thick navy sash, held my face in her hands, kissed me twice; she smelled of Vaseline and talcum.

"Rema," I said.

"Yes," she said, a misleading affirmation.

"Rema?" I said.

"She is coming?" she said.

"No," I said, waking up more fully into something.

The woman laughed.

Fortunately the drunkenness of longing didn't last long; I quickly sobered into true perception. This woman looked older than Rema, yes, but not so much on account of any particular feature, more because her hair was more neatly pulled back into a low wide clip, her eyebrows were more perfectly sculpted, and her lipstick was impeccably tamed into the cupid's bow of a '40s film star. At her side was a leggy, dignified greyhound.

"Her name's Killer," Magda laughed. Taking my hand, Magda led me inside a home that seemed already all wrong compared to the Rema's childhood home of my mind—too narrow a hallway, too few mirrors, a heavy and wrong potpourri.

What I would like to take, or drink, was what she asked me before leaving me alone on a velvet sofa overcrowded with tasseled pillows. Everything looked old, the velvet's nap diminished in patches. Maybe Rema has touched these things, I thought deliberately, as if I were planning to take fingerprints, and then: *I'm here in your pocket* came to my mind, a swatch of a song that Rema likes to sing, *curled up in a dollar, the chain of your watch around my neck.* And I petted the too-smooth upholstery of the sofa, thinking of thin wales of corduroy.

From a brocaded floor cushion, the greyhound watched me.

Magda returned with a tray bearing a teapot and two maté mugs and diminutive glasses of water and a plate overloaded with small cookies pressed into different geometries, some covered in chocolate. She said to me, "So you are a friend of Rema's husband?"

I was silent. Killer shifted her gaze to Magda.

Magda set the tray down. "Actualmente?" she punctuated, meaning "currently" but making me think "actually."

I had distinctly not presented myself as a friend of Rema's husband; I had presented myself as a friend of Rema. I had not known that Magda knew Rema was married—and maybe she didn't know. So I felt suddenly pressed into revealing something I perhaps oughtn't—a not unfamiliar situation for me since in the course of my practice I have often found myself in "situations" with patients' families, situations in which I am being pressed, with more and less subtly manipulative locutions, into revealing what I ought not reveal. But this particular moment with Magda was complicated by the fact that I did not quite know what exactly it was I did not wish to reveal, knew only what I was trying to discover. As I sat on that worn velvet nap, my overwhelming ignorance—about Magda, about Rema—seemed to materialize as the smell of my clothing, not dirty exactly, but overheated, and exhaling parts of itself.

So you are a friend of Rema's husband? repeated in my mind.

And Killer—she looked like a larger version of the doppelganger's dog.

"Well," I began. "Well. Well, yes, I am a friend of his," I concluded, which when I thought about it I decided was true, or true enough, and I was relieved to get to say something true because trying to maintain a lie, well, that becomes increasingly difficult over time. "That's how I met Rema. Actually. Yes. Through him." Which is also arguably not untrue. I reached for my tea with studied casualness. It was a maté, served in a special gourd with a straw, like Rema often made for herself at home, and I knew the drink was associated with several whole countries but I'd always thought of that gourd and its filtering straw as Rema's own personal eccentricity. "But of course," I said, sipping, "I'm now, currently—actually—also, very much a friend to Rema herself."

The maté tasted terrible, like socks. I eyed the tall chocolate cookies, then lifted my eyes to the woman; the coffee table's candle had cast her shadow up, against the ceiling, where it in turn loomed over her. "I'm curious," she said, "to hear what you think of Rema's husband?"

I had removed myself—parts of myself—from the conversation; a few cells were listening to Magda but whole factions of me had been devoted for some time to the question of whether enough time had passed to enable me to graciously reach for one of the oddly tall chocolate-covered cookies. "Well," I found myself saying, as if the word itself had formed a well-filled well within me, "well he's nice enough, isn't he?" I made a move to the cookie, realizing that my small half-truth was already tangling my investigation.

"I only met him once," she said without making eye contact, and reaching out a hand to pet Killer's head. "But to be honest— and I'm an excellent judge of character, I'm an analyst—I didn't like him. I didn't even like him a small amount."

I was busy trying to deal gracefully with the soft caramelly inside that I had not been prepared to find within the tall chocolate-covered cookie. Was she talking about me? Or some other me? Or someone else entirely? I had to wipe my mouth with my sleeve— I had no choice, she had not brought out napkins—and as I did, I thought, in a brief and stupid moment of mistranslated indignation, *Did you hear the news about Edward?*—another swatch of Rema song that I could not place—and then I swallowed my over-running cookie too early, causing a pain in my heart (originating in my esophagus of course), as I wiped more crumbs from my mouth, recovering myself. Saliva had rushed to greet the caramel. "Oh?" I asked carefully, belatedly. "*When* did you meet him? Was he good-looking?"

Did this other husband know the doppelganger's dog, the dog who was like an echo of Magda's dog?

"You can tell him what I said," Magda said, nonresponsively. "I don't care; it's not a secret, my feelings. I'm not one to keep secrets. Not about those sorts of things."

"When," I asked again, "when did you say—when did you meet him?"

"But that's okay if you like him. Beneath your awkwardness and reserve you fall upon me as a nice man. There's nothing wrong with liking somebody, at least not necessarily," she said.

"How long have you had this dog?"

Then Magda looked closely at me for what may have been the first time—maybe I still had crumbs on my face—and she did not seem to recognize me. "You're dressed rarely," she said.

"Me?"

"You're wearing heavy wool. And it's summer. You're dressed all wrong. For the weather."

"Yes, well, the weather was different. It was cold where I came from."

"I should apologize," Magda said, pushing her hair back over her shoulder. "For my behavior. I'm so rude to not be asking you more about yourself. Just going on about Rema's husband. Not making you comfortable. What a terrible host I am," she said, laughing girlishly, performing happiness. "Let me at least go and bring us some pistachios—" And she rose from her chair, which made her shadow terrifying to me.

"No really, it's all right," I said.

"You don't like pistachios?" she asked, pursing a heartbreaking pout beneath her monstrous shadow.

"Oh I love pistachios," I said. A gross exaggeration.

"Oh good," she said, and disappeared again down the hallway. The dog chose not to follow her, chose instead to watch over me. It was wholly obvious, her avoidance of the other husband issue.

But me too, I might have been focusing on the wrong issues. In my training, years ago, I had met a patient jaundiced to a curry who had never thought to worry about the changes in his skin and eye color but instead had arrived at the hospital extremely anxious about an insignificant nevus. That yellowed man, displacing his worries onto the meaningless sign, came to my mind then, in Magda's brief absence, as I worried about pistachios. Did Rema really have some other husband? Maybe she could have deceived me, I'll admit that—I can admit that—but how, what with sleeping in my bed every night, could Rema have tricked him, whoever he was, Anatole or not Anatole, purportedly (purported by me) my friend? In my mind—I knew it was just in my mind—I heard terrible laughter. I ate another cookie. And then another cookie, before I'd even swallowed the previous.

Magda returned with a bowl of pistachios, the kind dyed red, and before I could say thank you she began speaking.

"It's been years since I've seen Rema," she said. "She calls exactly once a month but won't give me her phone number and won't really say anything of substance, just talks instead about things in the news, only the most random things, like new discoveries about Saturn's moon she brought up recently, as if these are somehow personal events. I can't bring up anything real, anything personal, because then she shouts at me and hangs up the phone. You must think I'm terrible that she isolates herself from me but really it's not that at all, it's just that I can't have those kinds of conversations that she feels comfortable in, I can't have them; they are too ugly to me. When you said you'd seen Rema so recently, well, I didn't want to tell you everything on the phone because I was afraid that then you wouldn't want to come over here to speak with me, that you'd have a horrible misimpression and then my chances would be lost—"

I might note that Magda was crying through most of those words. People cry in front of me fairly often, so I have had ample opportunity to consider how one ought to handle such situations, and yet still, I admit, I am not very gracious in responding to performances of emotion. Obviously one can put an arm around the other person, or extend a hand, or murmur sympathetically. Or be silent. In my professional situation, I have (I believe correctly) chosen to adopt the most reserved among these options, because even just a single kind word can turn a few tears into a torrent, and one certainly doesn't want to ungate such a flood: it's just not useful. One can watch movies on one's own time, alone, for that sort of therapy. So—and yes perhaps this was wrong, or at least culturally unacceptable—I just sat there silently pretending not to notice the woman's—Rema's mother's—Magda's—tears. I sat with my eyes downcast and averted, as if Magda were naked. This was my attempt at restoring her dignity to her. There's a downside, of course, to such a strategy. Dogs offer more comfort than I do. But there's also this efficiency in which, when you watch someone cry, it can wholly relieve you of the impulse to do the same.

"You're not Argentine," Magda eventually said, recovering herself.

I looked down at my fingers that were stained pink from the pistachios I'd just eaten. It struck me that while she'd been crying I'd probably been making a great deal of noise, cracking those shells, chewing those nuts, sucking the salt off.

18. EigenMe

I have never, for even a minute, believed myself a meteorologist. I wouldn't want certain concessions I've made to my current reality to undermine an accurate understanding of the predicament I was in, a predicament that gave me little choice other than to retreat into the kind of inventiveness that resembles deceit and/or psychosis. And that is why I have gone to the trouble of detailing all the seeming irrelevancies of my initial meeting with Magda. I would like the position I was in at that time to be appreciated. Just think: I did not know where my Rema was, I did not know how much to reveal to Magda about my true identity, I was being watched by a strange dog, and in addition to all the unwelcome data that had been accumulating prior to my arriving at Rema's childhood home, there was suddenly this unforeseen, somewhat unassimilatable information about Rema having some other husband. Not to mention that: my luggage was missing, my home phone had been mysteriously ringing, my patient had gone absent, someone claiming to be from the Royal Academy had offered me a fellowship, and an old meteorologic research paper had seemed, in its way, to have spoken to me. On top of all this an objectively attractive woman had wept before me, while I sat in sweaty clothes with red pistachio dye on my hands and the corners of my mouth sore from salt. Who, in such a situation, would be safe from slipping into a second small ego-protective lie?

"So—I'm sorry—how did you meet my daughter and her, well, and him?" Magda asked, after having recollected herself.

I nodded my head and held up a finger as if to say "one moment," and then I proceeded to put more pistachios in my mouth, then sip again of the horrible maté, and then eat another cookie, the second to last. Unlike Rema, I've no knack for spontaneously inventing stories. In fact, quite the opposite. I can hardly tell anecdotes that are true. Except for the refuge of asking questions, I find speaking very challenging. That's part of why I'm inevitably the first to finish my meal at any gathering, because my main delay tactic when I'm asked a question is to eat.

Through the echo-y internal din of molar pistachio devastation, I heard Magda say, trying to speak for me: "You are a colleague of her husband's? You are also a psychiatrist?"

I found myself shaking my head—a gesture that can signal either denial or sorrowful disbelief—and swallowing. I like so few of my colleagues.

"No?" she inquired gently.

I found myself saying in front of a woman whose trust I would have liked to have gained: "Actually I'm a meteorologist." Then: "A *research* meteorologist," I added, with that liar's drive toward specificity. "Not one of those guys on television, though. That's what everyone's always asking me."

I suppose I was and wasn't thinking of Tzvi Gal-Chen in that moment. Meteorology, quite simply, was the first profession that came to mind. But again I would like to emphasize: I did not believe those words. I had never planned to say them. Some unruliest member of that parliament of me—although admittedly a perhaps intuitively ingenious member—had stolen the podium to speak those irrevocable words, and the rest of me then had no choice but to devote itself to the task of trying to maintain that false face.

But anyway, at that moment, the lie worked just fine. I maintained, in one move, both my privacy and my politesse.

"Meteorology. That is interesting," Magda replied after a moment. "I met a meteorologist once," she said. "At a dinner," she modified. And at this, as if suddenly she'd reached some judgment—one that appeared to be positive—she stood up quickly and insisted, "You're welcome to stay here if you want. Even before the crisis I rented rooms. You should stay here. You can ask Rema. Even with everything, I'm sure she'll tell you how nice it is here. Maybe she'll come visit you. Maybe you'll call her. You'll think it over. You'll think."

19. Into the noise

I did indeed think it over; I did so by doing what I often do when I don't know what to do, which was head to a coffee shop. An aloof and pretty young waitress—she had a lovely mole near her thumb and a waist like Rema's—brought me cookies with my coffee even though I didn't ask for cookies. Not that I needed more cookies, but regardless, this small variation in the way I normally experience coffee shops—those gratis cookies—woke me up a little to my situation, recalled to me to not be so foolish as to search for Rema in only one way, by only one method—talking to Rema's mother. I had another lead. Dipping a cookie, I pulled out my xeroxes of Tzvi Gal-Chen's research for the Royal Academy of Meteorology, and I began by skimming: *The numerical models discussed herein (and elsewhere) are formulated as Initial Value Problems*, a phrase that already caused me trouble as I could not feel confident (yes not even *feel* confident) about what that might mean—*Initial Value Problem*—though it's not as if I couldn't surmise, though my surmises seemed all wrong to me. So I set that reprint—which contained no images—aside. What "Initial Value Problem" could there be, even via stretched metaphor, in my relationship with Rema? I continued on to: *A Method for the Initialization of the Anelastic Equations: Implications for Matching Models with Observations.* "Anelastic" made me think of the brittleness of psychoses. I read further. *An algorithm is proposed, whereby the combined use of the equations of cloud dynamics, and the observed wind, will permit a unique determination of the density and pressure fluctuations.* Fluctuations. Yes, that seemed right. And "unique determination," a compelling account of love. But I knew my brain was eager to perceive order, so

I'd have to be rigorous before conceding any genuine concordances—otherwise I'd just be like Harvey reading the *New York Post* for meteorologic orders. Nothing had yet jumped out at me as much as that image, that thumbprinty image from the retrieval paper, and retrieval—that was so precisely, so straightforwardly, so unmetaphorically what I was trying to do. I dismissed the fluctuations sentence as only seemingly relevant. Then in the middle of a third article a distinct change in tone and content undeniably signaled a clue. The article had begun by discussing numerical prediction models but then, suddenly, read: *Plato was apparently the first to state that what we are sensing are only images of the real world.* Clearly an unnecessary sentence in a radar meteorology article. Appeals to antiquity naturally, well, appeal, yes, but deploying such a rhetorical move in such a context was highly unusual; clearly it signaled something; it would be foolish to contend otherwise. And why the added play of "apparently"? *Gauss*, the passage continued, *was apparently the first to formulate a mathematical theory of prediction*—something then to do with the inaccuracy of our observations hindering accurate extrapolation to future states. Again the "apparently." Under a noise cloud of percolation I continued reading: *In Gauss's work observations and models were combined to predict the trajectory of a celestial body*—which struck me as a rather inappropriate way of referring to Rema. Although, I thought, immediately scolding myself for my single-mindedness, perhaps there were innumerable celestial bodies whose motions needed to be tracked, and then I thought further about that word, "meteorology," and how it must itself, from the very beginning, have referred to the study of meteors, of objects falling through the sky.

Tzvi's article continued: *Atmospheric modeling is computationally complex, driving a search for less demanding, nonoptimal approximate methods . . . The exact approach requires the inversion of large matrices of the order of $10^5 \times 10^5$ but the matrices are sparse so that many of the computations can, in principle, be done in parallel.* Nonoptimal approximate methods. Computationally complex. The matrices are sparse. The words ungated certain snatches of music, of time, into my consciousness, but nothing had yet crystallized. *There is hope that the development of massively parallel supercomputers (e.g. 1000 desktop Crays working in tandem) could—*

Suddenly my BlackBerry rang and without even thinking, without even checking to see who it was—lost as I was in a haze of a thousand desktop Crays—I answered. As I did, a previously unnoticed cat looked briefly toward me, as did the Rema-waisted waitress—she was beautiful, unusually so—and a man behind the coffee bar wearing a green soccer jersey with the number 9 in white, he also looked over at me—and this made me look down at my shoes, which I realized had a fine beige dust on them, and I felt like while I had been disappearing into those words of Tzvi, everyone, and everything, had been *observing* me, which made me see myself multiplied, as if in a hall of mirrors, or on the screens of thousands of Crays, though I think this was just a matter of perspective.

"Hello?" I alarmed into the phone.

"Hello?"

"Hello?"

"Hello?"

I had no idea with whom I was speaking, but I was welling up with unarticulated emotion, emotion preceding any thought, and I saw images—thin wales of corduroy, hairs of an ink brush, bruisy blue vein on a foot, a yellow cardigan, archipelagoed tea leaves, smudged newsprint, a pulley, the tendon of a neck—and the word that rose to the surface was "Rema."

"I miss you" emerged from my mouth unintentionally, before I could think or plan or be wise in any way; it's ridiculous, to say I miss you to someone when you don't know who she is. "Where are you?"

"Leo, I'm at our apartment but where are you?"

Her words collapsed me into a smaller number of selves, a knowable number, an unpleasant dinner party. I stepped outside, stood under a eucalyptus tree, to continue my conversation.

"Rema, I love you even more than I could ever have imagined—"

"I love you too—"

"Loving other people is really just loving you, I see that now—"

"Leo, where are you?"

"When did you return?" I asked.

"When did you leave?"

"Did they have to force you to leave, or did you just go along with them, because you knew you had to? I didn't touch that other woman."

"Leo, I don't know where you are. No one knows where you are. You haven't been answering your phone. You've abandoned your patients. Don't you think that's strange? Doesn't that preoccupy you?" To say "preoccupy" instead of "worry"—that was a studied Rema-ism. Rema, except for when she was very tired, had stopped making that error years ago. I said:

"You're the woman who came home with that leggy dog? That's who you are?"

"You're upset—" the voice intruded nonresponsively.

"That wasn't actually a greyhound you brought home." A ray of sun had found me; I felt clearheaded. "Instead a little greyhound look-alike. Like a little toy dog. Is that who I'm speaking with? The lady with the little dog?"

"Are you with someone?"

"It's not polite what you did," I said with discolored conviction. "To just bring a dog into someone's apartment. The dog might have a disease. Or fleas. He might have made me sick."

"Leo, I'd really like to know exactly where you are." The woman sniffled—everyone with their tears—in a way that was not at all attractive. "Where you are right now, and why," she went on in between snarfling chokes that did seem, I concede, genuinely emotional, if repellent. "I just feel so preoccupied." Even if she wasn't Rema, I knew I should try harder to be nicer to her; I didn't know why I was so offended by the dog.

"If you need to cry," I said to her, "it's absolutely okay for you to cry."

"You're lying," she said, now sobbing. "You hate it when I cry."

"But I really am so sorry," I said. Why did I say that? Well: sometimes the scent of Rema's grassy shampoo reaches me, but coming from some other passing woman, and I'm then filled with feelings that I don't know what to do with; that's how I felt on the phone, with that voice. I found myself continuing on: "It's not just you, my problem with other people's crying. When Magda cried, I handled that so terribly." That was a mistake, to mention Magda by name. Even if I had been talking to the real Rema—and it did sound just like her, and obviously a part of me really *wanted to believe* that it was her—such a disclosure would likely still have been a blunder because, to state it perhaps too simply, family is a sticky issue, often best left alone.

But my words did make the woman stop crying. "When did you talk to my mom?" she said with a desiccating cornsilky voice.

I felt suddenly evaporated and cold, even out there in the sun. "I don't feel obliged to share with you all the details of my life."

"What did you tell her about me?" the voice continued sob-lessly.

Having nothing to say, I said nothing. And anyway, other than having mentioned that I was a meteorologist, I hadn't really said much to Magda at all. "She's a very attractive woman," I finally said, which was just a meaningless commonplace making its own merry way out of my mouth. It meant nothing. Maybe Magda is an attractive woman or maybe she's not, but it's not the kind of quality I was in a frame of mind to notice. Certainly she wasn't as attractive as, say, the Rema-waisted waitress whom I could see through the window—she was really beautiful, distractingly beautiful.

"Does she like you?" the voice asked.

I said nothing. I watched the Rema-waisted waitress wipe down a table.

"Does she look happy?" the voice damply whispered.

Again I said nothing.

My mind was comforting itself randomly with the name Alice.

But not so randomly. I realized then that those snatches of Rema song that I'd had in my mind while I'd been sitting in Magda's living room, they were songs from an album titled *Alice*. "Listen," I finally said to that woman on the phone, "I'm really sorry about this, but I'm actually under quite a bit of stress lately. I'm engaged in some rather pressing and important work—"

"You left me some very strange notes—" she began, and I held the phone away from my ear during the ridiculousness that followed, "—and if you say there's not another woman I believe you. I'll believe you. Leo, did you hit your head on something? Did—"

When there was a pause in the woman's excessive and absurd jeremiad—I, squinting in sunshine while she, I assumed, stood in the cold northern hemisphere shivering—I asked: "Is it snowing where you are?" Then impulsively, "It's summer here, you know."

"You're in Buenos Aires? With my mom?"

I stopped watching the waitress through the window. "Did you know," I continued, feeling other voices clawing out my trachea, "that just to discover the state of things as they presently are, let alone to predict the future, is a problem so computationally complex that to solve it even approximately would require a thousand Crays working in tandem?" And as I spoke, I noticed the wrong mental image blooming across the radar screen of my mind, wrong because although *I knew very well* that Crays referred to supercomputers, I pictured instead a thousand long-necked birds. Craning their necks? Or is *cray* a type of bird? Or was I just thinking about *cranes*? Like herons? "Forget," I added, "about forecasting; even nowcasting is near impossible." When I heard this fake Rema's voice, was the Rema stream of images conjured in my mind correct? Or somehow subtly wrong, a series of wrong images that had already begun the process of extinguishing the real images of my real Rema? What if I was picturing the face of the simulacrum? Would it be better not to see anything at all, so as not to blanch out what I still had? Regardless, it struck me that maybe the observation about the Crays was now outdated, since computers are so much more powerful today than in the past; maybe now such computations could be made in real time; Tzvi's idea either had grown superfluous or had been superfluous all along, had been a means of saying something else. A code? Maybe I was meant to contact Tzvi and ask. All these thoughts ran through my head, at uncertain speeds, entering from uncertain directions. Beneath the din of the phone voice I argued silently to myself that contacting Tzvi Gal-Chen would be ludicrous; the relationship between us was not a reciprocal one; we were allied, yes, but only from my point of view, and only in a somewhat imaginary way, in a somewhat alternately conceived world that didn't really exist, or that I didn't think really existed, not then. *Don't get metaphysically and metaphorically extravagant*, I admonished myself silently while that Rema-like woman talked on. *Only Harvey*, I reminded myself, *believes in the deception. In reality Tzvi and I know nothing of one another.*

"Maybe we can speak tomorrow?" I pleaded, being as polite as I knew how to be, given the circumstances.

"What if I said yes?" the voice said. "What if I said I did know something about forecasting and the thousand crayfish? Did you take my clothing, Leo? Did you take my purse? You know there have been many telephone calls—"

I began to feel a particular kind of nervous, as when an unwanted thought makes its steady migrainous progress toward the surface, a sense of rising water drowning my lungs. So I disconnected. Then I turned off my BlackBerry entirely. It was the only proper thing to do. I needed to go back inside: to the waitress, to dust glittering like tiniest meteors in shafts of natural light.

I asked the Rema-ish waitress for an apple Danish; it tasted like real apple rather than like apple flavoring. Ironically this made the taste seem ersatz to me, on account of the fact that all my childhood the apple flavor I knew and loved took the form of fritters wrapped in plastic.

20. Least squares method of fitting functions to data

I practically ran back to Magda's home. She received me warmly and began showing me photos of Rema—the hallway was a veritable gallery—while I hummed to myself Rema music. Rema in a baptismal gown, held up by large hands, the holder unseen. Rema as a brunette, sitting in a depression of sand, in a green-and-blue bikini, at the beach. A black-and-white photo taken on the front steps of that very home, with a small child Rema, barefoot, holding sandals in her hand. Rema older, looking bored, or angry, at Carnival, a sequined mask pulled up onto her forehead. Rema in pale blue at first communion. Rema in heels, and glamour hair, sitting atop a tractor, her legs crossed, her eyes squinted and looking off to the side. Rema in a burgundy graduation gown, her face blanched by a flash, with a wreath of baby's breath on her hair. Rema in a rocking chair with a speckled greyhound crowded onto her lap.

Only: those photos seemed photos of other Remas. And I suppose, in a certain very straightforward sense—regardless of certain other possibilities—that was inarguably and precisely true: I didn't know those younger versions of her. But I was unsettled and didn't know what to do with that unsettlement, didn't know if it was an ordinary everyday kind of unsettlement, or the paradox that is simply the most visible part of a profound error in an entire worldview.

Anyway: there were no wedding photos of Rema.

And no men. No men in any of the photos.

"Only once, you said," I said to Magda. "Only once you met her husband?" I asked her, trying to behave casually, as if her gallery of Remas didn't resemble a mausoleum, as if my questions were just ones of mildest curiosity.

"So long ago. He looked like the kind of American who would get fat. Did he get fat? I could see it in his jaw."

"I wouldn't say so," I said, hoping she wasn't somehow actually talking about me. Then: "I would like to let a room from you," I blurted out.

She tightened the low ponytail that held back her hair. A scent of citrus escaped. "I usually charge two hundred seventy pesos a week," she said, blushing terribly. "Though I'll take you as a guest, of course—"

"No, of course not," I interrupted.

We both felt (maybe I'm projecting) more awkward, more space-occupying than before.

Shortly thereafter that awkward money moment resurfaced, transformed, when in asking about the best way to get to the airport I mentioned to Magda the loss of my luggage, and she said *So you have none of your objects?* to which I shrugged nonspecifically. Maybe I felt bereft though; maybe it showed on my face; but I really wasn't—not then at least—thinking about that other husband, or even the night nurse, or even Rema. I was just thinking of my suitcase, which actually is Rema's and which is pale blue. Magda put her hand on my back, which is such a gentle and comforting way to be touched; it's too easy to get into a vein of living where that no longer ever happens, where no one touches you in that particular kind way, which produces a very particular feeling, not precisely reproduced by anything else, except maybe by that hug machine that autistic woman designed in order to calm down cows on their way to slaughter. Magda brought me a handkerchief. She stood quietly next to me a moment, or maybe a few moments.

Then, with her arm on mine, she insisted on lending me some clothes; she said she had some very nice men's clothing, which she felt confident would not be too far off from my size.

"No really, I'm entirely fine," I said.

"No," she said.

I again declined the clothes.

"It's hot outside," she said. "And you're dressed for winter. At least for you to have a change for tonight. And for tomorrow morning."

So I consented to her offer. She showed me a mostly bare closet. The closet door rolled on rusty wheels. Inside: clothing hung on metal hangers, covered in plastic like from the dry cleaners. Thin pale button-up shirts with pearline snaps. Tailored pants pinned to themselves in grip around a cardboard rod. A tiny dresser of undershirts, socks, a shoehorn, a glasses' case. Only after a very late dinner that night did I wonder why Magda had men's clothing at all. And whose clothing it might be. And again who Rema's other "husband" was or had been. And what that might have to do with her disappearance, or her double, or, for that matter, with me. And I admit, I wasn't quite sure in which direction my investigation was or should have been proceeding. And I was surprised, unpleasantly, at how well the clothing fit me, even the pants.

I slept in that other man's shirt.

21. One mystery resolving

I must confess that the insignificant price of letting a room from Magda relieved me; nevertheless, perseveration over the price of my last-minute, open-return airline ticket disturbed my sleep; and yet when I would succeed in tripping my thoughts off of perseverations on my profligacy, I would then proceed to ruminate over my miserliness, worrying that, in agreeing to such a cheap rate, I was taking advantage of my wife's mother. Thus I'd be set in pursuit of relief from what had, initially, been relieving me. That's why, reading the paper the next morning, over the coffee and medialunas that Magda offered me, I somewhat surreptitiously surveyed the classifieds section so that I could get a sense of whether I was paying a reasonable rent—a difficult task because I couldn't decipher the significance of the abbreviations and the addresses.

Not far from the classifieds, in those back pages of the tabloid, I came across '70s-looking portrait photos (long hair, slender faces, tinted glasses, loud print shirts) set off in boxes like yearbook advertisements. Alongside the photos were names and the day's date, but of a different year: 1977, two from 1979, 1981. Then phrases like: *Your struggle continues to inspire us. We carry you in our hearts.*

The feel of those photos, the mood of them, brought to mind the Gal-Chen family photo. So that was what I recognized first, that very particular familiarity. It took me a few moments more—synapses having to wend a very circuitous path—for me to realize that these were not just late '70s nostalgia photos; these were almost certainly memorials to Argentina's disappeared, published on the anniversaries of disappearance.

Let me confess that—what with its being over twenty years since the end of the "dirty war" (a term that strikes me as a too-catchy euphemism for mass murder, "war" misleadingly implying that the paranoid fantasies of the junta were true, but this seems an issue for another time)—I hadn't imagined that the wounds would still be quite so obviously alive, so manifest. I can see now that I should not have been surprised—what with my experiences, professional ones I mean, I especially should not have been surprised. People naturally perseverate on their personal tragedies, even though such perseveration doesn't really serve anyone, neither the living nor the dead. I mean, there's research on these things. It's simply not a practical use of time to think constantly of the dead. I'm not heartless, and I do regret that I must sound that way, and I understand how resilience is in its way a demonic kind of strength, a strength not unrelated to a capacity for indifference, a strength that is discomfiting evidence against the existence of true, eternal love. But is it better for the living to burn themselves in others' funeral pyres? As I wrote, once, "Mourning should be mortal." And, well, I think it's worth considering why memorial writing is so awful, why it so entirely fails to communicate the feeling of loss. I at least feel that it fails. Those vague earnest words all seem so demeaning, so shameful, like strangers hearing the sound of you going to the bathroom.

I felt nauseous reading those memorials, almost all of them accompanied by those hazy now kitsch photos that seemed like material downtown kids iron onto T-shirts. Why nauseous instead of, say, sad? some analyst sap might ask me, and yes of course *sad* I suppose, but that's a separate question. I felt sick, I felt an incipient migraine, and that is the main thing I'm trying to say. That, and maybe society should more seriously consider the coping mechanism of not talking about loss, at least not publicly; a highly superior coping mechanism, I would argue, is to cathart over the sufferings of fictional creations. I realize that in these views I am deeply heretical within my field, but considering the company that makes up my field, I feel no shame in distinguishing myself.

I hear other voices, maybe some of them my own, pointing out the Orwellian nature of Silence Is Health. But I respond with: well, let's not aphorize. Maybe politically, yes, nations should remember, the world should remember. But the individual sufferers should not have to. Let the sufferers run. They have a good chance of dying before any grief catches up to them. Myself for example: if Rema had, say, died rather than just disappeared, well, I wouldn't be turning over in my head the problem of such unresolvable pain. Mysteries that can't be solved should be passed over in silence, or something like that. If Rema had died I would just not think about her at all—or at least that's the advice I would give myself. What I face now, Rema's absence, borders on the unfathomable, but it's not actually unfathomable, not actually without hope of solution, and that is why I allow myself to think about it, because there's hope.

So: I was sitting across from Magda, dressed in a pointy-collared pale green button-up '70s shirt she had lent me, reading that newspaper, with its classified ads and memorials. I ate two, then three medialunas and drank too quickly, and then had to suppress burps. Just as I was about to ask Magda about the memorials, about whether they were "normal," or commonly seen, I noticed she was fixated on the cuff of the shirt that I had on, and this somehow made me realize that I didn't want to be the kind of person interested in asking the kind of question I was about to ask. I had other, more personally pressing, questions that I wasn't asking.

I opened my mouth.

Then my BlackBerry—set there on the table beside me—trembled.

Magda held a hand up to her heart, as if she'd been given a fright, as if a real alarm had sounded.

"It's not Rema," I said suddenly, perhaps brusquely, I don't know why.

"Oh, no, of course not," she said, and "please," she added, gesturing toward my retrembling BlackBerry. "Be at home."

It was just an e-mail marked "urgent"; I've programmed these to ring even when my ringer is off because I usually receive such notes only when an outpatient of mine has been admitted to the hospital.

Magda looked decidedly the other way; she took a cookie and dipped it into her tea with an expectant look, as if waiting to see if the cookie would crumble.

The urgent e-mail appeared to be from Harvey.

Dear Dr. Leo,

I wrote to Dr. Gal-Chen of my progress against the 49.

I have not yet heard back from him.

Have you heard from him? I have sent him three letters.

I am in central Oklahoma and am unable to obtain a copy of the New York Post. *The National Severe Storms Laboratory here was unprotected.*

Please pass on Dr. Gal-Chen's phone number. It's urgent.

—Harvey

When I looked down at my hands, I saw newsprint smudged on the pads of my fingers. Touching the screen of my BlackBerry left a print. I shouldn't have been surprised to notice, when I looked up and over at Magda, that she had on full makeup, even already then, first thing in the morning. There is something about a confident thick streak of eyeliner that makes a woman look very emotional. I could also detect Magda's concealer, there under her eyes, shy about the fine wrinkles to which it clung. Her cheeks had a dramatic swath of blush that slightly sparkled, as if sifted with very fine grains of sand.

"Who was that?" Magda said.

"Did any of the disappeared ever reappear?" I then asked Magda, who ignored me for a moment, as if I were talking not to her but to my phone. "I'm sorry," I said, probably because I thought that was what she should have said to me, for being rude to me. "I was just thinking about it on account of these memorials here in the newspaper." I wasn't going to tell her about Harvey. "I mean, those are *memorials*, yes? I was just curious if maybe there were people who had been *believed* to have been disappeared, but who had really just wandered off, maybe had gone crazy, or maybe had a bout of amnesia. And then maybe one day, maybe years later"—I was all about the maybes—"those people unexpectedly return. Or are found. I've heard of that happening, of mistakes like that. You know, I read recently, in another newspaper, that an unknown, unshowered vagrant had been found playing virtuosic Debussy in a church in a Scottish fishing village; I think the man spoke German; when asked his name he said he couldn't remember; word spread and hundreds of people—literally hundreds—said they were certain they knew who he was, came to visit expecting to find their lost brother or child or friend—"

At which point I think she interrupted with something to the tired effect of: oh really? And I realized, heat rising to my face, that I had been going on and on. Still, I added:

"Someone might have been right. Someone might have found his, or her, missing man."

Or I was saying something like that, trying to keep myself from staring at Magda's emotional makeup and trying to distract her from any questions about the note I'd just received, seeing as I was even less ready than I'd been the day before to invent some story on the spur of the moment.

But: at least a mystery, if not *the* mystery, was beginning to reveal itself. Harvey was not dead; he was in Oklahoma.

22. Method of maximum likelihood

There was a time when the belief was prevalent that all those who cared for the mentally ill became mentally ill, and at the arrival of Harvey's message, that idea—infectiousness—stretched its cadaverous hand out from the past to touch my mind.

I had thought to contact Tzvi Gal-Chen.

And Harvey had actually contacted him, or at least had tried to.

But it wasn't the same Tzvi Gal-Chen we were talking about. That's why I was nothing like Harvey.

Magda gestured to my small, empty coffee cup, and I startled back into myself and gestured toward the object about which we were obviously not speaking, my BlackBerry.

"That was just a colleague of mine," I said as casually as I could manage, nodding my head about the coffee, which she refilled for me. "Thank you."

"She's all right? Your colleague is all right?"

"He. It's a he," I said. "Yes. Yes, of course. Yes, he's fine, more than fine."

Magda sat down again, wrapped both hands around her own mug. Her hands—they were so much older than Rema's—were thin and receded away from the knuckles.

"Yes, this colleague," I began, trying to set Magda, or really myself, at ease. "He just likes to send me the most random notes, does it all the time," I said with a little laugh; in truth it was the first e-mail Harvey had ever sent me. "I get the most wonderful e-mails from him all the time," I said. In truth I have no friends, except for Rema, who send me wonderful e-mails; my e-mails are dully professional. "He's such a lovely source of entertainment and happiness," I continued, finally falsely elaborating to true excess.

I folded up the newspaper like clean laundry. I cleared my throat and stood up. I began to gather dishes over Magda's protest. I began to wash the dishes and Magda asked me to stop. She told me I was using the wrong sponge.

I told her that after stopping by the airport, I'd be spending the rest of my day at the university.

"Which university?" she asked me.

I didn't know. It just seemed like the place a research meteorologist would be spending his days. So I just said, "Thank you again for breakfast," and left.

23. An alibi not invented by Rema

I called the airport and a woman's voice told me assuringly that my suitcase had been found. I splurged on a taxi, but then what they showed me wasn't even the right color. My suitcase—Rema's suitcase—is pale blue, baby blue, and hard-shelled with regularly irregular craters like the moon. The suitcase they showed me was periwinklish, which I suppose some people will call blue and some purple, and both camps will be pretty dedicated to their idea of what the real color is, and will see it, often, as, well, a black-and-white issue. Rema and I argued over this once. But how do people make those kinds of mistakes? I wonder if the periwinkle color is an undecided issue in all cultures, or if there are some cultures with so many things to distinguish along the blue-to-violet spectrum that a much more sophisticated and precise language has evolved.

Anyway, a miscommunication.

I made my way back to the coffee shop where the Rema-waisted waitress had been. The Rema-waisted waitress was not there. The waitress in her place was attractive, but not as attractive. I asked for a coffee and extra cookies, and I set my first priority: to respond to Harvey's e-mail, and in that response to come up with a convenient barrier between Dr. Gal-Chen and myself.

After that, I could (I told myself) with a clear mind return to the central matter—I didn't see then how they were related—of searching for Rema.

I took up pen in hand and began writing, with no plan of what I was going to say, just hoping an idea would come to me; something to the effect of what is reproduced below is what my hand wrote:

Dear Harvey,
    Glad to hear that you are doing well.
    Some news: Tzvi Gal-Chen and I have been moved to separate legions and can no longer communicate directly. I can only send notes upward to my superiors, who will contact his superiors—possibly—who might then possibly choose to contact him, but one can never be sure. YOU SHOULD NOT MAKE ANY FUR-THER ATTEMPTS AT CONTACTING DR. GAL-CHEN DIRECTLY. Who can know the ifs and whens of whether messages are transmitted, or if they are intercepted? We must always be wary of the 49.
    These clouds do not cast shadows, they scatter light.
    I am out of my office for an undetermined length of time, but please, keep in touch.
                                         Dr. L

Terribly hokey. And not very believable? Why did I use that word "legions"? The use of all caps for emphasis embarrasses me. And I cannot even express the nausea evoked by recalling my feeble attempt at mysterious wisdom. If only I'd had Rema's help; she would have come up with something so much more compelling.

    I ate a cookie—slightly almond—and considered whether to type in and send my note. I did send the note. Harvey soon sent me back some quite surprising news.

24. In 1990, Tzvi Gal-Chen publishes "Can Dryline Mixing Create Buoyancy?"

So there I sat, wearing borrowed clothes, in the southern hemisphere, in a coffee shop near Rema's childhood home, the Rema-waisted waitress not there, my awkward missive to Harvey sent, time moving at an uncertain rate as sunlight flooded continuously through the window, inducing a not so subtle dew along the plane of my back, and when I glanced—at some moment—back down at the slightly reflective screen of my BlackBerry I saw—in addition to an orangutan-y distortion of my forehead—that I'd already received a response, of sorts, from Harvey.

He had forwarded me a note from tzvi@galchen.net.

Dear Harvey,

Thanks for your compliments. Sorry I'm responding to your e-mail rather than snail mail address; I know you said you were worried, but let me reassure you that e-mail as a form of communication is plenty safe for our purposes here.

As per your request, let me first say that I have no doubt that you've been extremely dedicated in your work as a covert mesoscale operator for the Royal Academy. For that reason and others, I agree with you that you definitely deserve more freedom as regards your assignments. Yes, New York can get dull, especially meteorologically speaking. I also love severe storm season in the plains. Anyway, from here forward consider yourself autonomous; I (and my superiors who must remain nameless) trust your judgment entirely.

With continued gratitude for all your atmospheric labor,

Dr. Tzvi Gal-Chen

P.S.—Yes, please do pass on my regards to Dr. L.

A breeze then entered the coffee shop. I looked up and saw a striking old bald man enter; I took a sip of the fresh-squeezed orange juice before me; then somehow I spilled the glass of orange juice; the pulp mosaiced through the liquid as it spread across the table; the Rema-ish waitress emerged seemingly out of nowhere carrying several white waffled rags with trim of pale blue stripes; she smelled of baby oil; with a paper napkin I patted at the splash on the screen of my BlackBerry, but flecks of pulp remained, looking like scraped cheek cells smeared out on a slide.

But beneath those not actually cheek cells, the e-mail from Tzvi to Harvey and then on to me, remained unchanged.

The door had swung shut; the breeze as if it never were; the man seated; a chill still on my dewy back; the Rema-ish waitress again vanished.

Recall: at that time in my life, the only Tzvi Gal-Chen I knew, really, was Rema. Rema, Rema, Rema, Rema. The Tzvi language didn't seem like hers, but certainly the note seemed like a clue. I didn't feel safe typing into my pulpy BlackBerry, but I found an old, very old, receipt in my pocket, and wrote on the back the following list:

Unnamed dog?
Anatole?
Royal Academy?
Rema's husband?
Tzvi Gal-Chen?

Then I folded the receipt over many times, making a compact little nugget out of it, so that I could reach into the deep and narrow pockets of my borrowed pants and feel the contours of that folded paper; I figured that would help me stay focused in my thinking, stay focused in my search.

25. A wrongful accusation

"You're here," a voice said, and looking up I again for a moment thought it was Rema, or the Rema-waisted waitress, but it was not the Rema-waisted waitress, nor was it Rema. It was Magda, there in my coffee shop.

"I'm here. Yes," I said, feeling suddenly like a child caught skipping school. Magda may have been standing there at the side of my table for rather a few moments before I remembered to offer her a seat, an offer she did not refuse, and we then sat there quietly for a few more moments, as I felt along the contours of the crumpled clue receipt in my pocket. My impersonation of a meteorologist—it was off to a bad start.

With a nod toward the damp BlackBerry, Magda, breaking the stillness as uninvasively as possible, said simply: "That's something." Then: "Before this morning I'd never seen anything like that."

"Yes, it's kind of a new thing," I said.

"Something I've never seen before," she repeated.

"But it's common," I said, deciding to let that small electronic device cloud over any false explanatory rays of my not being at any university.

Then it was quiet again, at least quiet between us. There were other sounds, I suppose—probably milk was steaming, and silverware clinking, and newspaper crinkling—but I wasn't noticing.

"Do you know what I'm wondering about?" Magda asked. I did not proffer my guesses, which were my dreads. "Rema's hair," she said. "I am wondering how is she wearing it?"

I must have looked at Magda strangely (but not on account of her question, instead mostly because I had my hand on that crumpled clue and I was still discussing Tzvi and Harvey and everything within the privacy of myself) because Magda began to explain herself: "It's just that we used to fight over her hair. She'd hardly brush it, and she'd let it hang in her face and you couldn't see her sweet features and she was making herself look vulgar and it would be this big argument. Between us, it really was ugly, what she'd do with her hair."

I offered cautiously, "Her hair looks very nice these days." And having the chance to say something that was simply true—it was not as much of a relief as I thought it would be. I coughed. Strands of Rema's cornsilk hair seemed to be snaked at the interstices of my bronchi.

"And so now—well—so how is she wearing her hair now? She looks pretty?" Magda asked, rolling her eyes and smiling derisively, at herself I think, not at me.

"She's very smart. Rema is very smart," I said to Magda, but—and this just struck me now—I suspect it was myself I was accusing with that blunt comment.

"I smell oranges?" Magda said.

I said, "I'm sorry. You'd like her hair, I think. The way it looks now. It's very tidy. And a beautiful color. Blonde like the inside of corn. She wears it usually in a low—" I demonstrated a ponytail with a gesture. "Holds it in a wide gold clip. And it's long and trim. And in the summer she pins the flyaway hairs back with neat little parallel hairpins that are a natural color instead of just plain black. But she still gets these pretty little loose strands; they get kind of extra bleachy blonde-ish and wavy in the summertime, I think naturally, or maybe she does that on purpose. My mom used to do that with lemon juice, little highlights like that." I unpeeled the pads of my fingers from the sticky surface of the table and saw the whorled print of my own grease, and it looked like the image from Tzvi's research paper. "More or less like that, anyway, is what her hair looks like," I added quickly. "I mean it's not like I see Rema every day, so who knows what she's doing with her hair on just any old day."

"You love her, don't you?" Magda said.

I re-adhered and de-adhered my finger pads on the sticky table. I patted at the cookie crumbs on the plate where there were no longer cookies. I think I said nothing and looked nowhere, but Magda, like Rema, knew how to crowd up the silent space. "I apologize if I have made you uncomfortable," she said. "Please understand that I am not narrow-minded in these ways. It makes me happy to see that you love her. It would make me happy to know that she has a lover. I'm just saying this, about this love you seem to have, partially because, well, her husband: I never saw it in him. I never saw that he loved her. That is why you came to see me, yes, because you love her?"

I spotted the Rema-waisted waitress, re-emerged from the back, attending to a nearby table.

"Rema," I declared, "isn't the type to have affairs under any circumstances."

No perceptible response in the spine of the waitress, no twitch of attention.

Then I dropped a spoon I hadn't realized I was holding. I reached out to my sticky BlackBerry and put it in my pocket. Soon afterward Magda left the coffee shop.

I love you, I wrote on the bill when I paid it, wrote as if a kind of test, in case somehow that waitress might really be Rema.

26. Lola

That evening, after watching the TV weather and reassuringly or disappointingly, I'm not sure which, receiving no signals from the forecast—I needed to verify constantly for myself that I wasn't perceiving patterns and signals that weren't actually there—I finally placed a call to the Royal Academy. I somewhat lost control of the conversation. This proved in the end fortuitous, perhaps even destined, or at least, I might say, *determined*, as in the folding of certain proteins according to the dictates of RNA.

I dialed what appeared to be the main number. "Yes. I'm returning a call?"

"Are you calling about the marital tension?"

"Someone called me."

"Yes. Do you know your party's extension?"

"Well, really, like I said, I'm *returning* a call. I was the object of calling, not the subject."

There was a bit of confusion, since I really didn't know to whom I was returning a call. So I mentioned that I was calling from Buenos Aires in hopes that the receptionist would then be put in mind of the expense I was incurring. Our "conversation" was not progressing well, and then on impulse I dropped Harvey's name—which I of course immediately regretted doing—but suddenly there was a little bit of tender piano music, I was being transferred, and then, abruptly—

"You're calling about the dog?" a trembly, almost theremin-y voice swelled.

"Yes," I said quite surprised, "I think I am."

"But the job is in Patagonia, not Buenos Aires. In El Calafate, right on the Moreno Glacier. You know that, yes? I think it wasn't clear on the posting."

"Excuse me?"

"El Calafate," she repeated with warbling irritation. "Patagonia."

"That's where the dog is?" I asked.

"Listen. Calling four times in a row doesn't help. We have your phone number—"

"But I'm not at my home phone anymore—"

"But like I was trying to explain, if you're willing to be based in Patagonia, then there's a real chance—"

"Is this related to the offer of fellowship—?"

"Listen," she said, the pitch of her voice dropping, "the truth is—what the truth is—well the truth is that I just don't know. And everyone's been calling with questions. The person before you asked me how we knew that information could be retrieved from black holes. Was that a joke? Why ask me? Was he mocking me? This is not my regular post; this is just a temporary position for me and I'm feeling really overwhelmed—" she said, her voice flaking.

"I'm really sorry to hear that," I said, with genuine emotion, because I was sincerely moved by this stranger's circumstances, even from the little I knew of them, just from the timbre of and tremble in her voice. "Really. I am really sorry."

"No, I'm sorry," she said, obviously crying—lately everyone crying to me—and even laughing a little bit as well at the same time. "How ridiculous," she said. "I don't know why I can't just keep my selves together," she said.

"It's all right," I said then. "It's okay to cry," I said. And the strange thing was that, not having actually to see this woman, not having actually to feel responsible for her distress, I really did feel it was more than okay to cry. In person, to be honest, I generally find weeping people repulsive. What can I do? I don't have other antisocial personality disorder traits. I went on, "Crying can be like squeezing the pus out of a gluteal abscess. I mean, listen, some wounds just grow larger and more infected when you expel them, but with others that may be the only option. It's a risk. You just don't want to get obsessed with the wound; you don't want to be looking for pus every day, poking and prodding, and making an ugly mess of your skin . . . but shedding a few tears over the phone to a stranger . . . well, maybe that's just right."

She was giggling during my little improvised analogy. "You've been really sweet," she said. She sounded very attractive. "I already feel a little better. You're funny," she added.

Then there was a silence. Was I supposed to cry too? Then she broke into the silence, as if with the sudden opening of a faucet, and said: "Listen, I think we're done with this call. Did you say you had a different contact number now? Let me just get that from you and when the regular person returns, the real person, they'll get back to you."

"And who are you?"

"I'm Lola."

I gave Lola my number.

She went on, "I really think there's not that many people able to go to Patagonia on such short notice. Apparently the person who was originally supposed to take the position dropped out at the last minute, so it's a bit of a scramble. So I think you have a real chance of getting the job. But listen, I'd really suggest that you don't keep calling. Some of the staff here are really petty and irritable, and that'll get used against you; I've even seen them purposely put CVs in the wrong pile, just to get them lost—well, listen, bye sweets," she said finally.

I thanked her for her advice and hung up in a haze of inexplicable happiness and confusion.

Progress may not lie, I told myself, where I might think it would lie. And this made me think of swapping beds, of Baudelaire's point about life being a hospital in which every patient is possessed of the desire to change beds. Not that I was actually ill, or swapping women, or projecting feelings from one space to another, or harboring unrealizable desires—just that the conversation with Lola had unsettled me. Our phone call seemed like the most substantial advance I'd had yet toward the goal of finding Rema. The waitress, the simulacrum on the phone, even Rema's mother—they gave the feel of closeness, but this was clearly much more promising.

27. Dog man

I went for a walk, in order to think, to pass the time, to not be alone, to not notice that Magda was still not home; even Killer was not at home. I dodged dog deposits on the sidewalk, was barked at ferociously by a rottweiler behind bars, was approached with love and trust by two skinny beaglish mixes. Then, not having noticed that I'd returned to right across the street from Magda's home, I saw: congregated, more than a dozen large dogs, all on leashes, connected to an unsettlingly pacific man who was leaning against a wall, smoking.

The dogs: relatively large, vibrant, healthy-looking. None like the miniature greyhound that the double had toted home.

But packs of dogs make me—this truly is entirely normal—very nervous. My feet stopped advancing.

The dog man nodded at me.

I echo nodded.

Then he called across to me, "The sin is yours, huh?"

I did not answer or nod but only looked at him amidst his pack of curs. I hadn't been flirting with Lola. Or the waitress.

"La señora," he said, now louder, and emphasizing the second syllable of señora, "no está?"

Magda's dog, the greyhound Killer: I spotted her among the mob.

Would you believe that I then looked up and immediately saw Sirius, the Dog Star, which appears to be one star but is in fact actually two, or possibly even three?

Then a woman's voice—it proved to be Magda's—on the other side of the street, nearing the beasts. She kissed the dog man on each cheek, then beckoned me over, as if not to a dangerous den, so what could I—if I was to maintain decorum—do except cross the street and join the humans and animals?

"I present you my friend," Magda said in English, pronouncing "present" so that it meant gift, and then giggling.

I bravely extended my hand out over the dogs, toward the dog man, who instead of taking my hand grabbed hold of the back of my neck and pulled me forward, and I nearly fell, save for his having hold of me like a wolf's grip on its cub. I felt his plump towelly lips press against my cheek. I was in an awkward tilt position—suspended out over that pack of dogs that I imagined looking up at me—and upon my return from the greeting I again almost fell over.

Which returned me mentally to: why so many dogs in my life all of the sudden?

"Dogs are not your dear friends," the man said to me.

"No, I love dogs," I said. "I really love them. Some of them. The gentle ones."

Magda and the dog man laughed. I thought of the vein on the night nurse's forehead. Amidst the unpleasant moment, I realized that I'd never had to deal with living in a community full of men who might possibly in the past have kissed Rema. At least, I didn't think that back home I had to be concerned, since Rema had been in the country only a number of months when I met her, since I'd never seen her, during all those months of just looking at her, with anyone else. Though I had at one time wondered if she was trying to avoid someone that first night when she couldn't decide where we'd have pizza.

I don't know why I thought she might have kissed, or loved, this oversized man with the dogs. He was hairy handed, much more so than me. When he spoke something more to me, in Spanish, I wasn't sure what he said, and so in response I just smiled. I guess one might say he was ruggedly handsome.

"Very, very nice to meet you," I said, then went inside the house. Alone there, I reexamined the gallery of Rema photos, and indeed, as I reconfirmed, Rema was standing next to a man in absolutely none of them. But there was a photo of Magda with a man. Just one, a wedding photo. Maybe this was Rema's father; maybe not. I really had no idea.

Very late that evening, I came across Magda in the living room. She was wearing a full-length, high-necked Victorian nightgown that was somehow immodest in its extreme modesty. "He's also an analyst," she said to me as I held my gaze down at the delicate eyelet of her hem. "He walks dogs only because nobody can pay for analysis anymore. He lets his patients pay just symbolically."

Which sounded dirty. And why could so many people pay to have their dogs walked while so few could pay for analysis? The long nightgown, the high incidence of analysts, the apparent manlessness of Magda's life—I found it all rather suspicious. And yet I could not cast out the ludicro-banal hypothesis that that man—whatever his name and economic status were—was an earlier object of attraction for Rema and that I might be—for her—a mere reverberance of him. Why? Just because we were both kind of hairy?

This is irrelevant to your investigation, one parliament member of me said to another.

I raised my gaze to Magda's still eyelinered eyes. "How long have you known that man who walks the dogs?"

"The analyst?" she said. "Since forever. His practice is unusual," and I was again suddenly anxious that she was going to talk about sex. "He works mostly with relatives of the disappeared. You should understand that he's very, very respected. He only walks the dogs now in order to be able to continue seeing his patients. And because he loves dogs. He really does," she added, as if to emphasize his moral superiority over me.

"Yes? Does he especially like—" but I didn't know the Spanish word for greyhound. Maybe it was just "greyhound." "Well, is there a special kind of dog that he loves especially?"

"Is there a kind of dog that you love especially?" she answered, stretching out her hands, catpaw-like, on the surface of her gown, over what I deduced was her midthigh.

But I really hate mirroring; I especially abhor the notion that whatever I say is secretly about me. So I didn't answer her, pawing there at her gown.

Then Magda said, "I should have thought—he also knows the American. I should have thought of that connection, that you know someone in common. Do you want anything? I'm going to bed now."

She believed I didn't love dogs, but her dog came and slept in the bed with me that night.

28. What would Tzvi Gal-Chen do?

I really do like gentle dogs. And when I petted the velvety crown of Killer's head the next morning, when I lifted one of her silken ears and held it like fine cloth between my fingers, she then lifted her gaze to me, which re-reminded me why I suspect people love dogs so passionately, for that loyal devotion of theirs that manages to be simultaneously easy and profound. Or at least their love appears to be like that even if only because I so desperately want to believe in such a love.

My pants were draped over a chair near the bed; the little nugget of paper upon which I'd written my notes had fallen to the floor. It looked like ordinary trash. I felt ashamed about a certain sort of slapdashness converging upon my mission. I put on the foreign pants. I picked up my crumpled note. I sat myself with proper posture at the desk. Killer arranged herself in a curl near my feet. And I uncrumpled:

> Unnamed dog?
> Anatole?
> Royal Academy?
> Rema's husband?
> Tzvi Gal-Chen?

Now there were Lola and the dog man to consider as well. There might be duplicates, though: the dog man might be Anatole, Lola might be Tzvi Gal-Chen. And maybe Tzvi, Lola, and the Royal Academy should all be one category. Or Tzvi and Lola just subcategories of the Royal Academy. And what of Harvey?

But this "system," in terms of action, was getting me nowhere. I felt acutely that I didn't even have, like, say, Harrison Ford in *Frantic*, a suitcase to rummage through. My life—so much less compelling, so much less organized, than even a movie. But I knew that was a uselessly vain thought, utterly beside the point, an influence of grogginess, and I did have this lead with Lola at the Academy, surely that would turn up something, sometime, and yet, here I was, indefinitely doing nothing in pursuit of Rema. That's when I heard in my mind—and I knew it was just in my mind—a Rema voice giggle-accuse-whisper: *What would Tzvi Gal-Chen do?*

I resolved to look again more closely at Tzvi's research paper, "A Theory for the Retrievals," a work that claimed to be retrieving "thermodynamic variables from within deep convective clouds," but that I suspected—or hoped—might be about quite a bit more. As I combed through the pages a small Rema memory came to me: I had once taken her to a performance of *Hamlet*, but the antique English of it had meant that she'd hardly followed a word, so it was less than a spectacular evening, and I'd apologized to her for not having thought of how the language would be difficult, but said that maybe it was kind of appropriate to the play, since the play was about, I said, what happens when you grossly overestimate what thinking can accomplish, and she'd said, no, really the play's about the long influence of dead fathers, that's how I like to think about it, she said. It just came to me, our little trades, her small indignancies, and I missed her so acutely. Regardless, Tzvi's paper, despite the difficulty of the language, did indeed reveal to me what was quite compellingly a reference to my situation with Rema. It argued for the validity of introducing into atmospheric models two types of errors: white noise, which referred to errors "on all resolvable scales," and blue noise, which referred exclusively to "errors on the smallest resolvable scales." These errors, he argued, enhanced "the realism of retrieved fields."

Did Tzvi know all about those "errors on the smallest resolvable scales" that characterized the doppelganger? Did he know how this related to retrieval? Certainly he knew about how Crays working in tandem could solve problems of increasing magnitude. So arguably it was as if I was a Cray, and he was a Cray, and . . . well why, I thought, shouldn't I turn to Tzvi for help?

That image from the first Gal-Chen paper I'd seen, back in the library: in addition to reminding me of Rema, it also looked to me like a lonely man, in an alien landscape, glancing back over his shoulder as if to ask something of someone whom he was not sure was there.

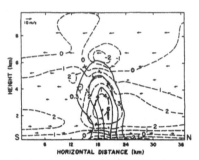

Fig. 3. Vertical *y-z* cross section at 90 min. at *x* = 14.25 km through the model storm showing the rainwater mixing ratio contours (g kg⁻¹, solid), the velocity vectors in the plane, and the potential temperature change from the initial base state (°C, dashed). South is to left and north to right. Wind speed proportional to vector length; areas void of vectors indicate very little flow in this plane.

"Maybe I will write to Tzvi," I said to gentle Killer, who did not seem to disapprove. "Maybe I need to make progress on the mesoscale, that is, the human scale." And so, sitting there in my mother-in-law's room, a mother-in-law I hardly knew and who hardly knew me (and who had been given the wrong clues for getting to know me), I turned my BlackBerry on, switched it to silent, and tried to be professional, direct, and sincerely warm at once. After thanking Tzvi for his correspondence with Harvey, I wrote to him about: the erroneous Rema, wanting to retrieve my own Rema, the inexplicable intrusion of dogs into my life, my most recent contact with the Royal Academy of Meteorology. Then I simply asked, making reference to his work that had wisely directed me to Buenos Aires in the first place, if he had any suggestions for how I might progress in my attempts at retrieval.

29. A mysterious misrepresentation

Dear Leo Liebenstein, MD:

I'm sorry. I suspect this is kind of my fault. I don't actually know Harvey. There's been some confusion. I really am sorry. And I'm sorry to hear about your wife. Unfortunately I don't know anything about her. Or her whereabouts. Again I'm sorry. I regret any confusion I've caused. For a few reasons none of which you should take personally I don't think I'll write to you about this again.

This reply arrived almost immediately.

I did think, for a moment, that maybe Tzvi had taken Rema. That, though, was just indignation speaking.

A better explanation for the cold reply: maybe Tzvi, like me, thought he had to work all alone because he didn't know if he could trust in me—after all, when he first received that note from me I was nothing to him but an e-mail address, and anyone can be behind an e-mail address, regardless of who appears to be behind it. (Years after my mother died, I would still receive mail addressed to her and occasionally I would answer her mail; once I went and picked up her glasses prescription.) So I can understand Tzvi's mysterious misrepresentation of himself and his knowledge—he couldn't be sure with whom he was communicating. And he knew what I didn't then know, which was that his own position was ontologically dubious. So he was experiencing, in a sense, an *Initial Value Problem* in response to having received a communication from me; he didn't know whether *I* was a parameter he might safely rely on, in order to accurately infer forward to a forecast of the truth, to reliable predictions of possible futures. Perhaps, all alone as he was then, as he maintained himself, working in isolation for the Royal Academy, he may have worried that he was, proverbially, "going mad."

I was alone too. If only Killer—very little white shows in dog eyes, so it's more difficult to tell where they're looking—could have offered me a second opinion, a second interpretation of the situation. Yes, retrospectively I can certainly understand Tzvi's retreat from intimacy as a manifestation of his anxiety, but in the chill of the moment I reacted less pacifically. Feeling that I had been condescended to, I responded immediately with:

Dr. Gal-Chen:

I was just kidding. Wrongly believed you understood. Sorry! Ha-ha. Again sorry! I thought you might enjoy this Adorno quote: "The unreality of children's games gives notice that reality has not yet become real. Unconsciously they rehearse the right life."

—Leo

So a rather petty and passive-aggressively pretentious move on my part, arguably brought on by the underclass feeling evoked by my own temporary dishevelment and isolation. Or maybe by examining too closely the worn nap of the velvet upholstering of Magda's desk chair in which I sat. (Her wardrobe so immaculate and yet her furniture so Miss Havisham.) To my credit, after sending that note I then immediately turned off my BlackBerry in order to protect myself from further impulsive communication.

I later lay around in that living room for what seemed like hours, waiting for someone—anyone—to pass through. But no stirrings. I felt that if I couldn't get into a terrible argument I might have to shred reams of paper into very, very tiny pieces. And I hate that feeling, of having a feeling within me that just vibrates but that has nowhere to go, like sound in a vacuum, never being received. Then I suffer the self-hatred of having allowed that undesired feeling to pile up, so that adds another layer of ugliness.

In the kitchen I found a tin of butter cookies, some with crystallized sugar atop, crystallized in a way that made me feel, by comparison, hazy and unresolved. I ate many of the cookies. Then overfull, and as if half the cookies were still in my esophagus waiting patiently to become part of me, I stared at the ceiling of the kitchen. It was painted in drips and drabbles—"spackled," I think is the word, the real word, not just Rema's riff on "speckled"—and the shapes that normally morph and merge out upon the random pattern of such a ceiling did not morph and merge for me as I sat there, though I waited for them to do so, even just playfully, but they didn't, which made it seem as if I'd become the worst kind of literalist and could no longer be startled past the surface of things. As if I really believed in a world where Tzvi didn't know about Rema, a world where people, oddly enough, meant just what they said.

30. An ersatz return

Did I think of going home? I thought of going home. Did I go to
the coffee shop and stare too much at the Rema-like waitress? I did.
After all, in the aftermath of Rema's disappearance, it had been
Tzvi's work that had directed me to Argentina in the first place.
And actually, it was Rema who, in the aftermath of the beautiful
ordinariness of our days, had sent me, as a corrective of sorts, to
Tzvi Gal-Chen. Now I suspected the circle of referents might be
meaningless. Or at least unsolvable, despite my turning round
them again and again. Why had I automatically cast Tzvi in the
role of heroic leader? Why had I expected him to tell me what to
do next? I could see that he was relevant to my mystery, perhaps
even central, yes, but that didn't mean he was necessarily, say, good.
Maybe his work was important, even while he himself was not. Or
so I tried to reason, through seven coffees, eleven cookies, and two
rounds of toast with marmalade. It was imperative, I eventually decided, that I undertake a more thorough study of Tzvi's work. Regardless of what he had written in his e-mail. His research—I had
just skated on the surface of those words, had turned for help prematurely. Surely, even on my own, I could yield more clues than I
had so far. And what with the Lola-arranged meteorological labor
that lay on my horizon, I needed to grow more fluent with meteorological vocabulary. Tzvi's abrupt dismissal of me only emphasized
the relevance and import of the work, I decided, as I left a sizable
tip and wrote *xoxoxo* on the merchant receipt.

   With impressive resolve, I headed back to Magda's home, to
Tzvi's research. I really was ready to go straight to work.

   But outside Magda's home I saw a woman. Without urgency,

ascending like a lava lamp bubble, a tamped thought: *she looks just like Rema.* Far more so than even the waitress. This woman was just sitting on the front step, her feet turned inward, elbows on knees, chin in hands, fringe of cornsilk blonde hair hanging over dove dark eyes. Next to her a dog. But not the small nervous dog from New York. Instead Killer, the magnified version of that orphaned dog.

I stood dead still, considered turning and never returning. Why was I instinctually afraid of her? Why had I automatically cast *her* into the simple role of antagonist? If my casting was so off to begin with, then my hopeless forecasting, wasn't that wrong too? She looked so forlorn and pretty.

The simulacrum—not aware of me—then moved her arms. She crossed them over and held on to opposite elbows as if she were cold. This flattened out her upper arm—pressing it against her side—made her arm look larger and also exaggerated its shape, distorting it, funhouse mirroring a form that I love, an ideal form, a just-so curve. This woman was definitely not as pretty as my Rema, not, at least, with her arm all flattened out that way, looking chubby. And that tincture of unattractiveness—well, it made the simulacrum seem to me suddenly harmless.

I stepped forward, into the woman's view, and said, with an admirable affect of nonchalance, "Isn't that the wrong puppy?"

Before I knew anything, she was holding on to me, and had her arms around me at the shoulders, and her cheek against my cheek, and there was that smell of grass in her hair, which really made me see in blurred triplicate, and then she was kissing my face, the manys of her, and to be perfectly honest this was all reminding me far too acutely of Rema (I felt her teeth on my cheek), of my Rema of the pecans and tea topiaries and foreign newspapers, and frankly it was all making me really too sad. I didn't like feeling sad, only perverse people like to feel sad—I hadn't been feeling sad, I had put that off for more important emotions—I wanted to push that woman off of me but couldn't because I felt like I'd lost control over my limbs, as if they were someone else's.

31. A call not for me

She was kissing me; then when I opened my eyes a moment I saw, in a sideways glance, Magda. It was strange to be seen kissing; it was a very not-me situation in which to be.

"Rema!" came Magda's voice. "Phone call!"

Not a single muscle of the simulacrum responded to the sound of Magda's voice.

"I'm coming," I called out, willfully misunderstanding whom Magda was addressing.

"I was having so much fear," the simulacrum said, kissing my eyelids—and I couldn't help but think about the eyelid kissing, and how this is a thing Rema always liked to do, and though I understand that eyelid kissing is a fairly standard part of any amatory repertoire, I remember how it really needled me at the beginning, needled me for being a sort of *learned* behavior, which therefore pointed to that whole world that was Rema before I knew her, and pointed to all those people who were not me who had gone into the creation of her as she was, and—well, in that way she was like some alien sedentary rock formation, some meteor fallen to my planet, and it seemed a violation of me to have no choice but to love some charred castaway, with all its strata—I guess I am very jealous and possessive—I just found it very difficult those moments, like eyelid kissing, when I couldn't help but perceive her duplicity, her triplicity. She took firm hold of my wrist. "I started by writing down a long list of mean things to say to you, but—"

"It's rude to Magda—"

"And I almost thought this was just an ordinary fight we were having, and I went through in my mind all the people who are more nice to me than you are, because many people are very nice to me, but then—"

"You can't be nice to Magda only when it's convenient for you," I said to her. "And it's not right to treat people as interchangeable, to replace one for another however and whenever makes you feel okay—" I don't know why I was saying all those things. I definitely wasn't thinking about my own behavior with other women. But as I said those random things, I was pushing that woman away from me—which was easy because she's smaller than me—and I turned to head into the home, and I think the simulacrum started shouting at me. But I am the kind of man who treats mothers very well. I wasn't going to pretend that I hadn't heard Magda calling to us. I don't know if I believe that our relationships with our parents establish patterns we are doomed to repeat and repeat but—I am surprised that I was not more anxious about marrying a woman who very well may have just abandoned her parents. For all I knew Rema had misrepresented and cheaply blamed this beautiful mother whose only fault may have been accurately perceiving the ugly truth—even with little information—about the rude American whom Rema had chosen to marry before she had chosen to marry me. I should at least have learned more about how it had come to be that Rema had abandoned her mother, before I asked her to marry—and hopefully not abandon—me. But I saw Rema all prismatically, all fractured and reconstituted as if seen in the valley of an unshined silver spoon, and actually I'm glad love does that, I shouldn't complain about love, or love's perspective—distorted or no, to feel superior to it would be wrong, as if there were some better way of seeing.

32. Measured radiances at various frequencies

Whoever the caller was had hung up, not waiting for the simulacrum to reach the phone's cradle. In the kitchen, Magda shruggingly informed us of this, and then the three of us just remained there, leaning against the kitchen counter, with nothing to say. Killer slurpled at her water bowl, then lay down, head between paws. She raised her gaze to us humans; we were in a row; I was in the middle.

"She's with a friend," the simulacrum said suddenly but without looking at anyone. "If you're wondering where the dog is. I left her with a friend from work."

"A dog," Magda echoed.

"Friend from work," I repeated.

Then another bruisy quiet, in which I felt my feet swelling, my ears growing, my vertebrae pressing down upon the cartilaginous disks betwixt and between, myself growing just shorter enough, just slow enough, to invoke a vaguest unsettlement, of everything, the whole world, looking a little bit off, a little too large.

"All for whores?" Magda erupted cheerily.

Turning toward the simulacrum as if I kind of knew her—and I did kind of know her, we had spent a couple of rather intense days together—I whispered, "Whores?"

"And Nescafé?" Magda added to my back.

"Alpha," the simulacrum enunciated to me—I watched her lips—in a cold, dry voice. "Alpha. Whore. Rays."

Was this a meteorological term? A military code?

Magda pulled down a package of cookies. She set to boil the teakettle, whose sound I had already, so quickly, become familiar with, although it was an electric teakettle, so instead of a certain trembling there's a more cavernous gentle rumbling sound, and one waits expectantly for the understated click that means the thermostat has been thrown and the water is boiled, though electric-teakettled water is never hot enough for me, never as hot as from boiling on the stove, though I know that it's impossible that it's not hot enough, I know that all boiled water should be, barring major atmospheric differences, equally hot.

"Go sit in the living room," Magda said, shooing us off like children. "I'll bring."

We didn't go. Were we both listening to that sound?

Killer rose to her paws and loped out.

"El es mi esposo," the simulacrum burst out in Spanish with a nervous laugh and a shrug of the shoulders. "Esposo" meaning "handcuff." But also "husband." Which is, I assume, what she meant.

"Who is?" Magda asked.

With a head tilt, the simulacrum indicated me. But she did not look at or touch me. The real Rema: having kept a secret from her mother for so many years, she wouldn't have hastily disclosed it so gracelessly.

"Him?" Magda said. "This man?" she added, pointing, as if I were just a statue. "Your lover I thought maybe he was."

"No," the simulacrum de-affirmed. "Not my lover. My husband."

"Those terms," I said in English. "They're nonexclusionary. They overlap. Often substantially."

The teakettle clicked gently. No one moved. Magda said, "It is like I am not hearing well?"

What surprised me during all of this was that Magda—and at this thought I couldn't help but picture her uterus—showed no signs of suspicion toward this false child, this woman whom she had never borne. I had overestimated Magda's ability to account for the redshift of her own desires, to account for Dopplerganger effect. I had miscalculated the internal error of the other observer

I was observing; I should have known that a mother who has not seen her daughter for years, who so desperately wants to see her, well, one could put Kim Novak in front of her and she would likely "recognize" her as her daughter, and it would all feel very right, and very profound, when really all that was being recognized would be a sense of recognition unhinged from its source, a misinterpretation of data, a forcing of facts into a model they didn't match. "I don't understand," Magda continued as if I weren't there. "Are you saying that you are married to the meteorologist?"

And I—I thought of a fork tine vanishing into lentils.

"Meteorologist?" the simulacrum echoed.

"What happened to the psychoanalyst?" Magda asked.

I was craving—craving instant coffee.

"Are you talking about Tzvi Gal-Chen?" the simulacrum said to Magda, alarmed. And then the simulacrum actually turned to me, looked at me, took hold of my wrist—and that made all the vastly spaced particles of me seem to crowd together—and she loud-whispered at me: "You told her about Tzvi Gal-Chen?"

"Of course I didn't tell her about Tzvi Gal-Chen," I murmured in a tense voice that, when it returned to my ears, sounded too high-pitched.

"What," Magda asked, "is chewy galleon?"

"I'm absolutely not in contact with him," I announced firmly to nobody.

More noncommunicative communication went on. To be honest I could no longer really listen, my head filling with the fluttering as if of a thousand mothers, or moths, emerging from an old winter coat not pulled out of a closet for years; I began to think of stepping out to return, again, for the nth time, to the coffee shop, where I could have a properly hot coffee and some cookies and a look at the pretty waitress. But I did not leave. "Doesn't she look strange to you?" I said, finally breaking into the blue, or really white, noise and speaking directly to Magda and only to Magda and not feeling bad about turning my back on that other woman.

"No," Magda said, reaching her hand past me, toward that woman. "I like the hair, Rema." I found myself imprisoned behind Magda's arm. "The color—it's more natural than your natural color."

The simulacrum flinched, as if it were winter and sparks had flown between them. But it wasn't winter, not there, anyway; it was warm outside, and there was a real chance that someone was going to cry, or snap, that was the feeling I had, and that sort of thing takes up so much space in a room that I thought that I should leave instead of suffocate, but I didn't know how to exit gracefully—leaving in the middle of a movie is an offense to the director, though I'm not sure, analogously, who was the director I was worried about offending—but then, thank God, or at least thanks to the most powerful institution of which I know, my phone rang, after which point the rudeness of staying surely outweighed the rudeness of stepping out, so I ducked under Magda's arm and headed out the front door.

33. Synoptic meteorology

Isn't it strange how conveniently timed my incoming phone calls were?

But isn't it also strange that the Gospel According to Matthew ends with Jesus on the cross saying, *Father, Father, why have you forsaken me?* Who could have foreseen that ending?

"Hi, this is Lola?" a voice said.

I was still stepping out front, to the courtyard full of dusty bougainvillea. "Who?"

"Lola?"

"No, I'm not Lola. Leo here."

"Leo? This is Lola. I'm calling for Arthur. Arthur Corning. About the job in the South."

"Arthur?"

"Yes. Arthur. Twenty-seven. Bowdoin College. Recreational ice climber? We talked about wounds?"

Then I finally, sun heating my back, relaxed enough to recognize that sensually quavering voice. The simulacrum's appearance must have temporarily blotted out my imagined image of Lola from the Royal Academy. "Oh," I said, my palms beginning to sweat as random sensuality carbonated up to my cortex. "Yes. That's me. Arthur."

Why did I say that? Say that I was Arthur when I was not? Well, the name was bestowed upon me, I did not come up with it myself. I had to be open to the disguised ways in which progress, clues, might present themselves to me. Lola and I had established a real connection; it would have been foolish to disregard that; that personal connection was what mattered; maybe paperwork had been randomly mixed up, but maybe it had been randomly mixed up on purpose; maybe this would lead nowhere, this name, but I couldn't reject it out of hand just because I remained ignorant of the details behind it, and just because I was, in a sense, lying.

"We want to offer it to you," Lola silked. "That position. Down South." Lola's words sounded dirty to me. I don't believe this was just because I suddenly imagined that she imagined me as a sexy, well-built, young ice climber. Nor do I believe those words sounded dirty because I was projecting my own anxieties—or hopes—about what likely never happened between Rema and the dog man, or Rema and Anatole, or Rema and no one. I think it was just over-stimulation; it was just as if I had been watching night skies and a new planet had swum into my ken, and a new planet naturally throws off one's calculations about the movements of all the other celestial bodies, and that made me think again of the Dog Star, Sirius, that had appeared to be just one star but was later discovered to be two, or maybe even three, and when they learned that, that must have changed everything, all the calculations. My mind was running like that.

"You were very sweet the other day," Lola continued. "I was feeling very—"

"Can you review again for me the exact details of the job?" I said. I wasn't trying to be mean, cutting her off just as she began speaking about her feelings. I wasn't actually developing the detachment of a disordered psychotic—I just wanted to concentrate, to stick to the business at hand.

"I'm sorry. Of course. Are you mad at me?"

I'm mad at Tzvi, I didn't say. And I heard myself saying to Lola: "Well, it's like what Tzvi Gal-Chen says in his paper 'A Theory for the Retrievals,' when he says, 'It should be emphasized that the thermodynamic retrieval concept does not involve marching forward in time by means of prognostic equations . . . Rather the retrieval method is a diagnostic procedure using the same prognostic equations, but in a different way.'"

"I don't understand what you are saying?"

I didn't quite know what I was saying, either; those words had arrived whole from Tzvi's research writings, writings I hadn't thought I had so nearly memorized. "Oh, that's just a thought that comes to my mind now and again—about retrievals, about improving predictions. Oddly enough, introducing errors into models makes for more reliable predictions. But I'm digressing. I really just wanted to hear about the work."

"But what did you mean just then? I mean, what's the meaning behind what you said?"

"I'm not really sure." But I did feel somehow relieved, as if I'd made progress. "But it's like Professor Gal-Chen's other point, about how we cannot tell what the weather will be tomorrow because we do not know accurately enough what the weather is right now. Like, how can we forecast when we can't even properly *now*cast? You know, an Initial Value Problem."

"What's the weather right now?"

"Sunny," I answered. "A light breeze from the southeast."

Lola laughed.

Lots of serious things get dismissed as jokes; that's a respectable coping mechanism.

Then Lola proceeded to fill me—as Arthur—in on the details of the meteorological job that I had apparently been awarded, that I could take if I so desired. I said I so desired. I desired to work for the Royal Academy of Meteorology.

34. Mesoscale phenomena

That night the double came into my bedroom (that is, whoever's bedroom I was staying in, maybe even Rema's bedroom). The double's hair carried a scent, in the faintest way, of bacon. I was sitting at the desk chair; she sat down on the bed.

"Those clothes you're wearing aren't yours," she said. "I am just now noticing that."

She had made a true observation. I was wearing the clothes that Magda had lent me. An attractive pale green button-up with a stain of unknown origin on the left breast pocket. I began to pick at that stain which I had not earlier noticed; it seemed like a gravy of some sort, powdery bits precipitated out of the goo. "It's because I lost my luggage," I said.

"You've lost your luggage?" she said, which felt like an older and more familiar accusation than it could possibly actually be. As if the simulacrum and I had often been in situations in which I had disappointed her in just this way.

"Really *they* lost my luggage," I explained, while keeping my attention focused on the old stain and not on her. "I mean: it was out of my hands when it was lost, so it's really not my fault. Others are to blame for having lost it. Though naturally I'm the one suffering as a result. Not that it's whose fault it is that matters most, that's just one thing. I mean I just said that, about who is to blame, because it happens to be true, because it's true that it's not *my* fault." I continued on, still picking at the shirt, though there was little hope for change. "But whose fault it is isn't the main point. Let's say it's Tzvi Gal-Chen's fault. It's just gone, the luggage. Anyway, they're supposed to call me." I didn't tell her about my job offer.

"I'll buy you new clothes tomorrow," the woman said abruptly.

Reaching one hand into a deep and narrow pants pocket, I told her, "Don't worry about it. I like what I'm wearing."

"No," she said shortly and with authority. Then softer again: "I will buy you something else." She was staring, like Magda had, at the snap on the cuff of my sleeve. She put her hand on my knee, making all sensation rush patella-ward, and she said: "So that's something that we'll do together. Tomorrow. Buy clothing."

Then a quiet again, hot at the knee, and I found myself saying boldly: "So who *is* taking care of that undernourished greyhound puppy? Is it Anatole? Is Anatole taking care of her?"

The mattress was sunk ever so slightly beneath the woman's weight, and this made the blanket crease out in radii in a way that made the simulacrum seem like the carpel of a flower, and she looked to me very beautiful, also very deerlike, as she said, withdrawing her hand from my knee: "Who said that name to you? Something is wrong with you." The woman looked—I only then finally noticed—as if she had not slept in days. The skin beneath her eyes was so dusky, as if the blood there had never breathed. The hair at her temple curled damply. "What," she sharped, "have you been talking about with my mom? She lied to me, didn't she? Did she lie to me? She didn't tell me she told you about him. I should tell you that she's kind of a crazy liar—"

And I felt sad, I felt a key change within me, and I involuntarily imagined myself zipping up a dark blue rain jacket—or was someone else zipping up that coat?—that I'd had as a child, and I said, in a dry and professional tone of voice: "She really hasn't said anything to me of which the truth-value would be considered the most important quality—"

"And what," she interrupted, "did you say to her about Tzvi Gal-Chen? What was that about?"

"Are you," I asked, feeling like I'd realized something, "the reason Tzvi sent me such a cold reply?" Unexpected emotion lined my throat like a medicine. Just speaking Tzvi's name to her had made my eyes water. "Are *you* working with *him*?"

Those questions definitively stoppered her rising irritation. That exhausted flower stared at me for seconds or minutes or years. Then she stood up from the bed and approached me. I scooted my chair back. She stepped again toward me. I rose from my chair and went and sat on the far end of the bed. Like eddy fronts we were, forming katabatic winds. She turned and again stepped toward me, and frowned gently at me, and then, her still standing, me still sitting, she moved her hand very, very slowly out toward my cheek—making me tremble—and I let her place her hand tenderly on my face and leave it there, which is what she did, and my face was level with her waist. I—well, I could see her beauty clearly for a moment, the beauty of her waist, at least, and it affected me, probably powerfully—I found myself whispering, as if a secret agent might be in the closet listening to us: "Can't we work together? Maybe we can help each other? Except that I don't know your story, I don't know your background, which makes for an Initial Value Problem, which makes it difficult for me to trust you, just like it must be difficult for Tzvi to trust me. I can't tell which errors of yours are intentional. It must be so exhausting for you to have to pretend all the time. I want you to feel that you don't have to pretend with me anymore. Don't worry yourself with pretending, because, listen, I already know you're not Rema. I already know that."

She moved her hand from my cheek to my forehead.

I wanted to press my face against her beautiful, beautiful waist.

She echoed, "I'm not Rema?"

I didn't reply.

"Can we go back?" she asked. "When you said Tzvi and 'cold reply,' what did you mean?"

Though I was still thinking about her waist, by considering how the dent I made in the bed might look different from or the same as the one she had made, I cooled my urge to press myself against her. But I wasn't—as much as I regretted prematurely disclosing my suspicions of her association with Tzvi Gal-Chen—thinking about the dent in the bed just in order to avoid answering.

"When you say," the simulacrum said, soldiering very slowly into the quiet, "that I am not Rema, what do you mean? This is just an expression that I'm not familiar with?"

I said, "Cold reply is an expression, yes. Or really, a dead metaphor." Rema and I had talked about that, about dead metaphors, about how, when her English was less good, she used to bring dead metaphors back to life by saying them incorrectly, by startling me with phrases like "chill down" for "chill out," and "weird chicken" for "odd bird." That had become less frequent, though.

"And I am not Rema? That also is a dead metaphor?"

"No," I whispered, full of regrets. "When I say that I am saying exactly what I mean."

"You are saying exactly what you mean?"

"Yes. What I mean."

"Mean," she repeated, mostly to herself, dropping her hand from my face.

I'd lost track, I realized, of that originally mysterious scent of bacon.

The simulacrum wrapped her arms around her own body, and then she sat down next to me, and it was ugly latticing in the bedspread between us, and her upper arm was again pressed into an unappealing shape.

"Tell me," she said without looking at me, "how am I not like Rema?"

Somehow I wasn't afraid of her; that was just a feeling I had. I sincerely wanted her to understand. Maybe I thought her errors could be useful to me. "For example," I said, "she's more emotional than you are. And more nervous."

"What about," she proffered, "when she had the ectopic pregnancy? She was very calm about that."

"That's true," I said, refusing to be baited by drama. "But she also smells different from you."

"But you smell different from you too."

"She smells like grass."

"You smell like my mom's shampoo today," she tried to counter. "But I'm still here next to you."

"And she's indifferent to dogs. It's hard to explain how strong a characteristic that is—"

"Those are the things that you love about her?" she said, raising her voice in impatient judgment. "Her smell, her nervousness, and her indifference to dogs?"

"Love is a separate issue," I clarified. "I'm just telling you something of who she is. I don't even know why I'm telling you." I'd felt, briefly, tenderly toward her, but now she'd begun to irritate me. "You probably can't understand."

"It must seem so strange to you," she said darkly, mockingly, and flushing red, and without compassion, "that I know so much about her, that I look so much like her, but then you don't love me—"

"Don't do this," I said shortly. "Don't get emotional." .

The blue beneath her eyes had grown even duskier. Then she started—all of a sudden—to cry, and not even as if just to disobey me. But I don't know if I'd call her cry a sad cry. And really I suppose one might even call it a sob, but more of a distressed sob than a devastated one. And in between heaves I think she eked out something to me like: "I know all these little things about you, like I know how you sit with a half a watermelon and a spoon and eat the whole thing, and that you read magazines while you brush your teeth, and that you throw away socks for no reason at all, when they're still perfectly fine. That you never seem to really like anyone, except sometimes me. And I know how much you loved that photo of Tzvi's family, how much time you spent looking at it, and talking about it, so much so that it made me uncomfortable and I had to take it down, and I like to think that all this knowledge I have of you, that it means something—"

"Aren't you tired?" I asked, unaffected by her little show. "I'm so sleepy. Are we expected to sleep in this same room tonight, together?"

"You don't make any sense," she said, still sobbing. "It's you. It's you who's not yourself."

35. The ghost in the machine

I should explain about the renewal of contact between Dr. Gal-Chen and myself.

We, the simulacrum and I, did share a narrow bed that night together in Magda's home, but the simulacrum did not permit the dog, whose napping company I had grown accustomed to, to join us. She, the simulacrum, wore Rema's green nightie boxers and an undershirt of mine; I was fully dressed save socks and shoes. Sleep did not visit me, but stray strands of the simulacrum's hair gave me the continual illusion of fleas mutely festivaling on my body. And the way the simulacrum's sleeping fingers searched for the water bowl of my clavicle gave me the feeling of Rema. And the way her knee sought the thick slough of my thighs. And her foot the freedom of the edge of the bed. And though the simulacrum seemed to be in a paralysis of REM sleep, my body, as when it is near Rema, waited nervously for the slightest regularly repeated movement, for the slightest seemingly unrandom touch. I didn't like that tense waiting feeling. She slept like one exhausted; I slept not at all.

Who, I thought at one restless point, *sleeps with Tzvi Gal-Chen?* It was the first note of a discordant thought orchestra tuning up within me. Was the simulacrum, I wondered, in some parallel world, really Tzvi's wife? In some worlds Tzvi was married to the doppelganger, in other worlds to other women?

She had a hand on my hip.

Or: was it possible that it wasn't the double who was Tzvi's wife, that maybe the marriage I was perceiving wasn't one in a parallel world, but in this very world in which I lay in bed with the doppelganger, and it was my Rema who was, or once had been, the wife of Tzvi Gal-Chen? But surely that was just my own mental shuffling; Rema probably had not been married to anyone else, and even if she had been married, it wasn't to a meteorologist.

The simulacrum's hand did not move, as if it were a mannequin's.

Still, maybe Tzvi—and not the night nurse, and not the analyst/dog walker, and not someone named Anatole—was the real unturned stone in the submystery of Rema's previous husband. And thus, by ripple, the central mystery of everything. Maybe he and Rema were involved with each other in some way.

Although Tzvi was probably—I thought then, before the category seemed obsolete—even older than me.

But maybe all that meant was that Rema loved him, might still love him, more than she loved me?

As the simulacrum sleep sighed, her whole thorax centimetered out against me—then receded.

And who was that in the photo alongside Tzvi Gal-Chen, with the creamy elbow crook? Wasn't she his wife for all time? And did he and she—the woman in the photo—love each other? Then? Now? And was his wife in any way, through some strange exchange, mine? And though Magda had let on that Rema's previous husband—or still current one?—was not a meteorologist, who was the meteorologist Magda had met who had led her to pass such hasty good judgment on me when I presented myself as a meteorologist?

The simulacrum's right hand lost tone, slipped off me. In a kind of inebriation of sleepiness, my mind just kept swapping and interswapping, this person for that, and that person for this, like some hapless turn-of-the-century dream interpreter. And although nothing in the cacophonous score of my thoughts made strict sense, one thing did seem obvious: my mystery converged upon the point of Tzvi Gal-Chen.

So I unlimbed myself of the simulacrum, grabbed my handheld, blindly padded my way out to the living room. The perhaps misguided action that I then took later revealed itself, I would argue, as the unexpectedly right step, if the right step executed for the wrong reasons, which when I think about it suggests that maybe my reasons were merely wearing masks and hosiery, that, undressed, they were likely the right reasons all along.

36. Chills

Despite having sent Dr. Gal-Chen that e-mail to which he had responded quite coldly, despite having more or less resolved never to communicate with him again, well: there alone in the not quite dark of Rema's childhood house, amidst the drunken sensuality of all that unseen velvet in the unlit living room, amidst the painful reminder of a Rema in bed with me without there actually being a Rema in bed with me, I found myself able to forget my and Tzvi's awkward exchange. Able to forget it and yet remember that I should not pursue any questions directly, that in seeking help from Tzvi I would have to approach from an angle. Because when I had asked directly after Rema's disappearance, asked directly about the 49 Quantum—that had made him nervous, that had made him uncomfortable. But maybe by talking about some seemingly irrelevant third thing, through a kind of misdirection, then we—the both of us—would be liberated to speak openly and truthfully—like getting a patient to loosen up, and reveal, by asking him to talk about his spouse, or mother, or favorite food, rather than about himself. Or, as in retrievals done by a single-Doppler radar system, one looks at a volume of air from an angle, then accounts for that extra distortion, so as to better deduce what's actually there if one could see it head-on, but one can't, because then one loses all dimensionality. Like that.

So I began composing a note asking how windchill is calculated.

As I typed, my BlackBerry's glow filled the room with a palest blue light.

Is windchill analogous to Doppler effect, I philosophized in a feeble attempt to sound atmospherically savvy, *but applied to the movement of heat rather than of light or sound?* I thought about making a further analogy, to movements in human relationships, say, to interpersonal coldnesses that feel much colder than they actually are. But then I decided that might be too much, that might feel intrusive.

How windchill is calculated obviously wasn't precisely what I most wanted to learn from Tzvi—what I most wanted to learn was what I had written in my earlier missive, whether he knew the whereabouts of Rema, and how to get her back—but I was, nevertheless, inquiring about windchill sincerely because I had indeed often wondered about windchill. It is one temperature, but it feels like another—how does one objectively measure something subjective? I think and thought it a cute question, a cute problem. One answered differently, I imagine, in every field. *Do you love me more or less today?* I used to ask Rema.

Before actually sending the note, I hesitated a moment. I was worried about seeming abnormal. But I reassured myself that windchill was an extraordinarily normal thing to ask Tzvi about. After all, I argued to myself, Tzvi is a meteorologist, a real meteorologist, and how many times in one's life does one have a direct line of communication with a real meteorologist?

I thought about New York 1 news.

I sent the inquiry.

Then I reclined, alone, on that velvety sofa.

Where was the dog sleeping? I wondered.

Unwillingly I pictured the simulacrum's sleeping position, her foot over an edge.

The screen on my BlackBerry self-dimmed, and the whole room went inky-black.

37. In the ghost's machine

Then blue suffused the room again.

"Windchill research got its beginnings in the US military during WWII," began Tzvi's response, which arrived so quickly that it was as if he'd been waiting there for me to contact him all that time, like a spurned lover waiting for any sign of reconciliation. "But the National Weather Service didn't share the information with the public until the 1970s." He included a link to a Web page that offered a brief explanatory treatise about the history of windchill research. "Nice that you're interested," he wrote. He made no reference to his rude earlier missive. He even signed off his note "Love, Tzvi."

What was he—or she? I wondered during the one ludicrous moment I again thought I might be communicating with Rema, who had, after all, posed as Tzvi Gal-Chen many times—inviting me to deduce? And why use that word "love"? Why bring up war? And the 1970s? And why the secrecy around windchill research? How was I meant to understand what he had said? How was I meant to respond?

I began searching the Internet on my handheld in order to do something I had long avoided doing, avoided perhaps because part of me had always felt that I was in some way wronging this stranger whose identity I had co-opted. I sought to learn some biographical, geographical, orthographical, political, diacritical, pathological, and/or other details about the real Tzvi Gal-Chen. Or Galchen. Or Gal Chen.

I found Russian jugglers known as the Galchenko brothers.

I found a Scottish rock band, named Galchen, reviewed on a Web page devoted to "Great bands with absolutely terrible names."

I found a blogger criticizing the grammar of Tzvi's use of the phrase "moving frame of references."

I found two photos—one in profile, one head-on, like mug shots—of a Tzvi-like man in plaid pants, standing on a balcony, holding a baby of indeterminate gender.

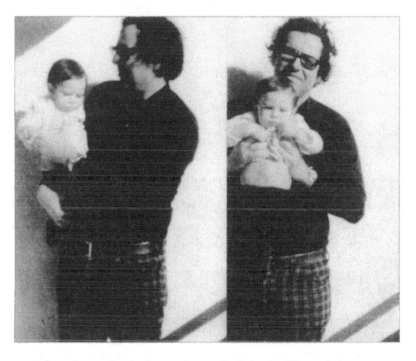

I found a geologic formation called the GalChen fach.

And I learned, from a purple Finnish Web page that began tinnily blasting a Mendelssohn dirge, that Tzvi Gal-Chen—most noted for his mesoscale work on downbursts and for his advances in single-Doppler radar research—had died of a sudden heart attack in October of 1994, at the relatively young age of fifty-three.

Then I noticed that next to Tzvi's name in that roster of the Royal Academy of Meteorology, there was a pale gray asterisk.

I reloaded and reread and reconsidered the pages.

38. Very normal conversation

If one wishes to be a true scientist—an explorer not in search of what one desires to be true but rather in search of whatever truth there is—then one must be willing to accept, to engage, even to pursue further the most unwelcome and confounding data. One must be willing to make discoveries that shatter one's most deeply held beliefs. Maybe it turns out that Earth is not the center of the universe. Or that monkeys are our relatives. Maybe we discover that a man is not an expert on himself, or maybe it turns out that we've been speaking to the dead.

A true scientist knows to explore, not dismiss, these uninvited discoveries.

So I wrote back to Tzvi, saying that I had recently received the impression that he was not alive.

"Oh. Yes. That is true, in most senses," he replied without subject heading.

I felt a breeze then, just very locally, a microclimate, like what happens in a movie when a ghost floats by. "Then why, or rather how, or rather from where are you writing to me? And to Harvey too?"

Tzvi wrote back: "If you'll remember, I didn't initiate contact. All I did was respond. I guess it was flattering when Harvey called me 'the mesoscale hero of the millennium.' So maybe I answered just out of curiosity. Or loneliness. But really I think it simply seemed like the proper thing to do. He wrote, and so I replied, as he obviously wanted me to."

Pressing Tzvi on the issue of his apparent death—that didn't seem like the proper thing to do. But those two photos, in mugshot form . . . and all the concordances . . . the retrievals work . . .

so I found myself typing from my heart: "Is it as if in some worlds you're alive, and in some worlds you're not? Is that what your retrievals work really is: not between reality and models, but between actual worlds?"

"How," he responded, "did you and Harvey come to be interested in my work in the first place?"

"If you don't already know, I promise to tell you one day. However, I suspect you do know. But can you tell me—is it that you're not really dead? Are you just, for some reason, pretending?"

"I would say more your earlier guess. Do I sound dead to you? I wonder if I talk like a dead man. My daughter once came home from school very excited about some lecture—this was years ago, before I died, though just right before—and she said her English teacher had talked about what the dead sound like in Dante. This funny thing about Dante's dead, which is that they know the past, and even the future, but they don't know the present. About the present they have all these questions for Dante. And that somehow is what being alive is, to be suspended in the present, to be suspended in time. She seemed to feel this really meant something. That and also that the dead know themselves better than the living do. When Dante the pilgrim asks, *Who are you?* the souls are able to offer these very succinct, precise descriptions, without provisos. I'm the one who was seized by love. Or, I am the one who quenched the doubt in Caesar. Everything very settled, you know?"

When is talking about literature not an evasion of the real question at hand? Although a nice-enough evasion. Into an honest and information-bearing kind of distortion. Was I supposed to ask Tzvi, as a kind of extended shibboleth that could separate the living from the dead, who he was? Was that what he was indirectly trying to ask me to do? But why should I care whether he was alive or dead if my main issue was finding Rema? And wasn't talking about literature also as straightforward an invitation to interpret his research as he could offer? Because I—I should admit—found my thoughts retreating to literature too. Retreating from what I'm not sure. I thought of the last of T. S. Eliot's

Four Quartets, a poem I'd once been made to memorize, in which the Eliot character chances upon the ghost of Yeats in the fire-bombed streets of London; upon recognizing Yeats, Eliot says they are "too strange to each other for misunderstanding." And the Eliot character says directly to Yeats's ghost, "The wonder that I feel is easy, Yet ease is the cause of wonder. Therefore speak: / I may not comprehend, may not remember." Perhaps the simplest interpretation of this starchy turn of my thoughts would be that I thought of Tzvi as of a dead master? One with whom I felt strangely at ease? Or that I should just ask Tzvi to speak and nothing more? And as I sat in that darkness, a cluster of competing hypotheses came to me as I thought how to proceed:

- maybe Tzvi wasn't dead at all (or, implausibly, I was)
- or maybe this was some mechanical residue of Tzvi, some part of himself translated into software of some kind
- or maybe he was dead inasmuch as I could understand the situation, but his death was a matter of perspective, of frames of reference, or a frame of references
- or maybe Tzvi was somehow Rema, since Rema had for so long pretended to be Tzvi

And none of these hypotheses dissuaded me from the belief that Tzvi could help me in my search, and so I resolved to ask him about Rema directly.

39. Conversation interrupted

But something clouded over my handheld electronic's moonlight glow, and I turned to see what, and although my pupils' contraction near blinded me, I made out the silhouette of the simulacrum. Her blotting out of screen glow made me think about the powder on sticks of chewing gum, then the powder in urns, and then gunpowder, and then the Chinese, and then fireworks, and the feeling was of my mind tripping along an infinitely winding and meaningless path.

"I had a nightmare," she said, her voice drawing my mind back to a starting point, "that I was in bed, and I reached my arm out to you, and you weren't there. And then I woke up and it was true." She was leaning over me; I think she was trying to read from my screen. But Tzvi Gal-Chen was for me, not her. Even if he was her, he wasn't this her. Or really just: I had a lot to think over.

I turned the screen off.

We were left in the dark, amidst all that velvet, and unaware of the location of the dog.

"Are you writing," I heard her say, "or are you reading? Or, what are you doing? What are you doing awake? Now? Out here?"

Her voice in the dark, so familiar—it was almost as if Rema was actually there with me, in the absence of luminosity, and maybe she really was there, paying me a visitation. Maybe it was, very briefly, Rema. But like a faithless Orpheus I turned the light—my BlackBerry screen, that is—back on again, to verify. And despite the familiar hip, despite the undershirt, it wasn't Rema.

"Do you not miss sleeping with me?" she breathed into the blue glow. "It is weird to me. I am no longer even an object of your desire?"

The cheapest of noir moves. Against my will, my ears filled with heat. As if she were some KGB blonde, distracting me while a spy, an agent, an assassin, stealthed out of a closet, a window, a gate. Or while my contact, my rescuer—quite possibly Tzvi—faded away. "Do you feel like there are other people in this house?" I heard myself whispering as I thought about what Tzvi might or might not know, about what important message might lie hidden in his research papers, translated into science, awaiting interpretation. "Or ghosts in this house?"

I believe she frowned at me.

"But of course you are very pretty," I said as a kind of consolation for what she'd earlier said. "But isn't it so strange that I had never met my Rema's mother before? That she didn't even seem to know I existed? Doesn't knowing—or not knowing—something about Rema at her initial value—about who she once was—doesn't that mean that all my predictions about what she's doing and what she will do and what she might do and what she absolutely will do and what she absolutely will never ever do—doesn't it seem like my predictions will inevitably be shot through with enormous errors? On account of the Initial Value Problem? I mean, we can't predict tomorrow's weather accurately if we have the wrong ideas about what the weather actually is right now. That's what Tzvi Gal-Chen says. I mean, it's almost as if I've married a stranger, if I think about it that way. Like if we think that it's one temperature just because it feels that way but actually it's really some other—"

Something like that I was saying, just saying whatever I thought the impostress might have expected me to say, nothing real, just filling up some space as if with a distracting puff of colored smoke, so that I could go back to messaging with Tzvi, but then the simulacrum moved her warm front of a body closer to me, whispering, further occluding the small amount of light between us. "Please," she said. "When I see you asleep I feel like we are the two happiest people in the world. I'm so happy when we're asleep together. Let's just sleep and see what comes to mind when we wake up tomorrow morning." She wiped tears from her eyes. The tears had arrived so slowly.

"Do you love me very much tonight?" I found myself saying.

"Why are you asking me this old, old question?" she sniffed. "Of course I love you. Even when I don't want to."

By then my ears felt more than hot, they felt painfully engorged. "Let's find the dog," I said. "Let's bring the dog to bed."

"No dog. I think she is sleeping with my mother. Just come to bed."

My screen, half Tzvi-corresponded, fell darkly asleep again; I tapped it to bring it back to life. "Please let's bring the dog," I almost begged, seeing again an image not of the simulacrum in front of me, but of the simulacrum as she had been earlier, entangled in bed with me.

"You'll stay with me tomorrow?" she pleaded.

It would be ridiculously unwise of me, I conceded to myself, to try to continue my conversation with Tzvi under the simulacrum's surveillance. "I'll stay with you tomorrow," I said, "if you let the dog sleep with us tonight."

And we eventually reached just such an accord. She, Killer, slept intercalated between us. She breathed hotly on my thigh.

40. The real point in space

But don't be distracted by my distress, by the simulacrum's distress, or by the dog's eventual sleeping position. The real point is that Tzvi Gal-Chen:

- who had first been (to me) just an oddly appealing name
- who had then become (for Rema and me) the unknowing centerpiece of the successful management of a delusional patient
- who furthermore (for Rema and me) rapidly developed into a relationship touchstone
- whom I'd regularly imagined taking leftovers from our refrigerator
- whose research proved to be my first substantial clue regarding Rema's disappearance
- who then later materialized as Harvey's correspondent
- but who, when I sought him out myself, had tersely retreated
- and who apparently no longer even numbered among the living

:yes perhaps, from certain perspectives, the real point of this entire project is that Tzvi Gal-Chen, in my proverbially darkest hour, he had, in his fashion, returned to me.

Part II

1. A Method for Calculating Temperature, Pressure and Vertical Velocities from Doppler Radar Observations

Before proceeding to a description of the more metaphysically extravagant discoveries I made in Patagonia, I'd like to openly engage my own worries, my own oscillating concern, for my, to put it in colloquial speech, sanity. Since naturally, from the beginning of this unwanted adventure of mine, I had borne such an anxiety. I had thought through continually, and rather extensively, the likelihood that I could attribute my perceptions to illness, to psychosis even. But over time I came to the fairly firm—and immensely dispiriting—conclusion that I could not. My thinking ran thusly:

Our vision involves—and one can produce myriad proofs of this—an interpretive leap. Consider the visual phenomenon of "completion" (that is what Tzvi's work does; it completes incomplete single-Doppler radar images), which sometimes leads to what is called "completion error" (which is what Tzvi's work attempts to avoid). I offer the following image from an old sign to illustrate the concept of completion and completion error. The sign reads:

VIᵥ/ALDI

Music lovers tend to see:

VIVALDI

While others tend to see:

VW/AUDI

The basic point—which can also be illustrated by considering the phenomenon of the blind spot—is that with any incomplete perception—and needless to say all perceptions are incomplete—the observer "fills in" by extrapolating from experience. Or from desire. Or from desire's other face, aversion. So basically, we focus fuzzy images by transforming them into what we expect to see, or what we wish we could see, or what we most dread to see. By what, in other words, already exists in our mind, what we already have available on file, however dusty the folder.

For example, when a person dies and we then repeatedly mistake strangers for that now-gone person, we are experiencing "completion error." We catch a few details of some far-off figure— a broad forehead, a certain slouch, some characteristic stubble— and our aforementioned wants, fears, and expectations fill in the gaps to make a familiar whole, a whole that is a decent but flawed interpretive leap based on the fragments. And it generally doesn't matter that this reconstituted "whole" is incorrect. We discover our errors soon enough, as the stranger draws nearer, becoming who he actually is rather than who we thought he might be. (How strange but reassuring that when the impostress entered my home that first time, that even when I saw her from a distance—there at the door, with that wet hair, and that pale blue bag, and that russet puppy—even far away like that, when I could have easily, and even from fatigue, filled in all the missing details appropriately— even then I knew she wasn't Rema.)

But we can do more than recognize our errors of interpretation; we can examine those errors as clues to the contents of—the preoccupations and desires of—our own minds.

We can similarly consider the "errors" of a suspected psychosis, the discrepancies between the presumably psychotic vision of reality and a consensus view of same. Such an examination could (occasionally, conceivably) reveal something other than prismatized fragments (taste of powdered milk + old woman with cataracts + holes in a navy sweater + fresh pretzels = navy poisons milk that the old pretzel factory workers drink down blindly) of the presumed psychotic's mind. Because although psychosis is often popularly conceived of as an infection or a kind of foreign body, a psychosis is in fact as personal, as eccentric, as interpretable as a dream. Its content comes straight from the mind of its victim, even as its form may be an aberration. (Consider the fact that over the past two hundred years the incidence of religious psychoses has significantly declined, while that of erotic ones has risen. Surely it is not the mental illnesses that have changed but rather the societies of people affected by them.) And so although we can call the process of transforming reality into an alternate reality "madness," we should not forget that the landscape of that alternate reality, all the molecules that make it up, come from the banalities of the life of the madman himself. Therefore each psychotic experience is singular, a fingerprint.

Investigating the origin of particular "errors" could, theoretically, solve the proverbial problem of distinguishing the prophet from the madman: if the "psychosis" were text, whom would you surmise to be the author? If the text reflects the fears, desires, or expectations of the "afflicted," then most likely he or she has authored his or her own vision. A man who fears rats may envision a rat king, and a fanatic television watcher may believe she has her own evening talk show, and a reader of tales of chivalry may believe himself to be a knight errant. But: if, say, an auto worker from Minnesota claims conscious blades of grass are plotting an overthrow of the Ecuadorian government, you should at least listen awhile before assuming it's another case of self-scripting. Because why would that be on his mind? What does he care for Ecuador? Or grass? If a story seems too random, or perhaps too brilliant, for a "madman" to have conceived of it himself, then consider that the "author" might be reality and the "madman" just the reader. After all, only reality can escape the limits of our imagination.

Why do I bring all this up?

When Rema disappeared, I chose to take myself on as my own patient, so I asked myself, did I "write" this new world, or was I just reading it? Reading what was "in reality" actually there? Well: I have never wanted or feared or expected Rema's replacement by a double, nor have I ever wanted or feared or expected my involvement in a weather-controlling cabal. If I were to have Rema-based psychosis, surely it would take a more mundane form: I'd be convinced that she was seeing other men, or women, or that she contemplated my murder, or that she moonlighted in a massage parlor, or that she had never existed at all, that she had always been just a figment of my imagination, an incarnation of all the women I've always wanted but could never have. Or that she was (gasp!) my mom—something banal and pre-scripted and conventionally Mad Lib–y like that. I would not have come up with this drama that is my actual current life. I just don't have those kinds of thoughts.

And since I could not detect my authorial hand in my strange new world, I could only conclude (at least, so to speak, with a $p \leq 0.05$) that it was being perceived accurately. That was the most valid extrapolation from the data that could be made. And that's why I felt so confident about my decision to speed south to

Patagonia, in anticipation of my meteorological labor, which I felt sure would bear some fruit, even if unexpected ones, even if ones I could not divine. It was kind of a wild plan, I admit, but one that came to me, and not from me, and one that therefore (I decided) should be heeded.

2. Variant case of Doppleganger effect in effect

Consider again that diagram from Tzvi's article. Is it not the image of a man leaving reluctantly? Is it not a portrait of me, leaving first my apartment, then the comfort of Rema's childhood home, in order to carry on my sad and uncertain search? How strange, the resemblance.

But isn't it more strange that in continuing my search for Rema, in (in fact) boldly pursuing a meteorological assignment (under the guise of a young ice climber named Arthur) for which I was in no way prepared, isn't it strange that through all this— sneaking out the bathroom window of Magda's home, paying full fare for a turbulent plane ride over Rorschach-y mountain ranges, enduring fierce winds off the silty blue Lago Argentina in search of reasonable shelter amidst the ersatz log architecture of El Calafate, witnessing the indignity of a sidewalk "impromptu" tango performance in that soulless tourist town, entertaining unnecessary self-doubt as I passed an establishment called El Quijote— well, isn't it strange that through all those obligatory banalities I gave hardly a thought to Rema, instead thought only, and obsessively, of Tzvi Gal-Chen?

I did ask myself if my oddly directed mental attentions were really just feelings for Rema transferred onto—translated over to— Tzvi. Well, if so, it wasn't as if I couldn't put that transference to good use. If I worked out an aspect of my evolving feelings for Tzvi Gal-Chen, I might—I reasoned—solve something about my feelings for Rema. And if I could determine the mysterious location of Tzvi Gal-Chen, then might I not learn something of the whereabouts of Rema? Or maybe there was no transference at all;

Tzvi had been so helpful to me, and perhaps my growing gratitude toward him was appropriate. I had, before leaving, written him more about the situation with Rema, and about the job offer from Lola; Tzvi had reframed my current life as a diagnostic-prognostic problem, like the one central to his own work in "A Theory for the Retrievals." And he made an ennobling comparison of my situation to that of a Greek hero. "Go south," he bid me. "Surely you'll learn something. About yourself. About the work of the Royal Academy." And he had listened so patiently to my detailing of how the doppelganger differed from my original Rema. Yes, he had listened as a true friend.

As I waited for my hotel room to be ready—Tzvi's paper affirmingly noted: "Remotely sensed data . . . can be grossly inadequate . . ."—as I warmed myself before a proverbial and actual hearth in the too-tastefully-homaged-to-ancient-cultures lobby of a serviceably nice inn, a vibration in my pocket disturbed me. I answered my phone.

"Hello? Hello? Hello?"

Rema's voice was what I recognized, maybe because I wanted to believe it was Rema, but also maybe because it really did sound like her, but probably just because a new stimulus extinguishes an old one with astonishing speed, and I had heard the simulacrum speak so much more recently than I had heard the real Rema.

"You disappeared again," the voice said through tiresome tears.

"May I ask with whom I'm speaking?" I inquired politely.

"It's me, Leo. You know that," continued the soppy sad voice, which, objectively speaking, was less sharp, less fiercely lovable, less accented than Rema's. The real Rema would have cut right to business, no matter how emotional—even because of how emotional—she might be. She would have asked me exactly where I was and she would already have been booking her flight, maybe mine too, and she'd furthermore already be befriending the manager of the hotel.

"And from where are you speaking?" I asked.

"You know exactly where I am, and you leave, and then you act like I'm the difficult one to locate," she said in an attempt to make, I have to believe, a frame-of-reference argument. But the frames of reference—they were obviously moving.

I was determined to remain analytical, to not be emotionally intimidated by the simulacrum's posturing as Rema. That would have been a bad kind of transference. "Please clarify? Where are you precisely?"

"It's crazy," she said, still crying, "and mean, to just disappear from me—"

But nothing and nobody just disappears. Not actually. Unless mass gets converted entirely into energy. But that doesn't really apply here, to people, basically never. (And especially an Argentine, it struck me, wouldn't use the word "disappear" so imprecisely; it would be like an American hosting a picnic on September 11.) So I think it must have been the silliness of the word "disappear," its rigged smokebox sentiment, that irritated me. Yes the silliness and also the wrongness. Wrong because generally people just leave. Or are taken. They only *appear* to have disappeared.

"If anyone has disappeared," I articulated into that telephone as I idly turned over a pamphlet proclaiming my presence in *authentic Patagonia!*, "it's not me. And if Rema has disappeared, if that is the correct way to understand this situation, and it seems increasingly likely that that is so, then it seems entirely possible that you're at least partially, if not wholly, implicated in all this. Tzvi thinks so, anyway. And by the way, Rema would have had a much better handle on this situation, she would have been in control, she never would have let me go—" at which point the woman interjected with some protest and tried to list memories that "proved" who she was—she even mentioned those oversized dogs from our walk in the Austrian Alps—but I soldiered on. "Just because you can deceive Magda, who hasn't seen Rema in years, and who sees whatever she wants to see, that doesn't mean you can count the sheep being pulled over my eyes—" And at the moment of speaking that mixed metaphor, an undeniably accurate image of the real Rema came to me, a sense of her body next to mine in bed, her arm around my waist, one of her knees beneath my own, her breath at my neck. Briefly, very briefly, Tzvi vanished from my thoughts, blotted out by Rema entirely. Or rather, by the painful absence of Rema. I said, "I've met complete strangers who remind me more of Rema than you do. You, you're really no good at what you do at all. What you don't understand is that this is a really close and intimate relationship, husband and wife. You're trying to be the woman who essentially saved my life, who made me feel like I really existed, the stuff of metaphysical poems, of all kinds of poems, we're talking about the first-prepare-you-to-be-sorry-that-you-never-knew-till-now-either-whom-to-love-or-how, that kind of love. I sent that to her once. You can't fool me. You don't seem to understand pretty close is not nearly close enough. It's nothing. It's not even a cigarette."

But perhaps it was a tad mean of me to say *you're really no good at what you do at all*. That was a bit much. After all, what did I really know about what it was that the double "did"? Impersonation wasn't necessarily her ultimate goal.

But about it not being Rema on the other end of that phone— about that I was definitely right. So I told myself as I stepped closer to the false hearth (gas and nonburning log sculptures) to warm myself. Wouldn't Rema on the phone have kept on crying? This woman had dried right up. So I hung up the telephone, not listening to whatever it was the double was saying to me, probably just listing more memories. I walked away from the warmth, felt something like dew forming on my eyebrows as I walked past the check-in desk and around a corner and to a cowboy-labeled restroom to run my hands under the hot water—which I believe I explained before is a very normal thing that I do—but it didn't get hot right away, and I waited for a while, and then remembered that it was the C tap that would be hot, C for "caliente," and I just felt so frustrated by the inane problems of even the simplest of translations. I just wanted to go back in time, to be home in

Rema's and my apartment back before we'd ever invented (or discovered or whatever we'd done) Tzvi Gal-Chen. I just wanted everything to return to how it had been before, even if that just meant Rema pouting on the sofa, reading a newspaper in a language I couldn't understand and being irritated with me for reasons unclear. Had Rema treated her previous husband better than she had treated me? And how had he treated her? How had I treated her? What nicknames did they have for each other? What language did they speak to each other? Maybe I didn't want to know any of those details. I was searching for Rema but I just wanted to find her, not find out too much else, not find out anything that I didn't absolutely have to know; about Tzvi I was open to discovering anything—his possible death had made that clear—but about Rema, not so much. (That was a little discovery I guess, discovering there were things I didn't want to discover.) I didn't want to think that her other husband, whoever he was, might somehow lie behind the circumstances of my strange new world. I didn't want to think that I might be wearing that other man's clothing. I didn't want to wonder if he and Rema had had sex in unusual positions, or with unusual objects. I didn't want to think about any men in Rema's life, actually, or any sex either. And in fact it was good that I so entirely succeeded in blocking those thoughts from my mind. And that I was somewhere cold, which keeps thoughts from associating so easily. Because in the end—or the state near the end, where I am now, ever approaching—they, those thoughts, could hardly have proved themselves more irrelevant.

I washed my face with hot water too.

3. A material intrusion

That conversation. It had laid down the absolutely wrong analytical tracks that my mind then kept running and rerunning over; so in an effort to derail the derailment—and thus clear my mind for rerailing—I voyaged into the cold. Walking that ersatz little tourist town, looking out at the pale blue finnings of the glaciers, feeling my skin desiccated by wind, feeling unreasonable jealousy of bickering families, I thought about Rema's old remark about Patagonia being considered the wild, uncultivated unconscious of Argentina. Well, I thought, if so, it was a tidy, brisk, unscented Lego-land of an unconscious. At least this corner of it. With clean glaciers, excellent signage and safety precautions, and full up with false gauchos offering pricey horseback-riding tours. Some unconscious. Although maybe that's what the "wilderness" of our minds looks like, maybe humans really are that dull and predictable.

My meteorologic labor wasn't scheduled to start until Monday—*that* might bring me out into the real atmospheric unconscious—but until then, frankly, I didn't know what I was meant to do to bring myself closer to Rema. When it began to rain lightly, I took that as a sign to return to my hotel.

Picking up an evening newspaper in the lobby, I began to read an article about chimp-human hybridization. That sort of thing (kind of) is on my mind often. Because whenever I feel sad, the sad feeling tends to manifest in my seeing humans (myself included) as orangutans. A human ordering coffee, a human offended when someone cuts in line, a human sprinting to refill a parking meter—

in my moods, all those people are orangutans. And this feeling doesn't make more real the secret emotional lives of orangutans—that would be one option. Instead it makes all the humans (with their loves, their hates, their haircuts, their beloved unconsciouses) seem sublimely ridiculous. Normal life, absurd. She loves you—who cares? She left you—so what? Scratch your armpit with your long, long arm and continue on, or not. The orangutan thing: it's just a feeling, not a rigorous thought at all. But still. Anyway, between that hybridization article and an article on legislation requiring the sale of larger-sized clothing in girls' boutiques, just as I was beginning to successfully forget about that phone conversation, I saw Harvey.

He was sitting near the gas hearth in a low, broad upholstered chair, his legs delicately crossed, his girlishly narrow ankles displaying wiry black hairs against paleness. He was wearing his suspenders over a sweater, with the cuffs and collars of two button-up shirts extending from beneath. He appeared occupied with his pocket mirror, seemed not to have noticed me.

I folded up my newspaper. This left the obituaries section facing out. Which seemed distasteful. And which reminded me of Tzvi. So I then unfolded and refolded the paper.

By which time Harvey had risen from his chair and crossed over to me; in response I rose too. He took hold of my entire forearm, gave it a firm, formal shake. I heard him say, "I thought I'd be more on your mind."

And yes I did feel like we both had unusually long arms, that our shake might have been observed in a zoo. "Wow. What?" I said.

"I've had so far," Harvey said, "a marvelous, marvelous time."

"Do you think," I said, stuck on his opening, "that I should have been more worried about you?"

He gestured that I take a seat. "Why are you asking me that, Dr. Leo?"

And I'd wanted to dismiss that conversation we'd begun, but then it was that feeling of some corpuscle of my bone marrow, some meek, undernourished corpuscle, taking the stand at the pulpit of my brain stem. "Do you think," came out of me in a whisper, and yes, I'd taken that seat, "that, if I really cared for you, I would have taken out an advertisement in the paper?"

Harvey sat down as well, then leaned forward conspiratorially. "Why would you take out an"—and here he stressed the second syllable—"ad*ver*tisement?" He also made a short vowel of the long "i" of the third syllable, which made him sound very affected— which made him sound very like himself—and which also I recognized as a move to gain ascendancy over me, as if I'd spoken incorrectly, or in a low-class way. "What," he went on, "would the ad*ver*tisement have said?"

I laughed loudly, to dispel any sense that I had been asking in earnest. Why had I said that? The thought of publicly declaring something, or even more specifically, of placing an ad in the paper—it was so strange to me, an intrusion, like how whenever I find myself near a high hedge the phrase *the secret life of dogs* pops into my mind, uninvited yet fully formed. Should I have taken out an ad looking for Rema? Was that the thought, cheaply costumed in generality, that I was really having? Did I think it halfhearted that I was looking for Rema all by myself? Perhaps it was that the image had partially risen again, as it does too often, of my mother looking through the newspaper classifieds. For notification of what? Of someone looking for her? Surely I had been misunderstanding. She always searched the paper so seriously, furrowing her brow just so, pursing her lips just so, and I would think—when I would see that—that maybe she was just terribly stupid. Or perhaps I was thinking of another echo of an advertisement in the paper, which is that a foolish friend once said to me, *You could place an ad in the paper, looking for your father.* One of the ugliest, stupidest things I'd ever heard anyone say. I wasn't looking for my father. I had no need to see him or speak to him or know where he was or what he was or wasn't wearing. Really, I barely remembered him, and I had no reason to believe that he was a particularly interesting or intelligent or good-looking man. (I can only surmise that it was the influence of the setting—the Patagonia of the unconscious that Rema had instilled in me—that prompted me to such banal and family-centered self-inquiry.)

"Yes," I answered finally. "What would an advertisement say?" I felt like I was delivering a line in a play. "What a silly question!" I gave out one punctuating guffaw, then imagined the newspaper issue, once a seeming bedrock, suddenly revealed to be just wrinkled butcher paper, now hole-punched, the resultant confetti fallen and swept under a chair.

I pulled my chair slightly closer to the hearth.

Harvey followed suit.

"I heard," Harvey said very quietly, "about your life, Dr. Leo. I wanted to express my condolences."

"There's absolutely nothing wrong with my life."

"Your *wife*, Dr. Leo. I heard. About what happened to her."

"But that's my private business, Harvey. That's not your affair. Who said what to you when?" When I tried to think whom I might have told about the doppelganger, I just saw in my mind an impassably thick hedge. Then a me, emerging out of a hedge, a double of me, speaking words and acting acts for which I was to be held accountable. Instead of recalling anything useful I heard the laughter of that night nurse.

"Dr. Gal-Chen," Harvey said, "told me."

"You mean Rema?"

"I mean Tzvi Gal-Chen."

"I suppose I did tell him." Though I hadn't explicitly asked Dr. Gal-Chen to treat my communications as confidential, I still felt, briefly, betrayed.

"And Dr. Gal-Chen told me."

"He told you?"

"Yes, he mentioned it. Also mentioned that you were here. Also that he was concerned for you. I didn't think it was a secret."

"Oh. Oh, yes, good. Of course. No. No, I certainly don't have any secrets."

"And I wanted to express my condolences. I wanted to tell you that I'd like to be of help to you in any way that I can."

4. Recent advances in epistemology

Of course he also wanted help from me. Harvey asked if he could share my room. He said he was out of cash. Naturally I accommodated; I couldn't imagine any unpleasant consequences, and, honestly, I felt obliged toward Harvey, as if I had abandoned him, as if it weren't he who had taken flight, or as if it had been my failures that had sent him away. Or maybe as if, obscurely, he were Rema. Who I was no longer, through some boyish idea of adventure, able to not miss.

"Your wife," Harvey said, settling himself onto my (temporary) bed. "I wonder how she's involved. What do you think the 49 Quantum Fathers are after? The whole journey here I couldn't sleep because I was worried they were going after the sheep; that's what you always hear about, Patagonian lamb; you don't think they'd go after live animals like that, do you? That would be unprecedented. Maybe it's just the fruit trees. I bet if you upped the winds on the pampa, not even that much, you could probably destroy all the fruit tree crops in one blustery evening. Cherries, peaches, apples—all smashed to the field of battle. Acres and acres covered in soft fruit flesh, just left to rot. Is your wife the silent, stoic type, or do you think this kind of thing might break her will? I'm sorry, I shouldn't have asked that. What's your current plan of action?"

Watching Harvey talk, I was reminded of a famous psychiatric case from the time of the French Revolution. A distinguished London tea merchant believed that a sinister "air loom gang" that controlled minds through mesmerism had foiled the peace he almost brokered with France. The merchant was placed in the asylum at Bedlam but in the end it proved true that the merchant was held there primarily at the request of a politician rather than for any medically indicated reasons. The details of the merchant's story were off—there was no air loom gang—but the heart of what he had been saying had a kind of truth to it. He had been lobbying for peace. What I mean to say: Harvey was an acceptable ally, despite everything. And Rema had always been fond of him.

I mentioned to Harvey (without divulging my pseudonym) that I—I and not we—was to begin a job for the Royal Academy that very Monday. That was my plan.

"But that's five days from now. Surely you can't sit idle until then," Harvey admonished, leaning then into an elbow-supported reclining position like the now-you-see-it-now-you-don't girl from those old Diet Pepsi commercials. Not unlike a common Rema pose. "What does Dr. Gal-Chen think you should do?"

Upon reflection I realized that Tzvi and I had spoken primarily of, well, poetry. And affairs of the heart. "I didn't quite ask him," I admitted. Curiously, Tzvi and I really hadn't had the most pragmatic of exchanges. "We did discuss windchill research," I proffered. "And its relation to war."

"Maybe we should call Dr. Gal-Chen now?" Harvey suggested in a voice decidedly un-idle, even as he lay himself out more fully on the bed.

I made clear—very clear—that of late Tzvi and I had restricted our communications to e-mail only.

"If there's been some sort of rift between the two of you, I believe I'm entitled to know about it." This statement Harvey directed toward the ceiling. For a second I thought Harvey was speaking again of me and Rema, but of course he was speaking of me and Tzvi. "We can't brook these kinds of interpersonal conflicts right now, Dr. Leo; what we're up against is too serious."

So I eventually consented to Harvey and I together contacting Tzvi via my BlackBerry. Much to my distress, Harvey started right up with his rapidly associating theories. One might have—I might have—thought Tzvi would have recoiled from Harvey's borderline nonsensical ideas, but instead—although Tzvi countered with many emendations—the two of them typed back and forth warmly, with a kind of exuberance, and I was reminded of (1) watching Rema develop Harvey's therapy, and (2) the absence of a brother I'd never had and whom I most likely would have hated having to compete with. But there they were. Within an hour, with minimal input from me, Tzvi and Harvey worked out that the Rema swapping most likely had been an early move to harvest chaos from our world to bring to a nearby one, that the dog was likely an essential determining agent, that the Patagonian crop-destroying winds—they weren't after sheep, just fruit—would be deployed soon, but not earlier than my Monday meeting with the Royal Academy, and that nevertheless it was essential to understand this not as a minor skirmish but as a pivotal battle that might be the tipping point to the full determination of our—Harvey's and my— world. At stake was the eradication of possibility. A fixed order loomed. If we lost, all would be set in proverbial stone. Time future as unredeemable as time past. No uncertainty. Rema still stranded.

"One thing I can't understand," I felt compelled to contribute, "is how you two can possibly know that nothing will happen before Monday."

That really was the single detail that didn't intuitively seem credible to me. Was I bothered by the parallel between Rema's therapeutic invention and the reality Tzvi and Harvey's communication seemed to support? No. I was buoyed by it and considered it a kind of verification by triangulation. What did intellectually shame me was the vivid realization that I had devalued the evidence of Tzvi's death. I'd breezed right past it, had simply resigned myself to it. But if I was communicating with a dead man—it did seem I was—then the world was radically different from what I had thought. And if I did in fact want to be a true scientist, I should have done more than just accept what had previously seemed unacceptable; I should have followed that new truth out to its logical implications. Where was Tzvi communicating to us from if not from another world? And how was he in our world if not through a kind of intrusion? And if such intrusions were possible, wasn't it obvious that there would be those who would capitalize on them? And, come to think of it, hadn't I had feelings, experienced coincidences, my whole life through, that had the character of such intrusions—of otherworldly order that seemed to make no sense? Nonsensical dislikes. Nonsensical likes. Even falling in love with Rema. Even occasionally getting mad at Rema for no obvious reason. And what of her unpredictable flashes at me? Who hasn't come across behaviors wholly resistant to interpretation—moods not reducible to serotonin or circumstance, Teflon actions that no theory sticks to—and such little unfathomables, wouldn't it make the most sense to understand them as uncanny intrusions of order from other worlds? Weren't Tzvi and the simulacrum both just such oddly familiar, not quite fathomable intrusions? And didn't Harvey and Tzvi's idea of an impending fixed order bear a strangely strong resemblance to the Eliot poem that talking to Tzvi had somehow seeded back into my mind? Why indeed had my ninth-grade teacher made us memorize that? *Down the passage which we did not take / Towards the door we never opened / Into the rose-garden . . . / But to what purpose . . . / I do not know . . . / Shall we follow?*

"I have inside information," Tzvi wrote, thus recalling me to the present. "Part of the brilliance of waging a war through weather is that the layperson doesn't notice there's a war going on at all. The layperson just shrugs his shoulders at the 'randomness' of it. Fortunately there was the dog this time," Tzvi added. "The dog was a real misstep, no? Either a misstep or the dog is central to all of this and they had no choice about introducing her, conspicuous as she was."

Harvey and Tzvi conferred about the possible "centers" of "this," though in terms of plans—that had been the original goal of the conversation after all—Tzvi said that all he could think for us to do until Monday was to monitor the weather closely.

"That's it?" I typed, on behalf of Harvey and me both.

"Frustrating, no?" Tzvi responded.

An interlude then. Of nothing.

"Who really," I asked, as a shadowy hope had blossomed within me, "do you think this work of mine with the Royal Academy will be with?" If I had a pseudonym, maybe my direct employer—a supposed Hilda—had one as well.

Tzvi responded that he couldn't quite say with whom. Then— and this surprised me—he asked again how I—I specifically, he did not include Harvey—had come across his work. Or rather, across him.

"My wife dreamt of you," I wrote. I accepted the melodrama of declaring that. Accepted the melodrama because the statement was, in its way, and in other ways, true. As Tzvi's research notes: add a little bit of white noise to the model, and a little bit of blue noise, and those carefully introduced errors will dramatically enhance the realism of the retrieved fields.

I left the bed to Harvey that night. "I feel so much safer," he said, "now that we're working together." As for myself, I slept, deeply, on the floor.

5. Without effort

Fresh snow the next morning made the light come in the window in a pink and quiet way, and in my dream, Rema was there; she licked a handkerchief and then wiped my cheek with it, near my mouth, where there was chocolate. When the room phone rang, this translated into a sensation that Rema, my real Rema, had left a teakettle boiling, and that we were in our apartment and that she was at her prettiest, and wearing pale yellow, looking like an afterimage of blue, and telling me something about Tzvi Gal-Chen, about the shirt he had on in that photo we had (once had) on our refrigerator, and about how Tzvi was a member of the 49, but the 49 were not our enemies. I used to have a simple recurrent dream, almost embarrassingly simple, in which I'd walk into a room and a woman would be there and I'd say, where were you? I thought you were dead. And she would answer saying, oh, I've been just right here, you just didn't look here, I think you didn't want to look here, she'd say, a little bit pouty with her lower lip, maybe with her eyes wet. It's like you didn't miss me, she says.

So I had the sense that Rema was near me, but when I opened my eyes I realized that I was on the floor with only a sheet and I saw objects that were not mine, that were not part of my apartment: a painting of horses, their manes blowing in a wind that moved nothing else, a faded photo of glaciers under a pink sunset. And I saw Harvey, his head under the covers, just a grip of fingers on comforter showing. And I remembered then, more or less, where I was.

The ring again.

"Yes?" I said, taking the receiver to my ear. Harvey stirred but didn't seem to wake.

"A woman is waiting for you," an unidentifiable and accented male voice said to me.

"Tzvi," I said, "is this you?"

"No. Here. Downstairs. She's waiting," the voice said and then hung up.

I didn't immediately rush down. I washed my face and the back of my neck. And I brushed my teeth and then flossed and then brushed my teeth again. I washed my hands vigorously to remove any dirt from under my fingernails. As for my ears, I had no Q-tips, but I did my best. And the trousers that Magda had given to me, I noticed that they had a small hole developing at the seam of the pocket, but I located a sewing repair kit—this hotel had foreseen everything—and neatly stitched the hole closed, reinforcing the edges, with a sufficiently matching gray thread. Also the button was chipped, so I went ahead and replaced it with a golden other. I just wanted to be very clean and well put together, for whoever that woman was, for whatever woman was waiting all that time, so early in the morning, for me.

6. The realism of retrieved fields

The woman waiting for me wasn't Rema, and she wasn't the doppelganger, and she wasn't—somehow—Tzvi or Tzvi's wife. She was Rema's mother, Magda. Magda: whom we hadn't even discussed the previous evening, whose role in the looming weather wars was unexplored, who might be inconsequential, but whose motherly/analyst presence nevertheless invoked in me a heightened and unwelcome self-consciousness.

"What a surprise," I said in a failing attempt at warmth. I wanted to return to my ignorance of moments earlier when the woman waiting for me might have been Rema. "I apologize for disappearing on you," I said, infected by the simulacrum's silly word choice. "I should have paid you in advance for accommodating me. I really did plan to get back to you on that." She was sitting, I was standing. Her gaze was level with the waist of my pants, with the golden replacement button. "I'm really—"

"No, no, I hadn't known that you were my son-in-law." Her laugh sounded strained, false. "There was so much knowledge hidden from me. I hadn't known who you were, you see? It is funny. Odd. Peculiar. The situation we were in."

I wanted to but didn't suggest "ironic" as a more accurate and succinct representation of our varied levels of knowledge.

Then Magda added, "Those pants; they really fit you just perfectly. That also is peculiar. Even the cuffs are exactly the right length. And the pockets are not deformed."

And it struck me that a more concise and precise description of my clothing would be to say that I was dressed like Tzvi Gal-Chen. Or, at least, like Tzvi once dressed, at the time of those photos.

"Listen," she said to me, "I wanted to talk to you about some things," and she looked around the lobby, where there was a tour group being beckoned by a white flag on a stick. "Somewhat secret things. Very secret things. Where can we go to talk?"

I should at least have left a note for Harvey, letting him know where I was. That would have been the proper way to behave. Even the simulacrum I had treated with such respect—the first time—but I just left, with plans to return as hastily as I (politely) could.

7. Sensitivity studies

"Listen," Magda said, reaching across the faux wood, faux knotted table of the nearest coffee shop we could find, a shop that claimed to be channeling the ancient Tehuelche spirit into its teas. She took my hand and whispered surreptitiously to me in her odd English, as if English were some obscure and therefore private Eastern European spy language—Hungarian, say, or Albanian—that nobody nearby would understand. "I have need to tell you that Rema has contacted me."

"What," I asked, "does that mean, that she 'contacted' you? Isn't she still staying with you?" I asked, feeling the need to engage in the earlier charade of the simulacrum being the real Rema.

"No, no," Magda said, choking a bit then, on saliva it seemed. "Not that woman, whom you saw in my house. The *real* Rema contacted me. I see now what you were trying to say, what you knew all along, that you were correct to suspect that other one."

Did I like having her confirm my difficult-to-fathom conviction? I did not. "How do you know it was the real Rema you spoke to?" I asked.

"I just knew. When I saw her. That it was her."

Judging by the visible pulsing of Magda's carotid artery, I suspected her heart was pounding. Tzvi, Harvey, now Magda too: the excess of corroboration actually undermined, rather than strengthened, my developing convictions. "You saw the real Rema?"

"Yes."

"Why isn't she here with you?"

"Well. Because." Magda reached out toward the clean and

empty mug in front of her, brought it to her mouth, sipped, and then set it down. "Why haven't they asked us what we want yet?" Scanning the room, she added, "Terrible service." A pause, then she turned her eyes straight on my unshaved chin. But I was clean in every other way; how had I forgotten to shave? "There's some. Well. I mean. Well, there are—there are complications."

As if it were a surgery gone bad, or a post-myocardial-infarction report.

"Medialunas?" I said to the yawning waitress who had suddenly materialized.

"For me the wellness tea. And huevos fritos. And medialunas. And some strawberry jam please. And a side of potatoes. And please extra napkins."

Her hunger struck me as suspicious.

"Let me just tell you exactly what Rema said to me," Magda announced after the waitress had left. "That way there will be no game of telephone problems." She removed from a vast purse one sheet of wrinkled graph paper—boxes outlined in pale blue—and she began to read. "Number one, she sends you her love. Number two, she says you are taking Harvey's disappearance too hard. And she wants you to know that whatever strange suspicions you may have, she is sure she can explain them. That's the main idea of number two, that she knows there are some things she needs to explain to you. I'm sorry I have no more details there. But then three. Three is everything important. She says she needs you to return to Buenos Aires. They have her working as a translator at the Earth Simulator, out in Tokyo, and something has gone terribly wrong. It is all just a miscommunication is what she is saying. But some of the scientists there are under the misimpression that she has powers for changing the weather—Rema said you would understand this—but of course she does not have those powers and she didn't know what she was getting into, and hopefully this will all be straightened out soon. She also wanted me to explain that she's sorry she didn't tell you about this job of hers earlier, but it was a new development, and she wanted to get a job all on her own, without your help, and then surprise you, and treat you to a trip all on her own money—"

"But we're married," I interjected.

Magda shrugged and went on, now reading more off her paper, "She says for you to help her. There's an office in Buenos Aires, the office of the desaparecidos. Her mother—that is me, yes—can take you there directly. And if you can get the paperwork started from the outside, and she'll be working from the inside, and hopefully everything can be fixed. Quick, quick."

Our food appeared.

Magda folded the wrinkled graph paper six or seven times, returned it to deep in her oversized purse. Then she looked at her sunny-side-up eggs that were looking at her. Then she glanced up from the eggs, and looked at me, and smiled.

I took a very tiny bite of my medialuna, to make things seem normal, even though I had no hunger. Then I asked casually, "Who told you to come down here?"

"I told you. Rema did."

"Why didn't Rema come see me herself?"

"What I said." Magda took her fork in hand; she broke the yolk of her egg; she startled as it spilled over. "She's stuck"—yolk rivuleting to the periphery—"over there. In Japan."

Land of the rising sun, her yolk made me think she was going to say. Which brought to my mind an image of Faye Dunaway gripped in the hand of King Kong. But that was the wrong Faye, the wrong monster, and the wrong country underfoot. It was the wrong image entirely. "But then how did you hear from her?"

Magda set her fork down. She reached again toward her mug, now full of special wellness tea, brought it to her lips, but I don't think she took a sip. "She visited me. Short time. Then she had to fly back."

The absolute lack of resonance of the story Magda told me—this confirmed for me that I wasn't just suggestible, that Tzvi and Harvey's assessment genuinely and singularly compelled me. I took then—there with Magda—a more sizable bite of my food. A dry edge of pastry scratched the roof of my mouth. "So what you are telling me is that Rema just flew down to Buenos Aires. From the Earth Simulator in Tokyo. To inform her mother—whom she barely speaks to—of her predicament. In order that her mother should speak to me. Then Rema goes back to Tokyo. Back to the arms of her captors. Without visiting me? Instead entrusting you with a wrinkled sheet of paper?"

Magda took hold of my right hand in a way remarkably devoid of any sexual undertones. "I made," she said with my wrist wrapped in her cold fingers, "a mistake."

"Okay," I said, using my awkward left hand to take another bite of pastry, to show my confidence, my ease in the situation, and suddenly I thought, obscurely, of Harvey sleeping, or not sleeping, alone, and maybe wondering where I was.

"I mean," she said, unhanding me, "I wasn't being clear. My words were not clear. I meant that Rema had a moment, there at work, in Japan, finally a free moment, and she used it to send me a message. Her message visited me."

"Her message," I repeated dryly.

Magda brought her own hand to her lap. "She sent me a message on the computer."

"Then why are you so sure it's really from her? Couldn't anyone be sending messages from an e-mail account with her name?"

Unlike Tzvi's and Harvey's and my theory, which had opened up for me, Magda's "theory" shrunk, retreated—even Magda's posture was worsening. "I mean not an e-mail," she said. "It was a message sent through another Argentine person. Through a friend of the both of us. Who also happened to be there with her. He's very reliable; he would know if it wasn't really her. I mean, thank God he was there. So that she could get a message out."

I noticed tattered strips of paper napkin amassed at the side of Magda's plate; the pile had taken on the look of some strange sea creature, washed ashore and dying. When had she torn that napkin? "Her other husband?" I intoned.

She ignored my words, then she picked up her fork and began eating from her plates round-robin style, fairly quickly, with pronounced deglutition.

We ate for a while, almost competitively.

Our hot drinks were refilled.

"You really believe you've received this message from Rema?" I asked finally.

A strand of Magda's tidy hair had fallen onto her face. "Oh, yes. Yes, definitely." When she brushed it away I could see the delicate print on the pad of her thumb; a few fibers of paper napkin clung there.

"I know," I said as sweetly as I could manage, "that we don't know each other so well. But I feel as if we do. That is a feeling that I have. So that is why I am going to ask you, again, directly: who sent you down here? Someone probably told you a pretty story to get you on their side. Obviously Rema didn't learn how to lie from you because you're really no good at lying at all. Lying can be appealing on young women, but not so much on mothers. Don't worry, I know, of course, that you are innocent. Understand that I certainly in no way blame you. On the contrary. Just tell me, was it the 49 Quantum Fathers? Or maybe a Quantum Father posing as a member of the Royal Academy?" I was trying to form an alliance with her, without really divulging anything of importance. "The more I think about this, the more I'm beginning to suspect there are some pretty powerful forces involved, much larger than just—"

"You're too old for Rema," she interrupted, raising her voice, becoming a shrill bird. "And you're a snob. And you're crazy. Crazy and not even very good-looking, especially not when I look at you from near like this. I'm happy to fail to bring you home. I don't care if she'll be mad at me. She'll always be mad at me no matter what I do."

I ignored her diversionary tactic. I ate as my own.

"Why don't you just come home with me anyway?" Magda eventually sighed. "It will make her happy."

"It's very kind of you to invite me," I said calmly. "But I have work here. I'm doing work here. I can't just turn my back on my responsibilities."

"But Leo. You don't have work here."

"That's not true," I said with conviction. "I'm doing climate change research."

"Leo, you're not a meteorologist. You're not. There's something wrong with you."

And of course that was true, what she said, that I wasn't a meteorologist, but it also wasn't true, because I was (in a way) employed as a meteorologist. Or would be soon enough. Her doubts did not disturb me.

8. Postprandial insights

I returned to find an anxious Harvey, who, upon my entering the room, threw his arms around my neck. Again I thought about orangutans.

"Where were you?" Harvey asked, with the trembling lip of a child.

"Nowhere important," I said.

"The snow flurries stopped so abruptly," he said.

"I'm so sorry," I said. "I'll never leave you without notice like that again." Saying that, to someone, felt nice.

"I thought maybe you'd already grown tired of working with me."

"I was just answering a phone call. A woman had called me. I had thought it might be important."

"You're not leaving me, then?" Harvey asked.

"Of course I'm not leaving you," I said, thinking of telenovelas but also of genuine tenderness.

And it was that easy to restore happiness. Harvey settled in front of the television weather report, while I set myself to the task of shaving. So I was shaving, and going over in my mind retorts that I hadn't offered to Magda, and not just vainly gazing into the mirror, when, upon close follicular inspection of (the reflected image of) a tender, raised, false pimple on my neck, the seed of the simulacrum's word—disappear—began to both germinate and molt in my mind, revealing itself as a two-toned postulating buzz; wasn't the simulation of Rema's appearance far more extraordinary than her disappearance? I had been so fixated on the disappearance, probably because it was more painful, but really it was the appearance of the doppelganger that was far stranger. Why not simply take Rema? This simulacrum, was she really deployed just to move a dog, or was she being deployed primarily for some other reason, to solve some other problem, to generate some other solution? Solution to what? Was the simulation of two observer Remas occurring in order to triangulate, in a perfectly coupled way, on the data of me? I had been comporting myself as if this mystery was proximate to me, but maybe the mystery actually was me.

If the dog was essential, but following me had proved more essential than staying behind with the dog, then didn't that mean I was more essential than the dog? And if I was deploying a meticulous methodology of being open to chance, while it was chance itself that the Fathers were working to control, then wasn't it me they were trying to control? The simulacrum had pursued me. As had Magda. Even Harvey had tracked me down.

I set down my razor.

It's a strangely impersonal feeling, to feel wanted for reasons one doesn't understand.

Half shaved, half convinced, I turned and said to Harvey, "I think the battle might not be being waged through the dog. It might be that it's being waged through me. I thought I was following the caprice of my own heart, but now I think maybe my movements might really be determined by some other force. Maybe the determination of the weather patterns is beginning—is getting its foothold into this world—through the determination of the patterns of me. I mean, maybe my movements really matter. Matter to a lot more people than just me. Maybe I'm the proverbial butterfly."

"Everyone's a butterfly, Dr. Leo," Harvey said, not even turning from the television set.

"I know, I know. But I'm saying—I think I might be the central butterfly. I don't mean to be grandiose; I mean I hope it's not true. But I just have a feeling."

"Well," Harvey said, now turning to me, "when I'm in a situation like that—as I think you know—I try to seek some corroboration, try to verify some hunches. Keeps me out of embarrassing situations, you know?"

Well there were all kinds of corroboration. "I think I should go try to find that woman who sought me out this morning. I need to understand her motivations better, even if she won't straightforwardly tell me what they are. Do you mind if I leave you again?"

"Do you mind if I order some room service? Go, go, but when can I expect your return?"

Well: it was a small town, that corner of the Argentine unconscious, and by evening I'd managed to refind Rema's mother.

9. The sensitivity of the solution to uncertainties

After I made a false promise to call the doppelganger after dinner, Magda conceded to sharing another meal with me. As soon as we sat down I began to explain that I of course understood that she was under the impression that there was something wrong with me, and I explained that I thought that was entirely understandable. I told her that if I didn't know what I knew, and if I didn't feel what I'd felt, then I too most likely would have thought there was something wrong with me. But maybe she felt, as I felt, that she knew things that I didn't know, and that if I came to know those things then I might see the world differently, as she did. If she wanted to, she could tell me those things that I didn't know; she could rest assured that I would handle well the coming to know of them.

The skin around her eyes: gray and recessed. She said nothing, just looked askance. Then sighed.

So I tried a different tack. "The landscape here is so astounding. What a beautiful country," I said.

"It's a broken, depressed country," she responded.

"Everyone seems so nice," I said.

She said how insincere everyone was. How it was all just appearances. "Even me," she said. "I'm only nice on the surface."

If she wanted to indulge in that common grandiose fantasy of not being a nice person, then that was okay with me. "You know more than I do."

"Yes," she said, "I do know more than you do."

"Yes you do," I agreed, realizing that she most likely hated me, at least for that moment while I had her attention. So I truly had nothing to lose with her, I could only gain. "So the man Rema left Argentina with? Her husband? Was his name, well, by any chance, well—what was his name?"

"I thought you were his friend?" she said, looking suddenly energized and disturbed, as if a bright light from an unidentified source had been shined on her through a window. "That was a lie also?"

"I've just been so confused lately," I said. "It has spilled, or I mean slipped, my mind. That means I have forgotten. I mean, well, was it—was his name—was it Anatole?" My plan was then to ask if she could recall Anatole ever asking after me, or after someone like me.

"Anatole?" she said back to me, pronouncing it differently, making four syllables of it, when I had been saying it over and over and over in my mind with only three. "Is that what you said?" she asked me, as if I'd let a genie—evil or benevolent I could not tell—out of a bottle.

"Yes?" I said. "I'm sorry I lied earlier. You're right. I don't know why I said I knew him. There was so much I didn't know when I met you. I think you can understand. I mean: you're an analyst. I mean: I was in a rather awkward position."

"When Rema tells me that you are now her husband, is she lying to me?"

I shook a little bit of salt onto the empty plate in front of me; I thumbed some grains into my mouth; I didn't want to give information, I wanted only to take. "You mean the woman I shared a bedroom with in your house? Well kind of, well yes, in the strictest interpretation, she is lying. But from a slightly alternate perspective she is not lying. I am Rema's husband. I am."

"But you don't know who Anatole is?"

I tried to picture an Anatole. He looked like me, but me as refracted in an ugly-making funhouse mirror; and then somehow that wavy Anatole took my place, and I had become the distorted him, and this revealed my original position to me as an intensely enviable one. "But you *do* know him?" I asked.

"Your marriage—if really it is a marriage—it's very strange. Cold."

I thought of windchill, as a kind of misdirected rebuttal. Magda went on about just what she thought my marriage was like. She talked on and on, and so confidently, and in such an ugly manner, until finally I interrupted:

"Aren't you extrapolating a bit too much, a bit too confidently, just from the single fact that I don't know precisely who Anatole—"

"I don't blame you," she said, which led me to understand that she clearly did blame me. "She is a strange girl, my daughter. Maybe that is my fault."

Then I was quiet as was she; I hoped she didn't read my silence as judgment. I broke a bite off a crackery breadstick; it cleaved along unexpected planes. As I listened to myself chew, I began to feel distant from myself, and, in that way, clearheaded. "So," I said, partly to Magda, partly to myself, "Rema left Argentina with this An-a-to-le person." I adopted the four-syllable pronunciation with confidence, feeling myself an Hercule Poirot: it was near the end of the story, the suspects were in the room. "I had thought he was the night nurse," I said as an engorging vein imaged in my mind. "But I am relieved to know that he is not the night nurse—"

"You think Anatole is a nurse?"

"No, no. I don't. Not anymore. I was wrong before," I said as I felt my investigation growing crystalline.

"Anatole was not Rema's husband," Magda said.

"Ah so," I said, gracefully turning on that dime. "Actually I suspected as much. They were only engaged then, am I right? It ended when they arrived in the States. Then the love just faded." I felt on a proverbial roll. "They realized it had been a matter of context, of setting. And though they were still fond of each other, it just wasn't enough for marriage. It was awkward in bed perhaps, pardon my French, and awkward at meals, he wouldn't eat lentils with her, and he couldn't handle arguing with her, and he never knew what to say, and he bought her the wrong gifts, things that revealed he could never really know her—"

"You are completely misunderstanding," Magda said, breaking into English. "These fantasies of yours are bizarre." She was not looking at me in the eyes—instead again looking at the cuffs of my shirt. "Anatole," Magda said, not hesitating in her pronunciation. "Well. He's. Well, really I feel rather strange saying this. Well, really. Well." I noticed Magda set down an accordioned tea bag label. Where had that tea bag come from? Neither of us had ordered tea. "Maybe it is wrong that I am the one telling you this. But. Anatole was *my* husband."

I guffed just one violent guffaw. But I felt in that instant that I'd lost all that had held me taut, whatever had tirelessly and praiselessly kept the shell of me from collapsing under the pounds of atmospheric pressure.

"Are you choking?" she said with concern, for me I think, more than for herself.

"I'm sorry," I said. "I'm always hearing the strangest things. Not the things people are actually saying." I could feel twitching in my face, and itching in my scalp, and laughter in my diaphragm. The room was too much there. I could feel the color of the wallpaper—burgundy—invading.

"You don't know," she said, "that Anatole was Rema's father?"

In the silence that followed I could feel the powdery softness of my button-up shirt, and the fullness of the veins of my feet, and the absence of Rema's hand on my forehead just where she likes to place it when she stands behind me while I'm seated in a chair and complaining of a headache, and I heard—maybe it was that accordioned tea bag label—a heated kettle, empty of water, not whistling.

I said, "I had a father too." I don't know why that is what I said. I find that sort of cheap identification shameful. I then immediately began forking food into my mouth.

"They took Anatole," Magda said. "Rema was very young."

10. Primate perturbations

I ate a delicious corn soup that night. Magda's meal looked tasty as well—a whole fish, head on, grilled—but I did not ask for a bite of it and she did not offer. My mashed potatoes were flavored with garlic and I imagine hers were too, though she did not eat hers while I did eat mine. (Why wasn't she hungry?) One might be inclined to lend too much importance to Magda's statements about Anatole. While such statements might be, of course, inherently important, they were not particularly important in my matter, the matter of locating Rema. After all, out of any assembled body of knowledge, there are many possible data points one might dwell on. That is to say, a piece of information may be important in some very local sense, but what does it have to do with, as they say, the price of tea in China? What with the recent discussion of Initial Value Problems, and of the Dopplerganger effect, surely some busybody will feel inclined to make cheap metaphors, or butterfly metaphors, but such metaphors would rely entirely on associations of only apparent depth. Really the details about Anatole were hardly relevant at all to my investigations, and there was no reason to believe they rippled out to increasingly dramatic effect. Never mind that the simulacrum later insisted that Magda was lying to me, that Anatole was not taken at all, that he simply left. Who knows? The point remains the same: people lose parents all the time, and in all sorts of ways, and if I perhaps did not know the very particulars of what had happened with Rema's father, it's not as if I didn't understand Rema herself, understand her entirely, see within her the exact contours of that disappearance even if I didn't know it was a loss I was looking at. What this—Magda's statement—was, was not a mésalliance like Rema's reaction to the threatening letter on mourning, but a misalliance of a different sort, and I was resolved not to let it derail my search, which it could easily have done if poorly interpreted. I was looking for clues that would help me find Rema, and then I stumbled across something resembling the truth about Anatole, which I had briefly mistaken for a truth about the other husband, something sizable, yes, but something I really had no interest in knowing, a stone I had continually, purposively, wisely even, left unturned. A clue, but to a different mystery. Regardless, I didn't want to know; I am not gentle enough to know such things; perhaps nobody is.

At some point during that meal I remember looking down at my hand, which seemed a terribly hairy paw, reached out from that delicate years-worn cloth.

Magda said to me, "I'm sorry, I did not mean to make you uncomfortable."

But I wasn't uncomfortable. Though it's true that I did fail to offer Magda any comfort whatsoever. Say what you will of me, but I would defend myself on the fact that (1) her grief, if there was any, was none of my business, (2) I could certainly do nothing to alter the etiology of it, (3) "comforting words" snag, like hangnails, and (4) we didn't have a professional relationship. Also, (5) disappointment distracted me from figuring out what my duties toward Magda might be, disappointment in learning nothing that seemed likely to bring me closer to retrieving Rema. I had been counting on the Anatole clue. Even if just to help me understand how I figured in all this.

Instead of following up on Rema's father, I eventually reiterated my question about who was the original husband of Rema.

Magda ate the eyeball of her fish. "Ask my daughter yourself. I am living in enough trouble already with that girl and the things that she does and does not want me to say."

"It was the dog walker?" I said.

"He's an analyst," she said.

"The dog walker is? Or the husband is? Or both are?"

"Stop," she said, closing her eyes, putting her hands to the sides of her face.

I whispered, "Was his name Tzvi?"

"This game is beneath you," she said, with her ears still covered. "It is, anyway, beneath me. So if you consider me to be beneath you, which you seem to, then I believe it follows that this game is beneath you too."

11. I always hated musical chairs

Harvey, amidst a mess of room service plates, asked me what I had learned.

"I'm not sure. But I think I'm not the central butterfly. Or I'm not the central man. This Anatole, for example, I wholly misunderstood his significance. And Magda just let me go. It seems like all my assumptions were flawed."

He asked me if I had learned that Rema was in love with Anatole.

I said no.

"Does the doppelganger love Anatole?"

"Why all this talk about love, Harvey? What's happening to your interest in the weather?"

"I often find that it's love that lies at the center of things, don't you?" he mewed sleepily. "One has to presume that the majority of the 49 Quantum Fathers once belonged to the Royal Academy, belonged until they were somehow burned by love. One of my old therapists pointed that out to me. How chance—"

"That doesn't sound right to me. Who was this therapist?"

Harvey shrugged. "You're the one who likes to talk about love to Tzvi."

"Not about love. About Rema maybe. About the doppelganger a little bit. But only as a kind of evidence."

"What about that man you told me about who you saw walking dogs? Is that who the doppelganger loves?"

"No, of course she doesn't love him," I answered in a quiet, calm, not at all irritated voice. Our room, with all those dirty dishes, had acquired the cheerless look of a bachelor pad. I set myself down in an armchair. I lacked the peace of mind to think of Rema's father. "What is sad of course is that even in this short time she has fallen in love with me. She can't stop calling me. So what can she do with her frustrated love for me, a love perpetually unable to reach its object? Maybe she will end up lavishing attention upon that other man simply because, at least superficially, at least in terms of profession, he resembles me, the forbidden fruit." I felt moved to attempt a love and chance lecture superior to that of his other unnamed therapist. "Maybe that's happening right now. But he—well, he wouldn't even really enjoy her attentions, since surely a man with his training would understand her interest in him as nothing more than simple transference, because he must know that a girl like her—I'm sorry, a woman—could never actually be attracted to him unless she was somehow unconsciously mistaking some superficial aspect of him for some earlier true love. He can be nothing more than the illusion of the recovery of that love; he can only be the ersatz love, you see; no other sensible explanation for her affection toward him would exist." I knew I was going on, but having arrived so dispirited, I now felt compelled to speak from a position of superior knowledge. "In fact, Harvey, this is all rather analogous to how Freud 'discovered' transference in the first place. Do you know? He had this experience, early in his career, of this beautiful young woman emerging from hypnosis, throwing her arms around his neck, and kissing him passionately. It haunted him. He felt certain, I suppose, that she couldn't really have been attracted to him personally, that he must have functioned as a stand-in for someone else. I mean, it's interesting—if Freud had considered himself attractive, he might never have made his discovery, he simply would have assumed the girl found him straightforwardly alluring. Surely that's what Jung would have thought. Although Freud takes his idea to an extreme—he seems to think that transference explains the origin of all love, that there's always a thicket of past people between any two lovers. There I'd have to disagree. As it goes contrary to my own experiences. Freud erred in universalizing his theory. That's the problem with calling psychoanalysis a science, because science shouldn't rely on authority, but—"

"You've thought about this a lot," Harvey interrupted with a glaze of deafness. He had begun to stack the various dishes. That's when I picked up on the scent in the room, one that went beyond steak and toast. I realized Harvey had been drinking. "I thought," he said offhandedly, "maybe you'd find out why your wife left you."

I had never said that she'd left me. Who had said that? Surely Harvey didn't actually think Rema had left me, but rather he was trying to talk about . . . what? My leaving him? Why did everything have to also mean something else? I wanted to be in a simpler, vaudeville world, where the jokes had to do with ladders being too short, or someone slipping on a banana peel. "Sometimes," I said to Harvey, "you see connections that aren't really there."

"Yes, you've often told me that," he said.

"And she didn't leave me. There's absolutely no indication of that. She just disappeared. Or rather, was taken. I don't know why, of all the people who could have been taken, why it was her in particular, but—that's another reason we're trying to retrieve her. I wish I understood better, but I don't. And I told you that I might be out all day, I gave you warning. Listen, why are we talking about me all the time lately? You and I should talk about you. Have you called your mom?" I asked.

Harvey sententiously set his piled dishes outside our door. "Dr. Gal-Chen wouldn't want me to do that."

"Why not?" I said. "You should call her. If you don't call her she'll be terribly disappointed. In you and me both."

"I'm not a fool," Harvey said. "I can see you're just changing the subject." He made his way over to the mirror, carefully fixed his hair. "I once received an MRI to rule out neurocysticercosis." He turned back to me. "You know sometimes when Tzvi would call you to pass on orders to me I would think I could hear your wife's voice in the background—"

"I don't know exactly what you're thinking, Harvey, but I'm pretty sure it's wrong," I announced calmly as my ears tingled, as if vigorously generating too much wax, "and whatever your suspicions are, they're not the right suspicions. And by the way I'm sleeping in the bed tonight, and you're not—"

"You think of me as useless, Dr. Leo. I can see that. That's okay. But Dr. Gal-Chen doesn't think like you. Soon enough you'll understand the essential niche I fill. Until then I can weather the indignity of your indifference. Dr. Gal-Chen knows I'm not just any serviceable cog in the Royal Academy's wheel. He knows my services are irreplaceable. Not like the object of affection of that patient of Freud's, the one who could have been anyone."

As Harvey rambled on, it became vivid to me that Harvey deployed Tzvi as a kind of psychotic patch, a mending of the rent caused in his universe by the unflagging perception of his own insignificance. Seeing Harvey so unable to understand Tzvi as a real person, seeing him misunderstand Tzvi as whatever Harvey most needed him to be—a new kind of sadness blossomed in me.

Under the spell of that glittery melancholy, I stayed up late that evening, composing a long and heartfelt note to Tzvi, in which I explained to him that though I had, naturally, been, at least once or twice, "burned by love," this had in no way tempted me to join the 49. Even Rema, I confessed, had at times been indifferent toward me. Not that long ago, for example, she had rented a miniseries of some sort—something with servants—and I had missed watching the first episode with her, and on those grounds she had then discouraged me from watching any of the rest of the series and she would just sit in front of the TV alone at night, spooning from a bowl of cereal and at the same time telling me she wasn't hungry for dinner, thus leaving me to eat takeout alone. (At other times nothing had made us happier than spending night after night watching rented movies and holding each other.) Or maybe it was I who had been indifferent to her. Usually we were tender to each other through moody periods, but sometimes we'd get struck by a dark mood at the same time and then we'd be lost. For example, I had recently taken to staying late at the hospital, not because I had to but simply because I'd find myself lying on my office sofa, reading every last square of newspaper and magazine. ("World Briefings" was often my favorite part, and it regularly pained me, the way it was over so quickly.) One night when I came home at 10:30 p.m. Rema asked me why I'd been occupied so late, and I told her, somewhat truthfully, that I'd been engrossed in a lengthy article about the discovery, in a cave on the Indonesian island of Flores, of a species of Hobbit-like people, *Homo floresiensis*: these three-foot-tall people who lived contemporaneously with *Homo sapiens,* separated only by geography. The archaeologists had also found, in the same limestone cave as *Homo floresiensis*, the remains of a Komodo dragon, a dwarf elephant, and stone tools. "Now," the article had noted, "that race of people is gone." But why, Rema asked me, couldn't you just read that here at home? And why did it take you so long? And why are you so interested in those gone people? When you called to say you'd be late, she lectured me, I assumed that you had no choice.

Anyway, I told Tzvi about these trivial incidents only because I wanted him to feel confident that I was unshakably on the side of the Academy, that I had endured unstable climates in the past, that I could do so in the future. But the simple fact of writing all that to him produced in me a new vulnerability. Too vividly the thought crossed my mind that the 49 had perceived the actual weaknesses in my marriage, that Rema and I had been targeted because the 49 wagered that given the attenuated state of our relationship, I actually might not notice, or respond to, the swap.

Perhaps just a phantom thought. But when, almost immediately after sending the note to Tzvi, I received an automated out-of-office reply in return, the feeling was one of devastation.

12. I didn't feel the way it seemed like I might feel

Again the room phone woke me from slumber; the message was the same as the day before; the message was that I was to come down to the lobby, preferably immediately, because there was a woman who wished to speak with me.

Casting about my room, I discovered Harvey wasn't there.

Okay, I thought, blocking out thoughts of a missing man, of an unidentified woman, of an absent father or two, blocking out possibly erotic thought, who knew, I was still half asleep. I dressed hastily, went straight downstairs. But instead of seeing Magda there I saw a woman (and at first I just saw her reflected in the mirror-lined wall) with hair blonde like Rema's cornsilk, but combed in a wholly different way, or rather, not very well combed, back in a sloppy bun, artlessly done, and greasy, with dark roots dramatically showing.

"Look," Harvey said—Harvey! looking tidy and proud, with his shirts tucked in just so, and even his cuffs properly buttoned—with a barely suppressed gloating grin, "I found her. She's a lily of the valley here to see you. A creamy daff of the dill. An atmospheric phenomenon."

I was looking at this blonde woman's image in the mirror; she was looking at that same image of herself in the mirror. Or so it appeared to me. But then I thought about the Doppelganger effect again, or at least that phrase came into my mind, and those words solved something for me: I realized I was misinterpreting my perceptions. That is: if I saw the blonde woman's face in the mirror, and if she appeared to be looking at the same point in the mirror that I was looking at, then actually she was looking at my face in the mirror while I was looking at her face in the mirror, that our faces could be in the same places (in the mirror) depending on just where one was looking from. So she wasn't thinking of, looking at, only herself. Nor was I thinking just of myself. That's just what it seemed like if one didn't account for anticipatable perceptive distortions. But hadn't I known all that about mirrors already? And yet right then it was as if I'd lost that knowledge and had to learn it again. Something about how we really don't understand how mirrors work, or what they are showing us, which is interesting to think about considering that mirrors are the main way we have of understanding what we look like—what was it that poetic charlatan Lacan said, something about how because we only see ourselves in mirrors we come to know ourselves "in the fictional direction"? I'm not sure why I feel so moved to clarify this brief moment so much; it just seems like an important case of misperception on my part, important because I caught myself misperceiving and immediately readjusted my understanding of the situation. This is not one of those cases when I am talking about an unimportant and unrelated topic, some random intellectual distraction, in order to avoid an emotionally laden topic. As if I was overwhelmed with emotion at the sight of that blonde woman. I was not.

Anyway, she looked at my reflection.

I looked at hers.

Quickly enough, my mind had done the corrective math, to realize that she probably could see and understand me seeing her looking at me, and so on and so forth, echoing, echoing, and the first words she spoke to me were, "I'm a better detective now; this time I just looked online at the credit card."

She also: I don't think she was talking about an emotionally less laden subject simply in order to avoid the main subject.

Harvey touched my sleeve and whispered, "Isn't she beautiful? She returns to us from another world."

She said calmly, "Harvey explained to me that the two of you have been working together this whole time."

"Not this whole time," I protested. "That's not true. Harvey and I haven't been together this whole time. I've been working very hard and for a great deal of that work I have been very alone. I have been completely alone. Have you been alone?"

"Harvey says you've been trying to find me," said the woman— she did smell like grass but also like baby oil and sweat—taking hold of my sleeve but turning away from me, turning toward Harvey. "Your mother still has you listed with the police as a missing person. Did you know that? And you are okay for her to be having worry like that? Do you know what that must be like for her, to not know whether you are dead or alive?" She then turned back to me, "Is this one of these disorders where the afflicted lacks empathy?"

I just looked at her.

"Well," Harvey's voice came in, "it has to do with someone I work for. That's the only reason why, unfortunately, I have to put my mother through this suffering, have to leave her, for now, in the dark, without knowledge, like, I mean, as Dr. Leo would say, some character in a Greek tragedy. Maybe after this assignment that Dr. Leo and I are starting Monday, maybe after that I will be dispatched back to my home base."

"Monday?" the doppelganger asked. "What starts Monday?"

"I think already I'm disclosing more than Dr. Gal-Chen would like," Harvey replied.

"But how," the ersatz Rema asked, glancing back over at me, "how did Tzvi Gal-Chen contact you, Harvey? Through this"— she raised my hand, as if it were a puppet's hand—"man?"

I stared sternly in Harvey's direction, shook my head ever so discreetly. But that is a characteristic of Harvey—that he doesn't read body language well. It's not what the doppelganger was saying; it's not that he lacks empathy. He simply misreads the person he's trying to empathize with, so in effect sometimes it can feel like a lack of empathy, when really there's plenty of empathy, it's just eccentrically directed. Even with me that happens sometimes.

"You are familiar with Tzvi's *real* work?" Harvey continued playing the fool for her. "You *do* know what I mean?"

The impostress raised her hands to her forehead, pressed in at the sockets of her eyes, as if something needed to be pushed back into place. "Yes," she said with fatigue, "I think I do. Harvey, you really should call your mother. But don't worry, if you don't want to call her, I won't call her. Even though she's been calling me."

"I'm glad," Harvey said, "you respect the delicate nature of my work."

"But please tell me," she continued cloyingly, "how exactly did this Tzvi Gal-Chen get in touch with you? Did you speak with him directly?"

"No, we didn't speak with him," Harvey said.

"No, we didn't speak with him," I said at the same time.

"JinxBlackMagicYouOweMeACoke," Harvey said.

We were all quiet a moment.

Then the doppelganger felt compelled to contribute: "And you, Leo. That girl in the coffee shop that you were leaving notes for—she went to high school with me. Also, she's not interested in you."

"I don't think the dog walker is interested in you," I said.

The exchange ended something like that, anyway. I'm uncertain how we finally broke off from that whole encounter. I'm not quite sure how one puts a cap, or really puts any sort of punctuation, any sort of finality, to those sorts of emotions, to those desires that lose their way and reach out to the wrong people, or those desires that get derailed on their way to you, leave you suffering a ludicrous and misguided jealousy, misguided because so often it can look—seeing events through the mirrors we see into—like someone is looking at, say, herself, or himself, or someone else, and being in love, but really he or she is looking at you just as you are looking at her while giving her the illusion that you are looking elsewhere.

"I haven't slept," the simulacrum said.

"You can sleep in our room," Harvey said. "I'll be out collecting data during the daylight hours."

She napped under my covers. I watched her. Breathing. Very slightly irregularly.

Needless to say:

The real Rema wouldn't have put her hair in a bun.

She wouldn't have held my wrist so tightly.

She wouldn't have criticized Harvey, nor, for that matter, would she have listened to him so attentively.

She wouldn't have had so private a conversation in so public a place.

She would have commented, in at least some small way, on my as yet unshaved morning handsomeness.

And if Rema had tracked me down by looking at our online credit card statement, she would have kept that information to herself.

13. A confession

I did not touch the simulacrum while she napped, but I did look at her closely. Her bangs parted down the middle and clung to her forehead in sweat and made me think of Mata Hari; she was beautiful in that moment, in her strangeness. Beautiful and also like Rema who, with her little secrets, her little silences, was often similarly wrapped in a thin but shimmering cloak of the alien. For a moment I thought of Rema and the simulacrum as genuine twins, or as the separate images that come together in a stereoscope. Shortly after she woke she sat on the floor and hugged my knees—I was sitting on the edge of the bed—and she said she would stay by my side until the end of time. That's what she said: the end of time. She said she'd thought it through under many conditions and that was what she had decided. Then she said she was hungry.

When we walked outside, the wind mussed up her hair and already she no longer seemed like Mata Hari, or like Rema, to me.

"We have a lot to discuss," she said like a schoolmarm.

The simulacrum received a menu in Spanish, and I one in English, or a kind of English. The first listing on my menu under Drinks was *Bloody Girl*. The next was *Bloody Great*.

"Will you come back to New York with me?" she asked.

"I'm afraid I can't," I answered.

"What's starting Monday?" she asked.

"My job."

"What kind of job?"

"I'm not going to discuss that."

"Did you receive the articles?" she asked.

"Of clothing?" I think I said; I was still busy wondering over the bloodiness on the menu. That's why it was difficult to make conversation. That and her interrogation style. If only she could have stayed asleep—it was so easy to think fondly of her then. "My luggage has still not turned up. They haven't called me."

"I'm talking about the articles I sent you in e-mails. Did you receive those articles?"

Another drink offered on the menu: *I crash.* That brought a smile to my face.

"Do you think," she said with a patronizingly patient tone, "those articles might have something to do with what's happening to you? To us?"

Then I solved something small, the bloody drinks. *Sangria chica, sangria grande*: they had translated themselves for me, but *I crash* still had not. I couldn't keep myself from giggling.

Stone-faced, the simulacrum said to me, "Nervous laughter is okay. I just want to know if you read the articles about the misidentification syndromes. And I want to know what you are thinking. What you are thinking of them. The articles. I'm being patient and not even asking you what you are thinking of me."

A fourth drink was *I crash Great.* My giggling grew worse. As some sort of excuse for my poor behavior, I passed my badly translated menu over to the simulacrum.

"Did you even read a sentence?" she asked again.

I used to ask Rema that about my own articles. "Did you read this?" I said, pointing to the menu.

"Don't copy me."

"Yes. Okay," I said, compressing my laughter into just abdominal pain. "I read the articles. I read them very seriously." This was true. (Rema used to lie about that sort of thing.) Then I noticed that the menu also offered *Popes Fried*, which really isn't even that funny, and which I recognized immediately as simply *papas fritas*, french fries better translated, but already the infection of laughter was returning.

"If you were in my place," she said dryly, "and I in yours, wouldn't you want to push me to think very carefully? To step outside of my body and look at this problem from the position of an other body?"

I tried to explain to her then that I did take my problem seriously, very seriously, and so of course I had read those articles, but it wasn't as if they told me anything I hadn't already considered.

"Do you remember seeing *Godzilla* with me?"

"I did see *Godzilla* with Rema, that's true."

"Do you remember her getting mad at you when you finished the brownie without offering her any?"

"I don't remember that, no."

"Okay. Remember how you tried to lecture her about the English phrases in the movie? About Geiger counter and oxygen destroyer, and she told you that you were too dominating?"

"Rema often likes my little lectures. That might even be what she likes best about me."

"But do you remember the little fight?"

"Listen, I differ with you on the details, but yes, I remember the incident you're referring to. But it was insignificant—"

"And yet I know all about it. Doesn't that seem to you strange?"

"Many things are strange," I said lightly and with confidence. "More things on heaven and earth, you know. Not necessarily all nice things. Nothing nice about a vengeful ghost, for instance."

"Maybe," she said gently, reaching across the table to brush some hair off my face, "it's more strange for me than it is for you. To see this face of yours but not really understand you. You have an absolute conviction that I am not Rema?"

An unintended glance at the menu revealed *eggs loins.* I had no idea what that might originally have been. "I guess so," I squeaked. "Yes. I'm certain. You know what I mean."

"All right," she said with the kind of quarter smile I associate with photos of people who have died. "From now forward, I'll be honest with you. I'll admit to you that I'm not really her."

The simulacrum had not shredded her napkin anxiously during this time of mistranslated anxiety; she had folded it up neatly, into a floppy fortune-teller.

"Okay," she further affirmed. "We are saying that you are right. We will say that. Okay?"

I looked away from the simulacrum's fortune-teller, and toward her hand, and I noticed that she was bleeding, ever so slightly, at the cuticle of her right index finger. Rema generally had ragged cuticles, but they rarely bled. There was just once when one, actually two, of her fingers were bleeding, and this was because Rema had been scratching a Tow Warning sticker off of our car; the car had been unmoved and accumulating parking tickets, but I hadn't known this because she had, for days and days in a row, taken upon herself the normally alternating task of moving the car, but I guess she would go outside and wander around and just not move it. She had been sad for a while then; that had been a very low time for her when she hadn't said or done much and once she cried because we were out of milk for the tea. In some ways I had left her alone, assuming she didn't want someone intruding upon her sadness. I would leave her behind in the bed in the morning. And when I'd come home she'd still have sleep in her eyes. I didn't quite know what to do for her. I bought her little things and wrote her notes. When she'd take a bath I would go put the towels in the dryer so that they'd be warm when she got out. I'd clip little articles out of the newspaper that I thought might amuse her, and I tried making her homemade marzipan, which I knew she loved, but it didn't work and I broke our food processor in the attempt. I had thought maybe she was disappointed in me, but in retrospect I see now what was fairly obvious and what maybe I didn't want to understand, what must have seemed worse to me than her anger: that often her mood had nothing to do with me at all.

The simulacrum reached out her only slightly injured hand and placed it on top of mine. "I'm sorry," she said, "that I didn't confess earlier. But I can help you find her. I'm not sure how, but somehow."

14. A reasonable theory

Did Tzvi think I should join forces with Rema's double? I wrote to him in detail about her confession but again received in response nothing but an automated out-of-office reply. At least the automated response assured me that my notes weren't strictly dead letters, not eternally. And even in Tzvi's absence I could still turn to his work for guidance. One of the triumphs of Tzvi's 1981 retrievals paper was demonstrating the real-world validity of results obtained through trials on models. For example, output from a three-dimensional numerical cloud model was used in place of observations to test a method for retrieving temperature and pressure deviation fields; then comparison of the theoretically retrieved fields to "real" data affirmed the robustness of the technique. Which I interpreted to mean that, by analogy, working with the model Rema would indeed reveal information about the real Rema.

But what kind of work were we meant to do? Had I accidentally meant what I said when, in anger, I'd quoted to Tzvi about children's games being a rehearsal for the right life? Harvey, the simulacrum, and I passed all of Friday and Saturday posing as ordinary tourists, blending in perfectly with the local culture of nonlocal pleasure seekers. Temperatures were unstable but the sun shone reliably. We took a boat tour of the lake and admired its protruding glaciers, their fish-scaly façades. When the simulacrum shivered in the wind, I gave her my wool sweater. The soda and chips on the boat were wildly overpriced, but I paid happily and no one felt cheated. I offered a compelling explanation of why glacial ice appears to be blue, and Harvey and the simulacrum both seemed patient, even possibly happy, to listen to my lesson. Later we ate strawberries and walnuts and tender lamb that had been cooked on a spit. We walked to cave paintings that proved disappointing but then were surprised by a black-necked swan on the walk back into town. The next morning we strapped crampons onto our shoes and—herded like ducklings by two young Argentine college boys—we crunched across glacial surfaces, felt awe at crevasses. Harvey sunburned and the simulacrum found an aloe lotion to apply. It was like we were a little family. It was nice. I almost forgot why I was there; I think we all did.

15. A case of mistaken identity

Saturday night just the simulacrum and I went out for ice cream. She ordered a flavor called banana split, one of these childish flavors with too many things in it but that she seemed to enjoy. She didn't thank me for the ice cream, or offer me a bite, instead she just sat there, smiling, spooning from her cone, humming along to the overhead music.

I myself ordered two scoops, one of chocolate and another of a flavor they called calafate that was colored deep blue, which somehow recalled to me the alarm that sometimes went off when I looked at orange foods. I regretted the adventure of my choice and was eating with considerably less joy than she.

"I don't want to be a finder of faults," the simulacrum eventually said idly, "but your way of searching for your wife doesn't seem to me to be the wisest, or the quickest, or, well—it hardly even seems like you're looking for her at all."

"Don't cavil," I said, and I admit being pleased to use a word that I suspected she would not understand. "It's not as if there's a trail of bread crumbs to follow. What I have here is a nonstandard problem, one that therefore demands a nonstandard solution. It's not easy to explain, but, for example, maybe eating this ice cream will prove to be useful. And there's always Monday. Rema may even be there Monday. There are indications."

"I think you should look for her back home." She was mining her ice cream for chunks. "Maybe at the Hungarian Pastry Shop if you want. That is the advice I would give to you, if you asked me. Can we set a date together for returning?"

I decided to change the subject. "You look nice in my sweater."
Then I asked the simulacrum how her newfangled flavor was.

"It's not new," she said. "Banana split is a classic flavor here. So
when should we go back to your apartment? Maybe after this
Monday meeting of yours? I really don't think we are making progress in this place," she said, gesturing around the room precari-
ously (for her ice cream) with her cone.

"I actually," I half lied, "expect to hear something important
from Tzvi Gal-Chen very soon." I started to spoon-feed myself
with more dedication. "I wish I could go back home. The problem
is that my actions, my work—they're important far beyond the
scope even of, say, just my own marriage. Tzvi sees me in this
very heroic light and I can't just let him down. It's hard to explain,
but even though I've sometimes had the feeling that my life was
insignificant, and even that my love was nothing more than an
accumulation of contingencies—still, all that ran contrary to the
enduring phenomenon of my own sense of great importance. Unwelcome importance really, an intrusion of importance. I felt central even though such a feeling seemed not to make sense, and to
be childish—"

And I was really beginning to open up to her, but then this short
young man, with '70s Warren Beatty hair and a five o'clock
shadow and a slouchy uniform on, appeared standing by our table,
repeating, in Spanish: *Could it be Rema?*

The simulacrum's capillaries dilated, her neck rashed, she emitted a series of sounds that I couldn't quite understand. She held
her cone out to the side as if it were a surrender flag. Then this
man was kissing her. Or greeting her, I suppose some people would
say, but from an objective point of view he was kissing her, he gave
her three kisses, alternating cheeks, so I'm not sure it really matters to what end he was doing this, why he was doing this, regardless the greeting was excessively effusive.

Excusing myself, I left for the bathroom to wash my hands. By
the time I came back the small uniformed man was sitting in my

chair. His triceps was vulgarly prominent, emerging from the rolled-up sleeve of a uniform shirt that bore as an insignia the Argentine flag. Was he a harbinger of an imminent battle? Could the 49 be so indiscreet? Just to make polite conversation I asked him, in English, as I stood over him, towering: "Did you participate in that hysterical invasion of the Falkland Islands?"

He seemed not to have parsed what I said. He announced in Spanish, "We were children together, Rema and I." Then he stood up and brought another chair to the table and offered it to me, as if I were the newcomer. "We lived on the same street. As children."

"Children," I said. "I was a child once too." I asked the man if she—I gestured—looked to him like the Rema of his childhood.

The simulacrum looked off to the side. As if it were a coldness in her eyes that would give her away. Although truthfully, her gaze was warm and full of emotion. She had set down her spoon and licked all around the base of her cone.

"Different but same," he answered, smiling. Then he looked over at her again and he repeated that phrase with variation: "Different but also exactly the same beautiful."

I asked the interloper if he was in the navy or the army or if he just liked to dress that way, and he said he was in the navy and then went on to say, "We used to have ice cream together almost every day, Rema and I."

I thrust my hands into the middle of the table to thwart what might have been his reach across to her unconed hand.

"We were children together," he repeated stupidly.

Then the small man—who still had not been gracious enough to offer his name, not even a false name, just for decorum's sake—said: "We used to run after the ice-cream truck. The ice-cream man would be yelling, 'Buy a cone and you'll be happy forever!'" Military man turned to me then, and he reached past my intercepting hands to point at her cone: "And she liked this same flavor, this same flavor of ice cream then as now." His musculature shifted grotesquely with each gesture, and he seemed to be perspiring nostalgia.

"That's wrong," the simulacrum said definitively to that other man.

I almost stood up and cheered.

"There's been a mistake," she said, switching her gaze to her cone. "I'm sorry," she said, holding that aloof gaze. "You are confusing me with someone else.'

"No," he laughed. "You're a little bit different but you're exactly the same."

"No, you're wrong, I'm sorry," she singsonged sadly.

She apologized even again; then she stood up, knocking over her chair in the process; she righted her chair, threw her ice cream away, then walked out.

That just left me and the uniformed man there at the table, with my ugly blue ice cream melting. "Is something wrong with Rema?" he asked.

I shrugged my shoulders, then excused myself to follow the simulacrum. I felt proud of her even as she distanced herself from me for the rest of the evening. And seeing that man hit on the impostress, seeing him miss her—it prompted in me a deeper kind of affection. Maybe his attention distorted the way I saw her. But maybe that distortion was valuable. Even corrective. Or maybe it was extinguishing my love for my real wife, wherever she was. I wrote Tzvi a detailed note about the whole encounter. Oddly, in his absence, I only felt closer to him. To everyone, I was feeling closer.

16. Materials and methods

Though she slept on the distant edge, she did share the bed with me that night. Her showered hair dampened the pillow, and I lay my hand on that cooling cloth. All that night I thought: I had left the simulacrum behind so hastily; regardless of circumstances that was wrong of me; it's never pleasant to be left behind though that's not really something that has happened to me much in my life, the case of my father not counting, since he wasn't leaving me but rather my mother. I really do try to leave people behind as infrequently as possible—I'd never, until this crisis, left a patient behind—but I think others will agree that when I left my mother behind, it would not really be fair to call that "leaving behind." I mean: I didn't leave her behind the way my father had. It was very different. I was eighteen years old and was leaving home for college. While it's true that I was essentially my mom's only friend, and that I could have attended school while still living at home, and that my mother's mood swings were increasing in amplitude and frequency and that our neighbor, this large woman who ate a lot of watermelon, kept sententiously saying *I just don't like the idea of her being alone*—apart from all of that, I in fact also remember feeling that it would be rather a relief for her to have me out of the way. And sometimes I think, contrary to popular belief, that being the one who is leaving is more difficult than being the one who is left, and I say this only because my mind has often stuck on the image of my mother lying on our yellow wool-acrylic blend upholstered sofa (the sofa had wooden armrests, where you could rest a mug of tea) wearing one of her very tailored outfits that entirely clashed with the idea of lying on a sofa in the middle of the day—and telling me that she'd always wanted upholstery of a different color, sky maybe, and of a quality that would catch a little bit of light, that was maybe a little bit satiny, or at least had a sheen, and that her whole life might look different to her if that was in her living room. And I myself was annoyed when she said this, not only because of her excessive aesthetic sensitivity, her ludicrously devout belief in beauty's ability to save us, but also because when I said, well, why don't you do that then, you could make those covers, she said that it would be expensive to get the kind of upholstery that would feel nice on your cheek lying down on it—and I said, well, maybe that wasn't something to save money on, that if that was what she really wanted, then that was what she should do and one can always find the money somehow—and she sighed and said, well, you don't care about what covers the sofa, do you? I guess I'm not thinking about that right now, I said, that's probably true, I probably don't care and I guess I'm thinking about other things, not fabric, not coverings—and she said yes that I was and she was glad for that. The skin around her eyes was sunken; her legs, which I could see up to the midthigh, were skinny and pale and streaked with blue; it was as if it had been months since she'd eaten a pigmented food. I didn't want to see that. But now I see it often, those wet cement eyes and her hand running across the fabric of the sofa. That's not actually the very last time I saw her, but I guess it was close to the last time; I think then I was just going out to buy some food, or go for a walk. But the only reason I am saying all this is to illustrate that I understood something about how the simulacrum must have felt, what with my leaving so hastily. And that maybe my mother would be pleased to know that now I was thinking about fabrics, about the look and touch and feel and necessity of them. Because I had decided to buy the simulacrum a nice and very warm coat; she had seemed so down after our ice-cream date and I thought a gift might cheer her up; and a coat seemed a wise idea if she was going to accompany me for Monday's meteorological labor, whatever it proved to be. And I wanted her to accompany me. I wanted her to be happy and to feel appreciated. I almost woke her up just to tell her how much I admired her, what a loyal and devoted and steadfast and adorable and loving companion agent she had been to me. Instead I thought a great deal about what kind of fabric the coat should be made of. I mean there was a nice symmetry there—thinking about fabrics—a nice reflection, some concordance, and one can't help but want to assign meaning to such things, or at least to want to luxuriate in the noise of possible meanings, even if there is no actual meaning there at all.

It was all brimming over with good intentions, the shopping plan.

That next day I found a heavy coat that I knew would look beautiful on the simulacrum; it was of a pale blue wool, not wholly unlike Rema's winter coat; I placed the coat in the simulacrum's arms with assurance. Although it was not a perfect coat, and not exactly like Rema's, I knew that later we could locate oversized buttons to sew onto it and then it would be spectacular. And meanwhile it could keep her warm.

"Doesn't interest me," the simulacrum said, seeming annoyed. "I'd prefer another color. And something more sporty, more like for climbing a little mountain." She tried on an ugly down jacket, very puffy, emergency yellow, with wide-stitch quilting.

"That would be a mistake," I said. I tried to explain to her about the buttons that would go on the wool coat and how nice it would look then.

She said it would look just like a wool coat she already had and that I perfectly well knew that. Then she petted at the sleeves of that ugly yellow thing.

Not wanting to cause trouble—she already seemed so short-tempered—I didn't point out that it wasn't actually her coat, it was Rema's, and I wasn't going to let her just take it. Certainly not for until the end of time. I mean, what I was thinking then was that even if I found Rema, she and I would probably let the simulacrum live with us, at least for a delimited period, if she had no other place to go; we wouldn't just kick her out on the street.

Who knew what her real circumstances might be? And who could say—maybe she and Rema would become good friends, and share clothes, and secrets, and dog-caring duties.

"You look like an alarm in that coat," I said to her. "Like a hazardous crossing signal." I carried the finer coat folded over my arm like a sommelier's napkin, and I followed the simulacrum all over the store as she tried on other unflattering jackets. Politely but firmly I held to my opinions. She steadily disagreed with them.

My pacific nature finally broke. "Why do you care so much?" I said. "Why does it matter to you, one coat or the other? Why can't you just take a gift graciously?"

The simulacrum looked right through me. A fluorescence above smoldered. "Why do *you* care so much?" she finally said.

I didn't respond.

"This is ugly," she said, looking at me, and I got the sense that she was referring to more than just the coat over my arm. She tried on one more item, traffic cone orange and far too large. "All right, this is it."

I quietly pointed out to her that the fabric looked like it was made from recycled tires.

"It pleases me," she said. "It's impregnable."

"But the color. I mean, maybe if you didn't dye your hair blonde. Maybe for a brunette, this color, but—"

Then—and there was a sweet bitterness in her speech, a bitterness like licorice pills: "Which do you think your friend Tzvi Gal-Chen would prefer?" She tilted her head. And this made me think of that night nurse laughing at me, and of that dog-walking analyst, and the way he had smiled at me that day, a laughing kind of smile, and even of Anatole I thought, and even of fireworks, and also I thought of me, of my unwanted laughter too.

"Why, which do you think he'd prefer?" I said back to her. She'd ruined the whole fun of everything, had reduced me to echoing.

"Can you not get him on the phone anymore? Poor thing. Although now that I am thinking," she said, "maybe he's not the person I would ask for fashion advice."

17. Attacks on the local steady-state hypothesis

That afternoon, Harvey approached the simulacrum and me with plans for going for "a constitutional." I agreed, but then the simulacrum backed out, saying she'd rather stay behind preparing for tomorrow's meeting, reading the research of Tzvi Gal-Chen. Her withdrawal seemed a kind of threat. But only kind of. At the time, I suspected nothing.

A few blocks out in that chill and Harvey ventured, "I'm concerned about the reality of Tzvi Gal-Chen."

"You're telling me that you're concerned about the reality of Tzvi Gal-Chen?"

"No, about the health of Tzvi Gal-Chen," he said into the wind.

"About the *health* of Tzvi Gal-Chen?" I said.

"No. About the *modality* of Tzvi Gal-Chen," he said. "About the modality."

"The reality," I said. "That is what you are saying?"

"Yes," he said.

"This is about the out-of-office reply? I got that too, and it distressed me, but I can't imagine it's anything serious."

"Out-of-office? What? No. My concern pertains to what the blonde told me."

I tried to think if I had earlier noticed him referring to the simulacrum as "the blonde." Instead sheep and fruit came to mind.

Harvey went on: "She told me that there is no Tzvi Gal-Chen. Not really. Not in any real sense like I thought there was. And then she said this. She said that if there was a Tzvi Gal-Chen, then you may as well say that *she* is Tzvi Gal-Chen. That's what she said to me. A bit arrogant, no?"

I heard a tremendous cracking sound: somewhere ice breaking. We had been told that chunks of glacier often fell, crashing into the lake. "Did you see that sound?" I asked.

"You're resistant to this information, Dr. Leo. All I'm saying is: do we really know who she is?"

I thought of the simulacrum walking out on that military man at the ice-cream shop, and I felt that pang of heartburn that I associate with, well, love. "She *is* someone, I suppose," I said. "Or not even suppose, but most likely. Obviously. Of course." And I did keep hearing ice cracking, sometimes even shattering. Off at a distance, but it made me feel unsteady. "Listen, Harvey—I think I know why she says she's Tzvi Gal-Chen. But it's a stupid thing that makes her say so, a very stupid thing, Harvey, and I don't want you to take the things she says very seriously. She is not a reliable source. Her data is shot through with error. Maybe blue noise, error on the smallest scale, but error nonetheless. Any data from her must be filtered—"

"But it's an interesting problem that she brings up, the problem of knowing Tzvi Gal-Chen. It's a problem that sounds epistemic but that may in fact be metaphysical."

"Which analyst used that phrase with you?"

"Doesn't it accurately describe the situation?"

"No. He's just out of his office. Being out—that's a totally normal thing that people can be. He'll return. And until then we know we have our meeting tomorrow. Don't get nervous over this. After all, how could Tzvi Gal-Chen not be real if you've been writing to him? If he has been writing to you? If he has been writing papers in journals since before either of us even knew him and since before the simulacrum was even born?"

"But he hasn't written any papers very recently; I even asked him about that, and he admitted that no, he had not. He's gone underground. But why—"

"Yes, well," I said, "the secret nature of some of the work? That's not something you don't understand." A cold, dry wind burned my cheek like a sunburn, or a slap. As I said those words that didn't quite convince me of anything, I was reminded of a conversation I'd once had shortly after my mother died in which I referred to my mother in the present tense. I said, "She works as a seamstress." But I should have said, "She *worked* as a seamstress." It was a pretty girl's question I said that in response to and this was during a time in my life when I had difficulties, much greater difficulties than now, talking to girls. Back then I had difficulties talking to anybody, really. Regardless, the girl said back to me, after touching my wrist, oh, will you ask your mother a question for me? Will you ask her if you can serge without a special machine that's just for serging? (For me the word "serge" heaved with sexuality.) My present-tense slipup grew increasingly problematic, because every time this girl saw me—she really was so pretty— she would ask me again if I'd talked to my mother, if I'd asked her about the serging. I suppose I could have tried to learn about serging on my own and just lied and said I'd asked my mother. Or I could have simply confessed to the fact that my mother was dead and that I therefore could not ask her about serging. But I did neither of those things; instead I worked harder and harder to avoid the girl, who grew lovelier every year (until at the very end of college she cut her hair short), and when I would spy her, at a distance, or in the cafeteria, I would feel a pressing at the walls of my heart, as if I were in love with this girl whom I didn't know, as if we might have been the happiest couple there ever was save for how I had ruined everything through my simple slip in language.

"I mean, it's not as if I've never been led astray, in my years of work for the Academy," Harvey broke back in. "I went back and looked more closely at the e-mails Tzvi had written to me, and to us, and I noticed something. He's extremely fond of saying 'rather' and 'suppose' and 'anyway' and 'regardless.' Which perhaps you've noticed are words you're very fond of too."

"That is peculiar," I acknowledged, censoring myself from saying "rather peculiar." "But not so peculiar."

"Yes, he likes 'peculiar' too. And he likes to repeat himself.

And like you often say to me—you've often said to me—peculiarity is something true rumpling the bedsheets of assumption—"

"I've never said that—"

"You said something like that," Harvey asserted. We had stopped walking; we were just standing out there in the cold. "Or maybe Tzvi said it to me. And I was just thinking that it was funny, that it was odd, but that probably you and he were just different possible versions of essentially the same person. That the two of you are supposed to be in separate worlds, but here you are in the same one. Maybe even vying for something? Just like the blonde and your wife."

"Is this an accusation? This strikes me as entirely ludicrous. If anyone is Tzvi, it's certainly not me."

"Not the same person. Just *almost* the same person. Maybe of varying provenances. Yes, it may seem impossible, but more possible than the other possibilities, no? I thought maybe these swaps might be a kind of prelude to—well, my working hypothesis is that tomorrow, before the storm, there will be a swap back. But maybe the simulacrum says what she says because she will be swapped for Tzvi, and you will be swapped for Rema, so it'll be a crisscross like that—"

And it strikes me now as worth recording that on account of Harvey's ramblings—I had been lulled into believing that I was working with a mostly sane man, my norms had redshifted without my noticing—we had lost our bearings. And it began to rain—sleet, really—rather heavily, and so we could not see far. I will spare you the heroics and dumb luck of our making it back to the hotel, but at one point, when the ground grew too icy, we crawled.

18. While we were out

Before we entered—somehow I just knew to do this—I gestured to Harvey to be quiet and I—soaked, cold—gently pressed my ear to the door of my very own room, my own hotel room, anyway, my temporary room. And I overheard the voice of my companion, my copycat companion that is, saying: "—but it's exhausting too, having to pretend about so many little things when I am with him, it's like I have to be not myself . . . I know you're right, I know I shouldn't have let him go, not even for an hour . . . now I'm worried and miserable . . . I wanted to see who he's been mailing with, but you're right . . . but I do want to stay with him . . . he used to leave me poems on the kitchen table . . . and buy me special fruits . . . and he says things sometimes like 'the foul rag and bone shop of my heart' . . . and I'm so happy when I sleep with my head on his chest . . . Saul didn't like to cuddle . . . let's say he is a little bit crazy . . . secret huge debts like David did . . . and so what do I care that he feels close to someone just because he thinks he's a meteorologist . . . it's better than sleeping with other girls . . . it feels nice to be the center of his world, even if it's partially because he's mean about everyone else . . . I think we love each other . . . I can feel him coming back to me . . . I feel—"

Or maybe what she felt was me there at the door . . . there was the question of whom she was talking to, and the question of whom she was talking about . . . and the question of whether I really went around saying "foul rag and bone shop" far more often than I might have thought . . . unless it wasn't me she was talking about with the poems . . . I'd only ever done that a handful of times . . . then the question of who didn't like to cuddle . . . the answers proliferated even faster than the questions . . . and what came to mind was a diagram, with each pronoun a blank box on a language tree, and each possible meaning shifting as I filled in the boxes with different names . . . and what also came to mind was Proust's narrator, attempting to talk to an elevator operator at Balbec, an elevator operator who did not reply, "either because of astonishment at my words, attention to his work, a regard for etiquette, hardness of hearing, respect for his surroundings, fear of danger, slow-wittedness, or orders from the manager . . ." But there I went again running into the wrong text simply because I felt intimidated by the lack of context for the simulacrum's words, but still I was able to generate quickly in my mind, by falling back upon my old list of clues, hypotheses about what this all might mean:

Unnamed dog—Not even mentioned and thus, as we had thought, either absolutely central (and thus appearing as an elephant-sized silence) or absolutely not.

Anatole—I knew now was Rema's father, but did he also buy her fruits? And did he leave her poems? Or was he actually not in her thoughts at every moment of every day?

Rema's husband—Or the simulacrum's. Maybe Saul. Maybe David. Or maybe she just used the names of ancient kings to refer to . . . who? Or what? Previous missions she'd undertaken for the Academy, or for the Fathers? Or, simply, previous loves?

Tzvi Gal-Chen—Her approval of my affection for Tzvi lent further weight to the hope or anxiety that she actually was Tzvi, or at least had played the part of Tzvi, which possibly even meant that she was, finally, Rema, and which possibly explained Tzvi's recent return to absentia. That, or she was unaware of the meaning of Tzvi.

Royal Academy and *Lola* and *Patagonian research*—I figured
I'd store these fragments and return to them after I learned
more at the meeting the following day.

All that, and yet. The real and unpleasant yield of that over-
hearing fell outside of my grid of previous clues. The real yield
was the unequivocal sense that I was not alone in my deficient understanding of the situation. She also was floundering—now me
with the fish—to understand. She clearly didn't know what to
make of me. I had preferred thinking that the simulacrum—while
she might intermittently deceive, while she might withhold—
that she, in the end, knew all the facts. But she did not.

I opened the door; she abruptly hung up the phone. I saw her
eyes well up with tears, and she just said, "You two were gone for
so long."

And I found that I didn't want to ask her about the dog. And
I didn't want to ask her about the Academy or the Quantum Fathers or Saul or David or poetry or Proust or anything. I found
that I just wanted to tell her that I loved her. This strange thing
within me, amidst all the other strange things within me, the intrusions from other possible worlds or simply from the recesses of
this one: I had thought I could love only my original Rema, but
maybe I was wrong. I felt within me those proverbial butterflies,
the desire to have her think well of me, the desire to lay myself out
beside her, the desire for the world to see her next to me, the flit-
tering conviction that she in fact was the whole world, was all
worlds, all those desires.

I didn't say anything like that, though; I knew we had to work
together.

Harvey went up to the simulacrum and hugged her.

19. The misrecognitions

Draped in her traffic cone orange coat, the simulacrum stood impatiently by the hotel room door, waiting as I finished shaving, as Harvey took down notes in front of the television news. What if we were a family? What if there were a school bus outside? What if I had packed our lunches, and she had always to hound us to leave on time? Or a different family altogether. She a charismatic alcoholic losing her beauty, he a painfully shy jazz aesthete, me a hardworking insurance man. Or she a no-nonsense nurse, and me a philandering musician of little talent, and he not existing at all. Or me a meteorologist, and she a computer programmer, and us settled down in Oklahoma with two spoiled children, both of them bad at soccer, both of them good in math. "Well, boys, let's go and we'll finally see," the simulacrum said, "about this mysterious Monday meeting."

I genuinely worried—I'm not sure why—that we were leaving to meet no one.

But at our appointed meeting spot in the central square, a woman was in fact there. Sitting along the edge of a fallow fountain, wearing purple oven-mitt-ish mittens, eating a lime green popsicle, her phosphorescent blonde hair held back with a fleece headband. Did I feel as a Greek tragic hero must feel at the moment of anagnorisis? Not quite. But why shouldn't that woman have been Rema? Why not her instead of the simulacrum? She had a dog with her, an exceptionally large German shepherd, with dirty snow-colored fur particularly thick and coarse, and I was reminded—so often—of those Austrian dogs that had seemed inexplicably strange, then explicably strange, once I realized they were simply dramatically larger than I was used to, which made being near them feel like being on a movie set with oversized props and doorways extra tall.

The woman bit from her popsicle. A chunklet fell to the ground; the oversized dog snarfed it.

Did I reach my hand into my coat pocket, as if I'd find something there—a swatch of cloth? a lock of hair? an old movie stub? a photograph? a piece of licorice? a special ring? a clipped news article?—something to identify myself to her, something that would prove, across the worlds, that I was really me? I did. But I found only a sugar packet. And a bobby pin that could have belonged to any girl. Nevertheless, I extended my hand to that woman confidently. "I'm Arthur," I said.

"You're not Arthur," she announced in a voice that seemed to me loud enough for the whole universe to hear. Then she laughed. "I'm sorry, I mean, you might be Arthur. But the funny thing is that I'm waiting for someone named Arthur. But an Arthur who isn't you."

"Twenty-seven? Ice climber? Bowdoin College?"

She looked at me almost cross-eyed. "You know him?" she said, beckoning her very large dog closer to herself.

"You know him?" I said, thinking about black magic.

"Do you know him?" the simulacrum—so intrusive—was saying to this other woman, intending, I believe, the "him" to be me.

Was this situation terribly disappointing and somewhat humiliating? It was.

Did that woman walk away? She did.

Maybe I expected she would eventually pursue me, but she did not.

20. Falsifiability

Maybe, as Harvey had been alleging, there was a problem with the reality of Tzvi Gal-Chen. Maybe that accounted for the failure of the Hilda encounter. Maybe that accounted for the lack of storms. Messages I wrote to Tzvi simply bounced back. Calls to the Royal Academy failed to connect me to any Tzvi or to any Lola. And a terrible migraine developed within me, as if to counteract the absence of external weather disturbances.

"Let's go home," the simulacrum whispered—though it sounded to me like shouting—in my ear, as I lay in bed with the lights out, with the shades down, waiting for my migraine to pass, waiting for Harvey to return from the field with news, even though I had no confidence that he would. "You'll find yourself so happy to be home," she continued. "You'll feel like yourself again at home," and the feeling inside me was of inhabiting a dark and uncanny fairy tale.

I asked her to please leave me alone. But she said that at my age I shouldn't be left alone when I wasn't feeling well. *At my age.* She said that more than once. I'm barely in my fifties, but she spoke of me like a man on his deathbed. In essence making a deathbed out of that oddly proportioned hotel bed, killing me in her imagination, in a room of false intimacy, with its horse and glacier images. "Most people of my socioeconomic status live quite a bit beyond fifty," I whispered through the yellowness of my headache. "I will get better. Tzvi will contact us soon enough."

Later the simulacrum began crying and accusing me more absurdly.

"Of course I love the original Rema," I murmured, trying to placate her into a shush, feeling a touch awkward about the simulacrum's excessive investment in my feelings for Rema. She continued heaping unfounded anxieties one atop the other. For a long time I said nothing, but finally I interjected: "No, that's not what any of this is about at all. That's not why I don't want to go home yet."

Undeterred from her perseverations, she went on saying things that don't merit transcription, saying that I didn't find her attractive, repeatedly confounding herself and Rema, lily-padding from irrelevancies to inaccuracies. In a slight ebb tide of my pain, I exhaled the following: "You don't understand. If anyone is, or was, unfaithful, if anyone is, or was, 'seeing' anyone else—maybe seeing many other people—it was her, it was without a doubt her, and it was only her. How many times have I picked up the phone only to have the other person hang up? Rema is very young. She is too young. She probably thought she wanted someone older, and reliable, and financially established; but in the end she didn't want to be married to a father. I could practically be her father. But I could never be enough of a father and a father is not enough. Maybe no one will ever be enough. Maybe she's not a person for whom anything will ever suffice. Well, maybe that is understandable, understandable even *to me*. So she finds someone else, someone younger, maybe. Prettier, maybe. He will disappoint her too. She'll return. I'm not worried. I have no worries—"

I didn't actually believe a word of what I said. Even if I did, briefly, that would have been purely on account of my distorting neurologic state. That's not what Rema's like. I was just talking. And women, they're always wanting to take the side of other women, and so somehow the simulacrum had put me in a position where it seemed like I was arguing against Rema, like I was in some way hurting Rema. I wasn't. I was loving her and I was looking for her. It was not, as the simulacrum kept alleging, that I wasn't really looking at all, that I was running away. And the truth of the matter was that the matter between us happened not to be the matter between us—that is, whatever problems we actually suffered within our own marriage were absolutely irrelevant to what was currently keeping us apart. "Tzvi understands what's keeping us apart," I declared. I didn't think he fully did, actually, but I wanted to appeal to an authority outside of myself.

Later the phone rang. Not my phone, but hers. She wouldn't answer it. "It's just my mom," she claimed.

"Why don't you talk to her?" I said, feeling unusually aware of other people's pain.

"It is difficult. I don't like it."

"The poor woman," I scolded. "Can't you spare a little kindness? You know what happened to her husband, don't you?"

"Did she tell you that lie too?" The simulacrum sighed. "He just left her. That's all. She likes to make it seem something else, something dramatic, but it is very ordinary. She likes to make her pain seem extraordinary when it is just ordinary, ordinary pain for an ordinary, ordinary person."

I turned on the TV, very quietly, to stop her mean talk.

21. A birth of comedy

In my dream she was there, then I awoke and she wasn't there, then I fell back to sleep and then woke and she was there. She was wearing, in addition to a frumpy alpaca sweater, a small, sad look of triumph.

"Where's Harvey?" I asked.

"He was called home."

From among the chaos she carried within Rema's pale blue purse, she pulled a folded piece of paper. The filmy folded sheet proved a faxed copy, printed in a powder that finger oils could smudge away, of a page from the September 1996 issue of *Journal of the Atmospheric Sciences*. Blue lint had collected along the fray of the folds and when I unfolded the paper it crackled slightly with what I believe were crumbs of rye cracker. I include the full text of the journal page she presented to me.

As most readers of *Journal of the Atmospheric Sciences* know, Dr. Tzvi Gal-Chen was its co–chief editor for about two years before his sudden passing in October 1994. He was also an influential and stimulating atmospheric scientist and a warm and much-loved human being. As his close friend and colleague, I accepted the task of standing in for him at the *Journal of the Atmospheric Sciences* for a year and also of collecting and editing papers for a special issue of the journal to be published in the month of his birth.

Tzvi aspired to be a multidisciplinary scientist, with interests and activities in largescale, mesoscale, boundary layer, and climate dynamics, and with a strong emphasis on remote sensing analysis techniques. As most working scientists know, "multidisciplinary" is a favorite word and expectation of administrators and journalists, but it is often regarded with suspicion in the academic community. Tzvi's earthy way of saying it was, "A multidisciplinary scientist had better be an expert in at least two disciplines, or else he is a charlatan."

I am not a great fan of special issues of an archival journal like the *Journal of the Atmospheric Sciences*. Sometimes the papers are premature, excessively delayed, warmed over, or accepted largely on the basis of their presentation at a conference. I agreed to edit this one on the understanding that the papers, though solicited to some extent, would be fully acceptable to the *Journal of the Atmospheric Sciences* under any conditions and that their subjects would be as broad as Tzvi's interests. The result is a nice mix. It includes one paper coauthored by Tzvi as the advisor of a doctoral student; two other papers authored at the University of Oklahoma; another by a close former associate using Tzvi's work as part of the foundation; three papers on geophysical fluids, including a major work in planetary science, an area which Tzvi was associated with in his earlier appointment at NASA; a paper on data assimilation; a paper on TOGA COARE, which was the last observation project in which Tzvi participated; and a boundary layer paper. I feel that all these are contributions that Tzvi would have liked to read. I must admit that in some cases the reviews and authors' revisions were slightly accelerated to meet the publication deadline. I hope and believe, however, that this issue will be found worthy of the high standards of the *Journal of the Atmospheric Sciences* and stand as a small but fitting memorial to Tzvi.

Douglas Lilly
University of Oklahoma

The simulacrum sat expectantly at the bed's edge, with her hands between her knees in that inadvertent prayer position kind of way, waiting for me to read the document. I found myself reading the document over several times. Yes, before looking up I had read it several times and so understood it quite well. When I made eye contact with the blonde, she tilted her head at me, like a puppy. There was then a pregnant pause for language, a repressed face-off of sorts, for who was going to begin with the speaking, me or her. I tilted my head in the opposite direction that the blonde had tilted her head, which thought of in a certain way is the same direction, like in a mirror. And the silence continued from that angle, but I'd like to clarify that it was not a reverent silence that was being maintained, not on my part, not a silence in the face of the greatest of mysteries. This "mystery" that the simulacrum had presented me with—in its own way—well, it was so very *small*. All she was trying to say was that Tzvi Gal-Chen was dead, and that we should therefore find it strange that I had communicated with him. At least, I think that was all she was trying to say. But that had become, for me, maybe the least of many mysteries, one that mattered to me only as a door to other possibilities, only as a passage through which I followed. Not as a thing unto itself.

The simulacrum tilted her head in the other direction and then, with an excess of gentleness in her tone, she asked me what I thought "this Tzvi Gal-Chen character that you have been communicating with"—she wanted to know what I thought he might think of this memorial issue of *Journal of the Atmospheric Sciences*.

I pointed out the problems inherent in such projective hypothesizing.

The simulacrum reasked me the same question. What did I think "this Tzvi Gal-Chen character" would think?

I answered that I thought it would be rather rude to ask such a question of "this Tzvi Gal-Chen character." I regretted employing the diminishing terminology that she—rather inappropriately—had taken to using.

What do you mean it would be rude to ask? she wanted to know.

I said that a feeling I'd often had was that it would be awkward to talk with people about their deaths after they'd died. There might not be much to say about it.

She said that what I was saying didn't make sense.

You mean it doesn't make sense *to you*, I clarified.

No, no, no, no, no, she said, standing up, moving too close to me, talking right into my face, her body so close that I thought I could feel the air move out of her way. She went on: "It doesn't make sense *to anybody*, at least not to *anybody else that I know*," she said, infected, I believe, with my admirable tendency to qualify. "Not even to Harvey. It's just you," she continued. "Doesn't that make you wonder when something is just only you?"

"I didn't come up with this craziness," I said. "It came to me, not from me."

22. Conclusions and future work

Toward the end of his retrievals paper Tzvi wrote: "Are these errors a reasonable simulation of those actually present in Doppler radar data? Is there any way to recover useful information from the resulting fields?" Naturally these questions came to mind when I was deciding whether or not to return with the simulacrum to the apartment that I shared with Rema.

Let's say that I agreed to return, that she agreed to return with me. We arrive. I imagine the apartment will smell musty and she'll open the windows and cold blasts will compete with one another through the length of the space; the curtains will billow. The thin dog—who will return her?—will retreat to the simulacrum's lap for warmth. An old newspaper will be out on the coffee table, as if still important, something circled in red pen. The bed will not be made. Four spoons and a glass will be sitting unwashed in the sink. Not sure how to behave, I will offer to make tea. The *click-click* of the gas stovetop will make a nice contact sound as I set the teakettle to boil. I don't want tea, she will say. So if you're doing that for me, don't do it, she will add. I'll ask her if she wants coffee. She'll say no. Hot milk? Do you want to rent a movie? Go for a walk? Eat chocolate? Lie under covers? She'll be inconsolable and I'll find myself curiously dedicated toward her immediate consolation.

"Sometimes you're not very mean," she'll concede, eventually, after dozens of suggestions.

We'll go out for dinner, which Rema and I never do, and the dinner will be okay. The butter will be unusually good, but neither of us will speak much, and I'll order a hamburger in an attempt to be cheap and will regret it. She'll finish less than half of her lamb. I'll mention something I saw in the newspaper—young Turks' voting patterns maybe, or the mummy of Queen Hatshepsut—and she will say that she also saw that—whatever it might be—in the newspaper, but we'll fail to turn our mutual reading into a conversation. When we decide to return home, the nearby subway station will be closed; we'll walk ten blocks to an open station and then descend and wait. She'll say she doesn't believe the train will ever come. I'll assure her that she is right, that the train will never come and that also the gates will close, and we'll be locked in the station, and she'll say that she is just so tired and regrets ever having thought that she wanted to go anywhere. Then the train will come; there will be plenty of seats; she'll lay her head on my shoulder. And in the dark glass of the subway car I'll see this gentle sleepy her leaning on me. We should have had pizza, she'll say. Even though there's no good pizza in the neighborhood.

The next morning I'll catch the grassy scent of Rema's shampoo coming from the shower. I'll walk into that steamed room. The dog will have preceded me, will be curled up on the bath mat waiting for her. Without saying hello but also without apologizing for my presence, I'll wash my face in the sink. Later I'll find she's wearing my socks.

Maybe we'll eventually get a second dog, one who dotes on me more than on her.

As time passes, I will begin to wonder how far my collaboration with the simulacrum might, or could, or should, or shouldn't go. Perhaps we'll eventually find ourselves wholly making believe as if she is the original Rema, as if nothing has happened. That is perhaps what we were meant to do. Be partners in solving a poorly defined crime. Appear normal. Share the wide bed. Take turns doing laundry, walking the dog (or dogs), parking the car. Cook lentils, watch old movies, fumble through the recycling to find a news story. Maybe we'll do the crossword puzzle together and she will be a little bit better than me. If one night she wakes up in an undefined terror it will be my responsibility to put an arm around her, pet her until she falls back asleep. Though of course then I'll be awake, from having woken to calm her; I will disentangle myself; I'll leave the bed to take a long hot bath; I will use her soap with its flecks of abrasive and I will use her pumice to scrape my feet, and when, still very awake, I bring my handheld into the bed so as to be able to read the news online—there will be conflict somewhere in the world, atrocity—the tiny glow will reawaken her, and she'll be furious with me for this, so the next day I will sweep, and bring home nice fruit, and then everything will be more or less okay between us.

This will repeat itself, in variations.

In many ways, I'll realize, this alternate life of mine will be a small but fitting memorial to my life with Rema.

One evening I'll put key to door but find the door unlocked. No creature will greet me. I'll hear only an inscrutable but distantly familiar, tinny, regularly irregular popping sound. Proceeding toward the noise, I'll discover the kitchen ceiling covered with soot; strangely, this sight won't make me think of anything else. My mind will stick just to that covered surface, but my heart rate will increase, my hands will feel cold, the popping sound will continue until I finally realize that the sound comes from the teakettle having been left on the burner empty, with all the water boiled away. I'll call out to her and no one will answer. I'll turn off the flame and try to transfer the kettle over to the sink, but even the safe rubber handle will have become too hot. I'll call out to her again. I'll search the space of the small apartment. That very slow way of drinking that she sometimes has, of putting her finger to the surface of the tea and then bringing her finger to her lips—that will come to my mind. That and yellow panic.

Then I'll hear the apartment door open. Then I'll see her. Unmarred, happy, with the russet dog in her purse, she'll pull several date cookies out of a brown paper bag and offer them to me. She'll tell me she just went for a walk and forgot; she'll go to survey the kitchen and wipe stripes in the soot with her finger. She'll smudge ash on my cheek and nose. She'll say let's clean it tomorrow, not today, I had this whole happy idea of having tea and these date cookies and reading the paper and that's what I want to do. She'll boil water in a saucepan. I could have fallen in love with this woman, I'll realize, just meeting her right that very moment, even if there was no history between us. I'll tell her that. Or something to that effect.

Yes, I will have the feeling that this life I am living with the simulacrum is real. And one morning I'll get out of bed first and set the kettle to boil and the heat will smell chalky, and the puppy, or dog—and I will know the creature's name intimately—will follow my every move in the kitchen and I will be speaking amiably with this creature, distracted, but then when I look up from those dog eyes she will have appeared, standing under the lintel, in green nightie boxers and an undershirt of mine, and her hair will be messy, and she'll rub her eyes and smile shyly.

One day, on the subway, she will peel a clementine and hand me slices. When we transfer trains, she will be showing me the pith gathered under her fingernails and this will distract me and then I will find I have bumped into Tzvi Gal-Chen.

We will all mumble apologies.

Tzvi will be wearing plaid pants. He will be holding an uncrying baby. He will acknowledge us—the recognition, the uncanniness, the whole situation—very discreetly.

Then I'll remember that something has been forgotten.

I will begin, again, to notice. To really see. Small errors in her performance.

I'll note fork, not spoon, marks in the ice-cream container. I'll think maybe it was a guest I'd forgotten about. But she'll be walking comfortably in heels; she'll drink her teas quickly; weeks will go by in which she isn't irritated with me; I'll meet people she works with who don't seem to be in love with her. We'll go to a movie and before it's over she'll tell me, without embarrassment or explanation, that she wants to leave. Later I'll come across her ticket stub in her jeans pocket, and it will be flat, whole, nearly unhandled. Of course I will want to deny such evidence. But when the lost luggage from Argentina, full of Rema's shirts, finally returns, this will excite her not at all. One evening I'll arrive home two hours late and find her unworried, eating blueberry yogurt. I'll begin to notice how often she gazes philosophically into the eyes of the russet puppy, as if no other creature in the world really understands her. One day she'll even stop dyeing her hair. And she'll cut it short. I'll run out of ways to deceive myself. And though all of this will be painful—it will be like losing her all over—I will at least know then, again, that I must find her, that I can only ever truly love the original Rema. I won't know what this means for me, or for anyone else, or for the Academy, or for the Fathers, or for the world; probably I won't even really be able to care. But for all that ignorance, still—that image of Tzvi in my mind, underground, holding that baby, dressed in a way that could make him a foreigner or a hipster or an accident or a transplant from another time—I'll at least know the purpose of the rest of my life.

Acknowledgments

My friends, teachers, and the perennially generous crowd at the Hungarian Pastry Shop have taken better care of me than I could possibly deserve.

I'm forever indebted to the profoundly gracious and tireless Bill Clegg, the endlessly smart and charming Eric Chinski, and the wunderkind Gena Hamshaw.

Also many thanks to the Rona Jaffe Foundation for early and generous support of my work.

And I owe especial thanks to my family: Yosefa, for a bottomless supply of pears and love; Denise, Tom, Heather, and Greg, for play and comfort; Oren, Viki, Gabi, and Rhone, for unending rational counsel and joy; Aaron, for mahmoul yojimbo moozu; and Tzvi, always my company through life's alien corn.

CPSIA information can be obtained
at www.ICGtesting.com
Printed in the USA
LVHW091601301219
642079LV00004B/508/P

9 780312 428433